This first English translation of *The Legend of the Ice People*
is dedicated with love and gratitude to the memory
of my dear late husband Asbjorn Sandemo,
who made my life a fairy tale

The Legend of the Ice People

1. Spellbound
ISBN: 978-1-903571-75-0

2. Witch-Hunt
ISBN: 978-1-903571-77-4

Further titles to be published in 2008

3. Depths of Darkness
ISBN: 978-1-903571-79-8

4. Yearning
ISBN: 978-1-903571-81-1

5. Mortal Sin
ISBN: 978-1-903571-85-9

6. Evil Inheritance
ISBN: 978-1-903571-87-3

Chapter 1

There was no warning of the catastrophe. There were no omens. Nothing appeared to be amiss. Life in the high Valley of the Ice People in fact was austere and hard for Silje, Tengel and the children – but they shared a simple happiness. As often as they could, they spent time together doing ordinary things. The children particularly liked to join Tengel when he went fishing on one of the lakes and today the oars of the boat, in which they all sat, creaked regularly in their rowlocks each time they broke the surface of the calm water. Seated in the stern, the children were chattering incessantly, their shrill voices carrying across the mountain lake. Sol sounded matter-of-fact, as usual; Dag was calm and slightly aloof; while Liv's piping fairy-tale tones were mostly drowned out by the other two.

Silje sat in the middle, watching Tengel at the oars; his unflinching gaze was on the children – he was always concerned that some harm might befall them. But they were responsible – unfettered but disciplined – and Silje knew that he really didn't need to watch them quite so closely, though she understood his concerns. Here was a man who had once resigned himself to an empty, lonely existence, but who now had four people depending on him, respectful and giving him the love that he had only imagined in his most secret of dreams. She was so proud of them all – her little family.

Her husband Tengel – the feared outcast whom she had met five years ago – only she knew that his frightening, faintly demonic exterior concealed an unbelievably fine human being. As for the children, her heart warmed just thinking about them. Sol, always cheerful and lively, presented them with a dilemma, tainted as she was by the blood of Tengel the Evil One and the threat of tragedy. Dag was a blond intelligent dreamer and Liv, the youngest, imitated the older ones in everything. Liv takes after me in so many ways, thought Silje. The same chestnut-brown, wavy hair – although maybe with a hint more copper than mine – the same shy, expressive eyes and the ready smile. She shares my imagination as well, seeing trolls everywhere, breathing life into shadows and everyday things, communing with trees. Oh, sweet child, thought Silje, if you continue in my footsteps your life will be rich and varied, but you may be too kind and generous-spirited to cope with all the heartache it will bring.

She was reluctant to turn around and look at the children. It always distressed her to see how poorly dressed they were now. Sol's dress had burst all its seams. Dag wore a jacket and trousers made from one of Silje's worn-out skirts, every stitch a testament to her lack of skill with needle and thread. Liv's dark heavy woollen dress, conjured from a pair of Tengel's old trousers, was an utterly worthless garment which had been openly ridiculed by neighbours' wives. The very thought of it made Silje cringe with shame.

They had set out their only fishing net carefully in a favourite spot and were now returning towards the shore.

Much to their delight, the children had been allowed to come along, because the weather on this early summer's evening was so mild.

As they rowed, Silje's eyes searched the mountains surrounding the Valley of the Ice People. They were thrillingly bathed in burnished gold by the setting sun and her gaze eventually came to rest on a fissure between two peaks. 'You know, Tengel,' she said musingly, 'I've often wondered if there's a way through the mountains up there.'

He rested on his the oars and looked upwards. 'Yes, there is, and a few of us *have* managed to find a route. I don't recommend it though. It brings you out onto the glacier on the other side. From there it's a hair-raising journey down to more pleasant countryside.'

'So you've really been right through yourself?'

'Yes, once, a long time ago. I swore never to do it again.'

The boat touched ground, and the children jostled to be first ashore.

'Be careful!' warned Tengel.

No other words were needed and they all did precisely as they were told. He had instilled unbelievable discipline in them – but it was a discipline that reflected only love and kindness. The children hung on his every word and were always careful to obey. It was not difficult to see that they worshipped him – but only Silje knew how much.

****

Each of them took something to carry up the hill to the cottage. The children had learned long ago that, to survive in this wilderness, everyone had a part to play. Liv grew tired, so Tengel lifted her up on his shoulders. Sol and Dag walked on either side of Silje.

Sol looked thoughtful. Her lively face, framed by dark curls, was uncharacteristically serious. 'Why do I call you Silje, when Dag and Liv call you Mother?' she asked.

Silje took her hand. 'It's a long story. You've always called me Silje.'

Both children looked up at her expectantly. 'The other children called Dag and me "bastards" today,' said Sol, her eyes wide and questioning. 'What does it mean?'

Silje felt a chill run down her spine. 'Did they? They had no right to say that.'

She stopped walking. 'All right!' she decided, 'I think you're both old enough to hear the truth. You're seven, Sol, and Dag is nearly five, but I don't think Liv will understand because she's only three.'

She called Tengel's name and he stopped and turned. They had reached their own land now, crossing the meadow beneath the cottage and outbuildings.

'The children were called bastards today!' she said quietly.

'What?!'

'You heard me. They want to know the truth,' she replied. Silje was indignant, but at the same time eager to tell them. 'You take Liv home, and I'll tell the whole story. They're old enough now, don't you think?'

Tengel hesitated, looking at them thoughtfully. 'Yes, I believe it's for the best. I'll come back and join you after I've put this little girl to bed. Come on Liv, You're so sleepy you can hardly keep your eyes open.'

****

They sat down beside the stream on some old logs where their pails of milk were placed to cool. In the background the water bubbled and gurgled softly as Silje began her story

4

and the children sat very still, eager to hear her every word.

'First I must tell you that I am not your real mother, Sol, nor yours, Dag. But I am Liv's mother – I hope that doesn't sadden you.' She paused, her expression anxious. 'I've tried hard to see that you wouldn't miss having your real mothers and I've always loved you both so much – every bit as much as I've loved little Liv. Father feels exactly the same.'

At first the children sat dumbstruck, then in a plaintive voice Sol asked, 'So Tengel isn't our father, then?'

'No. He's Liv's father. You, Sol, have always called him "Tengel".'

'But I don't,' Dag butted in. 'I say "Father".'

'That's because you were much younger when we took you in. Sol was older.'

This wasn't going very well, thought Silje, struggling to find the right words. It was becoming too complicated for comfort for her, but she made one more effort to explain. 'The thing is, we wanted you to be our children more than anything ...'

Sol interrupted her. 'So who is our real mother?' she asked, her voice uncertain. 'Did you just take us away because you wanted us?'

It was so typical of Sol to see right through her fumbled explanation and get to the very heart of the matter, thought Silje, sighing. Although she was only seven, her mind was already much sharper than was normal for that age.

'Of course not, dearest,' replied Silje at last. 'Anyway, you had different mothers.' Despite finding this very difficult, Silje knew without any doubt that she was doing the right thing and she decided to persevere gently. 'Sol – your mother was Tengel's sister, so that makes him your uncle and Liv your first cousin.'

Sol sat motionless, staring into the distance.

5

'Where is she now, then?'

'Your mother, do you mean? In heaven, Sol. She's dead. She died from something called the plague, a terrible sickness. It took your father too, and your little sister called Leonarda. Of course, you can't remember any of it, because you were only two when I found you. You were all alone, and so was I. So it wasn't just you who needed me – I needed you as well. Angelica was the name your mother gave you.'

Sol stared at her intensely, and then her face lit up. She had always been proud of her name, Sol Angelica, and now she was pleased to know why she had been given the second part of it.

Silje tried to think, but her mind wandered as she looked at the girl's dress. Far too short in the sleeves, it would not last much longer. The cloth had almost worn through in places and she had absolutely nothing from which to make a new one. Shaking off the thought, she dragged her mind back to the problem in hand.

'Your mother was very beautiful, Sol. Very, very beautiful. Her hair was jet black and wavy, just like yours, and she had lovely dark eyes.' The child said nothing, but her eyes were brimming with tears. 'Your eyes are lighter though,' added Silje hastily. 'More of a green or yellowish colour – almost like Tengel's.'

The sign that you are of the chosen ones, a descendant of the original Ice People, thought Silje bitterly. Oh, my dear children, what will become of you all?

'What about *my* mother, then?' asked Dag. 'And my father?' He sounded slightly reproachful, as if Silje and Tengel had deprived him of something.

This was more difficult. It would be impossible to tell him his mother had abandoned him in the forest to die.

'Your mother,' she began with a little smile, then waited

as Tengel walked soundlessly towards them across the meadow that was already damp with the evening dew. He sat down with them and Dag clambered into his arms at once, as if needing to reassure himself that he really did have a father.

'Your mother, Dag, was a fine lady,' continued Silje. 'A noblewoman – a baroness. We don't know her name or even if she's still alive – and we don't know where she lives. We only know that something very bad happened to her and she lost you. I don't know how it happened, only that I found you.'

The two children leaned forward, desperate to hear more. She would have to go on.

'It was a strange night, children. It was bitterly cold and bonfires lit up the sky over Trondheim. I had lost my whole family in the plague and was alone in the world. I was hungry, tired and homeless. Then I found you, Sol, beside the dead body of your mother. I took you with me, because I liked you and wanted to help you. You didn't want to leave your mother, but you would have died as well, if you had stayed. So you see why I had to take you with me, don't you?'

Sol nodded solemnly.

'Which farm is called Trondheim?' inquired Dag.

'Trondheim isn't a farm,' said Silje. 'It's a big town – beyond.'

'Beyond what?'

'These mountains.'

The boy looked at her, frowning. 'Is there anything beyond the mountains?'

Silje and Tengel looked at each other in dismay. Here was something they'd overlooked.

'All the great wide world is there,' said Tengel carefully,

troubled by the direction of the conversation. 'But we'll save that for another day. Now let's listen to Silje.'

The cry of a waterfowl, probably a diver, echoed across the lake as mist rose along the water's edge. No one was paying heed to the time, however, on this wonderful, glorious summer evening.

Silje glanced anxiously at Tengel. What was troubling him this evening? For the last few days he'd been so distant. He seemed to be listening for something. What was causing that anxious look in his eyes? She knew her husband well, and understood his ability to sense disharmony in the ley lines of the natural world around him. There seemed to be something that was just beyond his grasp and understanding, and it frightened her a little. She looked away from him.

'Then, Sol,' she continued, 'as you and I were walking along, we found Dag. He was all alone, just like us, but he was so very much younger.' Silje dared not say *how* young he was – that his umbilical cord was still in place! He must never know of his mother's unspeakable wrongdoing. 'In fact it was you who heard him crying, Sol. It's thanks to you that Dag is alive today.'

The children gazed at each other enquiringly, weighing up what they had just been told. Gently, slowly, their hands inched closer until they touched – then their fingers entwined.

It was most often Dag and Liv who kept each other company, Silje reflected. Sol was far too volatile, too mysterious to spend much time with the younger ones. Nevertheless, there was never any doubt that they were all devoted to each other, not least because the harsh conditions here in the wilderness had helped to create a bond of trust between them.

'So all three of us continued walking – well not Dag, of course; I carried him – and we had no idea where we would go or where we might find food, warmth or shelter. Then, suddenly Tengel appeared. None of us had ever met him before.'

A cold shiver went through her as she remembered the events of that night: meeting Tengel for the first time, the gallows, the executioner, the soldiers, the stench from the funeral pyre. She sat upright, straightening her shoulders as if trying to shake off the memory.

'Tengel took care of us,' she said softly, her voice full of tenderness. 'He gave us everything we needed and we've all stayed together ever since – just like a little family.'

Tengel smiled wistfully. He said nothing of his own loneliness, which had been far more wretched than theirs. For a while Silje and the children had suffered loneliness brought about by circumstances and the need to survive, but his had been like a deep wound that never healed. Being so different from other humans, he was constantly aware of how everyone shied away from him. Even now it distressed him to think about that first encounter with Silje and Sol – the way they had both recoiled from his mystifying frightening appearance.

It had been so difficult for him to forget that meeting. The memory of Silje's vulnerable innocent eyes had haunted his loneliness, drawing him to her. Had he wanted to preserve her virtue, only later to defile her himself, he wondered suddenly? No, he was being unfair to himself! He really *had* wanted to protect her, to be selfless and benevolent. His resolve crumbled, at long last, only when he come to realise, to his complete astonishment, that she was deeply attracted to him.

Oh, what a marvellous time that had been, filled equally

with yearning and pain, apprehension and desire, as each of them struggled to understand the other's feelings. All the while he knew fate had decreed that he should resist the attractions of women – yet how could he ever have resisted Silje?

Through his abstraction, Silje's voice came to him again. So swiftly had his thoughts come and gone, that he had missed nothing of what she said.

'Then Liv was born. You remember that, don't you Sol?'

'Yes. When you were sick.'

'That's right.' Sije paused, then said, 'If you like, you can call us Mother and Father, Sol. We feel as though we are your real kin, and we would be too, if it were possible.'

The seven year old thought about this for a while. 'I suppose I could,' she said, nodding wisely, 'but I don't think it would feel right, because I'm used to calling you Silje and Tengel.'

'I understand – and what's more we have always treated each other as friends – sharing things. You know that you have always been a great help to me, don't you?'

Spontaneously, Sol climbed onto Silje's lap and hugged her tight. Silje smiled at Tengel and the smile seemed to celebrate wordlessly the realisation that they had both been jointly accepted as parents.

Dag looked serious, almost brooding, but his long, thin face was so typically aristocratic that it lent an almost comical air to his expression. 'Did my mother come looking for me?' he asked dejectedly.

This was a difficult question.

'No one can say,' answered Tengel quietly. 'All we know is that you had a noble crest embroidered on your clothes. And that is why we believe you may be a baron or some such. We *tried* to find your mother, Dag, but I don't think she's alive any more.'

'Did she die from the plague?'

'Very likely. Which would explain why she lost you. And your father is certainly dead.'

It seemed best to Tengel to tell him that. All the evidence suggested that Dag's mother had not been wed and that he was the result of a short-lived encounter. In any event, right or wrong, Dag appeared to be relaxed about this explanation.

'My real mother and father are dead,' he said sombrely.

'So are mine,' said Sol, managing to shed a tear – but this was for no other reason than that she enjoyed the melodrama.

'I hope you'll both want to stay with us. You will, won't you?' asked Silje quietly, feeling more than just a little anxious.

Both children nodded solemnly.

'Other children's parents are always quarrelling,' said Dag in his ponderous, precocious way, 'as if they didn't like each other. You two never quarrel. You seem to resc… reps…'

'Respect each other?' Tengel finished the word for him. 'Yes, of that you may be certain.'

His loving gaze met Silje's and, without exchanging any further words, she knew that he could see the passion in her eyes.

****

Silje stayed up late that evening. After lighting one of their precious resin torches, she took out her diary – the one given to her by Benedikt the Painter so many years before. There were few pages left to write on and she knew she had faint hope of finding another up in these mountains.

She began the entry: *Todae we tolde the childrin about ther heritag …* and as always, her spelling was hopeless.

When she had finished writing, she snuffed out the flame of the torch and went out into the yard. The summer solstice was approaching and the valley was bathed in the magical shimmering light found only on a Nordic summer evening. The mist from the lake had spread across the meadows, where it fluttered like dancing elves, and a diver's shrill calls might easily have been mistaken for the cries of water nymphs or the souls of lost children. The breeze gently stirred the grass and made unseen eddies around her feet, sighing occasionally as it found its way into the nooks and crannies of the old buildings. In her mind Silje imagined it was the sound of small mischievous trolls or some other supernatural creatures. At that moment an old sway-backed horse plodded along beyond the dry-stone wall, making his way back to his own farm. Could it be that he too was enchanted?

It's almost unbearably beautiful here, she mused, remembering what she had written in her diary. And yet I hate it so much – the feeling of being shut in! I love Tengel and I love my family, but with all my heart I wish that we could leave the Valley of the Ice People. I have nothing in common with these narrow-minded people. They call our children bastards and Tengel a sorcerer, a devil, a wizard and much more besides, although he's never done them any harm – on the contrary – for he never resorts to using the powers I know he possesses. Yet still he remains an outcast in the eyes of many of his kinsmen. There are some that accept us, however, and I thank God for them!

Our best friend Eldrid, Tengel's cousin, is leaving the valley. Her husband wants to make a home in the outside world, hoping that people have forgotten his association with the rebels. If only we could go with them! I feel life here is draining our spirit. We know nothing of events beyond the mountains and, because of the hunger and sickness we have suffered here, we could send no one to help Benedikt and his people. I'd really like to see the King just once in my life, as well. But then he never comes to Norway!

I find my own language becoming poorer and more akin to the Ice People's. We've tried to tutor Sol and Dag, but not only are we reaching the limits of our skills, we are slowly losing what we ourselves have learned. I know Tengel also longs to leave, because he has told me so many times, but he will not put our lives, or the children's lives, in jeopardy. We would be seized at once if we ventured out of the valley and my loved ones would be condemned to be tortured and broken on the rack. Tengel and Sol can never conceal their faces and their kinship with the first Tengel, the evil spirit of the Ice People.

Thinking these thoughts, Silje let out a long woeful sigh. The winters! How she hated and feared the winters. Everything froze, including the food in their pantry, and they lived with the constant worry that their supplies would run out. Last winter's shortage of food haunted Silje like a nightmare – the bewildered look in the children's eyes when they went to bed at night, no less hungry than when they had woken up in the morning; the loaf of bread she had decorated for Christmas – it had been their only food that day.

When she thought of how many more such winters there might be in the years ahead, she felt her chest tighten as she was overcome with anxiety. The urge to run away, anywhere, to leave it all behind and not have to worry any longer, began to take hold. All she wanted was for her nearest and dearest to be safe and well.

She paused and took a few deep breaths to stop herself from suffocating. Whenever the children showed the slightest sign of any illness, she was almost beside herself fearing that they might die. Yet she dared not let anyone see how much it troubled her. The spring thaw, when at last it came, echoed with the awful lament of the melting ice breaking up, while the evenings made her feel despondent and she ached and longed for …

Tengel's gentle touch on her shoulder startled her. 'I saw your bed was empty,' he said quietly. 'What thoughts bring you out here, all alone?'

'Oh … nothing important,' she replied evasively.

'I know what it is, you don't need to tell me. You long to leave the valley, don't you?'

'Tengel, you mustn't think that I've ever had any regrets.'

'Of course I don't think that. I know you have been happy here.'

'Yes, very happy!' she assured him.

'But now, like me, I think you're growing restless, hampered by the way of life here.'

Silje waved her hand fretfully. 'If we had not been *forced* to stay here I would love this valley with all my heart,' she said fervently. 'Life would be perfect if we just spent the summers here. But I resent not being able to choose. It makes me so irritable. I think I both love and hate the place at the same time, Tengel.'

'Yes, I know that feeling well. When I was away I longed to be here, but as soon as I returned I wanted to be gone again. But now it's …' He broke off and fell silent.

Silje looked at him tenderly. 'You're worried. I've seen it in you for many days. I thought it was strange that you did not want to keep any of Eldrid's livestock here, despite their offer to let us have them. It made me think – and hope. Can't you tell me what's wrong, Tengel?'

The night wind ruffled his black hair. 'I don't know,' he

replied slowly, 'I really don't know what it is. Have you listened to the mournful wailing of the wind? Do you not hear the terror of the grass as it rustles or the houses groaning?'

'You know I don't hear those things,' she smiled. 'But Sol feels something. She's so fretful and she often has that faraway look in her eyes.'

'Yes, I sense great peril all around. It haunts me and torments me. If only I knew where it was coming from.'

Choosing her words carefully, Silje said, 'I think you decided to *let* Eldrid take all the animals with her, so some of them would be waiting for us away from the valley.'

'Perhaps,' he said absentmindedly. 'I can't remember what I was thinking of, although maybe I did say to her husband that *if* we were to follow them …'

'Oh, Tengel!'

He shook his head in another sudden gesture of indecision, then continued uneasily. 'Well, the people who are moving into their old cottage will let us have all the milk we want, so we really don't need any livestock now.'

'Yes, they are good people, I suppose, but I don't think I like their children.'

'What do you mean?' he asked quickly.

'Well, they join in with the others in the valley to scorn our little ones,' said Silje with hurt in her voice. 'They call them terrible names, as you heard this evening. What's more, their parents won't let them play with Sol and Dag and Liv. It grieves me so, Tengel.'

Through gritted teeth he said, 'They're scared of Sol, aren't they? Oh, I well remember that happening to me as a child! Always left out and feared by everyone.'

'Sol is dangerous,' Silje whispered. 'Do you remember what she did when the neighbours' daughter kicked Liv?'

Tengel shuddered.

'Don't talk about it. She has awful powers within her.'

'She made a doll that looked like the girl and held it over the fire. The girl burned herself on hot coals that very same day and suffered horribly.'

'Until I managed to make the doll harmless,' added Tengel grimly.

'Yes, but what made her think of doing such a thing?'

Tengel took a deep breath. 'Do you want to know what I've found out?'

'What is it? You're scaring me.'

'You know how Sol often disappears? And we used to think she was out playing. Do you know where she was?'

Silje shook her head.

'With old Hanna!'

'Oh no,' said Silje in a hushed voice, looking horrified. Then she nodded slowly. 'It's true Hanna has always been fond of Sol – and Liv too, since she helped to bring her into the world. Whenever we go and take food for her and Grimar she always calls them "my girls". She doesn't seem to care so much for Dag.'

'I'm glad that the girls have always meant so much to Hanna,' said Tengel nodding. 'But it scares me as well. I don't like to think of Sol going there alone.'

'Do you believe that the old witch is … tutoring Sol?'

'I fear she might be. She knows that Sol has powers, of that there can be no doubt.'

'Oh, but that is awful!'

Silje was standing with her back against the wall of the cottage. Tengel leaned forward and caressed her shoulders. 'Dearest Silje, what fate have I brought upon you?'

'Now, you stop talking like that. No one has brought me as much happiness as you. When I'm away from you, even for an hour, I grow sick just yearning for you.'

'You were no more than sixteen summers when I took you for my own. Now you are twenty-one and have toiled with us all these years. Yet still I know that your destiny lies elsewhere – not in the boredom and hard work found in a lowly cottage.'

'I hope you don't think I've been grumbling too much. I know my skills as a housewife are still poor. The children grow out of their clothes and shoes so fast that it pains me not to be able to find them new ones. I dislike housework so much that I grow tired at the very thought of it, Tengel. You know that. To be able to weave cloth, but not sew it properly into clothes for the children, depresses me. Anyway it won't matter. Since the winter killed off all the sheep in the valley, there will be no wool to weave. They mock Sol horribly for wearing that old coat I patched up last year – and often I have forgotten to wash the clothes … Oh, I'm sorry for grumbling again – I didn't mean to.'

His tender smile displayed limitless understanding, but also helplessness. He pressed his lips against her hair. 'Do you think I don't understand you? That I don't know how much you long to create things or paint pictures? Or that you write in your book at night when we are all in bed?'

'You know about my book?' she asked, aghast.

'Oh yes. I know where you keep it hidden as well – but I'd never allow myself to read it. You must let no one else know of it! A young woman writing in a book – now that's truly the work of Satan. They'd have you burned at the stake in the blinking of an eye.'

'There is so much evil in the world! I forget how this valley preserves us from it,' she said in surprise, as though this was a revelation. 'I really wouldn't have minded if you'd read it,' she continued hurriedly. 'I was looking through it the other night and every page was filled with love for you and all my family.'

'You like to write, don't you?'

'Oh, yes! It gives me room to breathe. What's more, when I read what I have written, I am surprised by how well composed it all is.'

'I'm not surprised at all. You speak very well, unlike the other people here in the valley. Now you're making me curious. I'd love to look at it.'

She giggled, embarrassed yet pleased and encouraged by what he had said. 'Oh, I'm sure all the spelling is horribly wrong,' she replied. 'I never learned to spell properly – I just write down the words the way they sound … Tengel! What are you doing?'

His hands had started to move down across her body and, with a soft chuckle, he pressed her harder against the wall. Still heady at the thought he might decide that they should leave, Silje made no attempt to stop his advances. Surrendering to the moment she relaxed gently against him.

As he leaned closer, his cheek brushed her forehead. Tengel was always clean-shaven. She knew this was because he was well aware of being sixteen years older than she was and did not want to look older than his years. A beard would do too much to emphasise the difference in their ages.

'We really ought to have kept an eye on Benedikt and his farm as well,' she continued, deciding to press home her advantage now that she sensed his attitude about travelling was changing. 'I worry about them a lot.'

'Yes, yes I know,' mumbled Tengel absently. 'If only I could decide what to do for the best – to take all of us away from here, or to stay. You know that beyond those mountains there is nowhere for us to live.'

The touch of his fingertips excited her skin; his caresses, light and sensitive, were creating small tremors all through her. Her body began to respond as the sensations grew and converged in one specific part of her. How was it that her passion never diminished for this man, who in the eyes of others appeared so frightening? It was not simply the fact that, as a man, nature had endowed him so well – she could not have known that when they first met. No, it was almost enough just to look at him, for an urgent craving to sweep through her, leaving her weak and completely at his mercy. Indeed at that moment she realised she was having great difficulty concentrating on her train of thought!

'But what about Benedikt?' she asked breathlessly, 'couldn't he find us somewhere to stay?'

'We don't even know if he's still alive – and that horrible Abelone woman will give us short shrift. No, Silje – I have thought many times that we ought to leave here, but the risk is still one I dare not take.'

Silje's voice was becoming muffled with her mounting passion. 'But another winter like this last one – I don't think I could stand it.'

'Yes, I know. That's what I have been thinking about.' Suddenly his lips were everywhere – on her forehead, her temples, and she closed her eyes ecstatically.

'What are we doing?' she giggled, finding it hard to catch her breath. 'We are a sensible old couple and we've been married for years! Still, it's quite exciting to be out here in the open.'

She eased herself up onto the low wall surrounding the cottage and pulled up her skirts. Instantly he grasped her hips, his hands hot and probing, supporting her. His kiss was deep and seemed to last forever.

'This isn't like you, Silje,' he whispered breathlessly in her ear, surprised at her unexpected enthusiasm. 'These past few years you've been so – well, so hesitant.'

'Maybe I have,' she agreed, surprised that he hadn't

already guessed what lay behind her eager passion. Her hands caressed his body until finally she guided him to her, gasping with expectation as she did so. 'I didn't mean to be, but I was frightened.'

Tengel's movements were unhurried and gentle. 'I know. You were afraid of being with child again, it goes without saying. I too felt that same fear a hundred-fold.'

'The memory of Liv's birth is the worst horror in my life,' she whispered. 'I didn't want to go through it again.'

'I understand,' he muttered. 'But we've been very careful – and it's worked.'

'Hmmm,' she murmured, and the sound could have meant anything or nothing.

As she pressed her moist lips against his throat, Tengel's memories of the first passionate year with her were rekindled. He pushed her harder up against the wall and lifted her legs, wrapping them around his waist.

With an embarrassed laugh, Silje whispered, 'Your spear has pierced me – pinned me to the wall – a sacrifice to my unbounded passion.'

'Oh, such language!' he grinned, but she could see that he was aroused and pleased by it.

Silje closed her eyes again, unable to speak, and a soft, languorous smile spread across her face. Tengel looked down at her and saw she was ready for him. She had not succumbed to her desires so completely for a long time and he began to wonder what had caused this. Then in another moment he could wonder no longer because the dark timbers of the cottage walls seemed suddenly clouded in a magical mist and a familiar, exquisite dizziness took rough hold of him. An unbearable urgency began to rage within him, mounting in a long, slow gradual crescendo before finally leaving him spent and helpless.

'Oh Silje,' he whispered. 'Silje, Silje – my beloved little

flower. How is it that one so delicate, so frail can hold such fascination? It must surely be a form of magic.'

****

Some time later, Eldrid left the valley. Without any ceremony she and her husband set off down the tunnel beneath the glacier, taking with them all their chattels and leading a train of livestock, bound for an uncertain future in a hostile world.

Silje sobbed after they had gone, and later that evening, she asked Tengel, 'Why didn't you want to keep any of their livestock? They're ours by right anyway. Tell me the real reason!'

The children were playing outside and Tengel was sitting quietly mending the fishing net while Silje cleared the supper table. Lifting his head, he sighed, 'You know you don't like hearing me talk of such things.'

'But this time I want you to.'

'Oh, as you wish, you obstinate girl. I felt that – hindrance again.'

'Hindrance? Oh, I see. Something within you made you resist when Eldrid offered to leave you some of the animals.'

'Yes. I've never felt it so strongly as I did then. So I let them go.'

'Yet still you don't want to leave the valley?'

'Even if I did, I would first have to go on my own and carefully search out a place where we could live. But there *is* nowhere, my dearest. The descendants of Tengel the Evil One are hunted everywhere. Oh, everything seems so hopeless!'

'I know how you feel,' said Silje quietly.

She stole a glance at him. Could he really know nothing? Had he not suspected or sensed her condition? With all her heart, she hoped not.

She felt so afraid – afraid for her life – but more than that, she was afraid Tengel would find out. After the awful, difficult birth of Liv he had vowed, 'Never again! Never – never! If it happens again, Silje, I'll kill the unborn within you, quickly and painlessly with one of my potions. Next time it will do no good to pray for the child!'

There was no denying that she had carefully and anxiously examined her food for signs that he had sprinkled a powder over it, but he obviously suspected nothing. Not even when they made love outside in the yard had he realised why she had thrown caution to the wind, despite being surprised by her apparent wantonness.

Of course she knew it was mad to try to nurture this new life inside her! She knew there was a chance it might turn out to be a monster, a half-human descendent of the first Tengel – a mutation like Hanna or Grimar – or worse still, the woman down by the lake. Silje had only seen her once when Eldrid had wanted some eggs and cheese taken down to the woman. When Silje left the lakeside dwelling she had been almost numb with terror, knowing that something so primitive, so unspeakable could exist. An aura of absolute evil had surrounded the woman. Although she was no longer alive, the experience had made Silje realise just how little Tengel and Sol had been tainted by their evil heritage, even though most people, apart from herself, regarded Tengel as hideous and terrifying.

There was also one more uncertainty. Silje would probably not live through another childbirth, and this fear was uppermost in Tengel's mind. Thankfully Hanna's intervention had saved her the first time, but should she try to give birth to one of those 'beasts' – one with Tengel's abnormally broad, angular shoulders – it would be impossible for her to survive. Tengel's own mother had bled to death bringing him into the world, although Sol's mother had survived, possibly because her daughter was of a more delicate build. Yet Sol too carried the unmistakable signs of the heritage that lived within her. The awful power of witchcraft and her face, with those cat-like eyes, immediately betrayed her ancestry. This was the seven-year-old girl that Silje was thinking of taking back to Tröndelag, where the Ice People were ruthlessly hunted down!

Eldrid would be all right. Her features looked normal and she was not one of the chosen, despite being a direct descendent of Tengel the Evil. Liv bore none of the signs either. But what did Silje know about the child now forming itself inside her? It had been growing for almost four months. Concealing her pregnancy from Tengel had been difficult, but luckily she hadn't suffered such dreadful early bouts of sickness this time. At the moment it was relatively easy to dissemble and disguise its presence, although soon, very soon it would start to show.

Then two days later they received a visit that was both unexpected and disturbing. A man who had hardly ever set foot beyond the boundary of his own farmstead and who had never visited them before came to see them. Nothing was said or done in advance to herald his visit. Yet his arrival, when he appeared, filled Silje with an immediate and dreadful foreboding. What on earth, she wondered, could this mean?

Chapter 2

At first, Silje couldn't make out who was struggling up the hill. But at last, as the bent figure came closer, she recognised him. Now she could see his protruding eyes and the grotesque wart-covered head that in her mind resembled an overgrown turnip. It was none other than Grimar.

Silje suspected the worst as she curtseyed and welcomed this relative of Tengel and Hanna. She invited him into the cottage, but he shook his head. 'Hanna bade me come,' he growled as he stood in the yard looking like a pile of filthy rags. 'She wants to speak wi' you – all o' you!'

'Thank you,' replied Silje calmly, although the unexpected invitation struck fear into her heart. 'We shall be pleased to visit her.'

'There'll not be feasting,' he added swiftly.

'Of course not. Not when old Mother Hanna is bedridden.' Silje hesitated, gathering her thoughts, then added, 'Tengel and the boy are out in the forest gathering wood and will be back before long. The girls and I will put on some better clothes. Will you not sit awhile, Uncle Grimar, and take food while you wait? We can all go back together.'

The repulsive creature, whose clothes might have been fashioned from mouldy cloth held together by spiders' webs, hesitated and gave Silje an inquiring glance. His amazed expression said silently, 'You're asking me into your home? No one has ever done that!'

'Well, I s'pose I might,' he muttered and shuffled inside, accompanied by an overpowering foetid stench.

Before they had time to make any embarrassing comments, Silje herded the girls into the back room to put on the somewhat forlorn Sunday pinafores she had made to hide their tattered everyday clothes. Straightaway she began to set the table for the old man with the best food they had. Sadly it was not much because, like so many other residents of the valley, they had run short during the harsh winter. Nevertheless she had ale, bread-cakes – made from the last sweepings of corn from the floor of the barn – and goats' milk cheese. She even brought out the last few precious cloudberries that she had been saving since the previous autumn.

Eagerly Grimar helped himself to the food and the noise of his eating could be heard throughout the cottage. Silje left him and went to see if the girls had finished dressing and quickly combed their hair.

'You two go out and talk to Uncle Grimar while I put on some other clothes,' she whispered when she saw that they were ready. 'Liv, you must say nothing about the way he looks or smells! Sol, you will behave won't you?'

'Of course, we know each other well,' she said precociously.

I'm sure you do, thought Silje wryly, and she was very relieved when finally Tengel arrived.

Almost at once they all set off with Grimar, who by now was a well fed old man, huffing and puffing as he tramped along at their side. Dag had not welcomed the unexpected visit – he was quite fastidious, and dirt and disorder made him feel uncomfortable. Tengel had found it necessary to place one hand hastily over the boy's mouth to stifle an uncomplimentary outburst. Now, suitably chastened, he walked in dignified silence at Silje's side, as far away from the old man as possible.

As expected, Hanna greeted them from her bed when they entered. By the dim flickering light of the fire, Silje could clearly see that she had aged greatly. The years were eventually catching up on the old witch – she was after all one generation older than her nephew Grimar and two older than Tengel. Silje was thankful for the lack of light, for while she considered Grimar repulsive to look at, Hanna was ten times worse! Here before her lay the very worst of Tengel the Evil's legacy.

'So – you've arrived at last!' snapped the old hag. 'I thought you'd never get here.'

'Silje offered me vittles, Hanna,' said Grimar excitedly. The rarity of the event had made him quite emotional.

Hanna was unmoved. 'And well I know it,' she hissed. 'They feed all their guests well and I have eaten there more times than you – when I pulled this little girl of Silje's out into the world. Oh, yes! I've seen how well they live.'

With the matter of prestige now firmly settled, she turned on her visitors. 'Tengel, you are a stupid fool! Why did you not take your family and leave with Eldrid?'

No one else but Hanna would ever have treated Tengel like an errant child. However, he did not seem to be unduly taken aback by the question.

'Should I have?' he asked coolly.

'You know full well that you ought to have gone. Sol knew it as well.'

The children stood in respectful silence at the door. Dag,

26

more sensitive than the others, was not enjoying the spectacle at all.

'I was filled with uncertainty,' Tengel answered. 'So many perils await us there.'

'Stupid! Always stupid!' she said scornfully. 'Always worrying about this thing or that. People like *us* cannot afford to be worthy! This you know. Yet you – you are both worthy *and* stupid. Stand up for your kith and kin, man! Now listen!' She leaned forward, adding weight to her words. 'I know that you have also sensed something, and that is why you let the livestock go. That was a wise thing to do. Now you must prepare to leave as well – without delay!'

Tengel stood motionless, his face showing no expression. 'But what of you, Old Mother Hanna? And Grimar?'

She sank back against the pillow. 'Aasch! We are old. But the children, and your wife … Come closer, Silje!'

The small dark room was filled with an unworldly aura, as though spirits lay in wait, crouched in every dark nook and cranny, watching them. Was someone weeping somewhere, mourning the loss of a way of life – mourning the past?

Fighting to hide her revulsion, Silje moved closer to the hideous creature lying on the bed. She kept reminding herself that Hanna had once saved her life, as well as the life of her daughter Liv. The next moment the witch's cold gnarled fingers grasped Silje's hands.

'You and your children, Silje, have been … they've been … Oh! It is of no matter!' Pointing to Tengel she continued, 'Promise only that you will make this half-wit of a man take you and the children away from this valley!' Her voice faded to a whisper. 'For this time I shall not be able to help you.'

Silje twitched – Hanna knew! But of course she did. Hanna always knew. She squeezed the old woman's hands tightly, as if to warm them. Then in a loud voice she asked, 'Why do you believe we should leave, old Mother?'

Hanna looked directly at Tengel. 'Do you not know?'

'No,' he replied. 'I sense great fear and anguish, but no more than that.'

The ancient crone nodded in agreement, adding, 'But I sense far more than that. I can feel that one of our kin from the Valley of the Ice People is in distress. Great distress.'

'Heming?' Tengel said quietly. It was a statement as much as a question.

'Yes, it *is* Heming – the worthless wretch! Would that he had been stifled at birth.'

There had been no news of Heming for several years and it was assumed that he had left Tröndelag – or perhaps been killed – long ago.

'Now perhaps you can understand why you ought to leave.'

'I can. But do you think there is danger? Here?'

Hanna threw back her head in a gesture of impatience and dismissal. 'Why have I called you to me, eh? Time is pressing. I feel it like a fire that burns inside me.'

'Then I shall give thought to what you say.'

'Then think quickly, very quickly! Now be gone and leave your – or should I say your sister Sunniva's – daughter Sol here with me for a moment. I need to speak with her alone.'

'But Mother Hanna!' Tengel objected.

'It does not concern you!' the old witch screamed in a voice that chilled the blood. 'That such fine girls should be related to such a cretin! Off with you! And mind you take good care of little Liv Hanna, my goddaughter.'

Awkwardly Tengel bade farewell. He and Hanna had never been able to agree about anything. She was the witch who fought to keep alive the evil legacy, while he was the friend of humanity, mercilessly afflicted by his ancestry, trying to prevent it from spreading.

On an impulse, Silje bent forward and kissed the old woman's withered cheek and as she did so, she saw that the crone's eyes were glistening – brimful of tears.

'You go on,' said Grimar, bidding them farewell. 'Sol will catch up with you.'

Once they had started back on the road home, Silje said, 'My heart is filled with sadness, Tengel. Your unease has touched me too! And poor Grimar – I know nothing about him; he has always stood in Hanna's shadow. Today I saw him as a separate being for the first time, and I feel so sorry for him!'

'Well, you shouldn't,' said Tengel curtly. 'Grimar is Hanna's lackey and when she commands, he obeys – with pleasure! The Ice People keep the secret of his deeds. Folk have disappeared and other terrible things have happened about which none dares to speak aloud. Yet nobody will challenge or stop him because he does Hanna's bidding – and everyone is wary of *her*. Only a fool would not be.'

Despite Tengel's outburst, she said, 'Well, I cannot help but feel sorry for him – for both of them.'

'No matter. It is fortunate we are in their favour,' conceded Tengel, 'and that is in no small part your doing.'

'Those people were horrible,' said Dag. 'Are we going to leave our home?'

'I don't know,' answered Tengel slowly.

'Oh yes we are!' interrupted Silje. 'We are definitely leaving …'

'But where shall we go?' objected her husband. 'Are our children going to suffer a life of utter misery because of us?'

Silje was deaf to his protests. 'We are going! And wherever we go, we will start to pack this very day.'

'All right,' sighed Tengel. 'As you wish.'

****

As soon as the decision had been taken, Tengel acted with feverish urgency. He spent the whole day sorting through the cottage and outhouses, carefully selecting and packing the things they would need. 'It will be a few days before we can leave,' he declared. 'I need to catch more fish and I must barter for more meat and other vittles with the neighbouring farms. The shafts on the cart need fixing as well.'

'That's good. Then I will have time to wash all our clothes.' said Silje. Looking at the pile of things to be thrown away she exclaimed, 'Good Heavens! What a lot of rubbish we have collected.'

'Yes,' Tengel agreed, 'it's hard to believe, but tomorrow we can burn it all.' Carefully lifting the pretty glazed, leaded mosaic from its shelf, he added, 'We must take this with us.'

'Oh, yes. You remember when you said it was destined for a different house?'

'Perhaps I was right after all,' he said, but his voice suggested he still had his doubts. Then he reached up and took down one more thing. 'And what about this?'

With a broad grin he held her book aloft. Silje reached out and took it from him, placing it among the items to be taken with them. 'Of course. But we don't need to take everything with us, do we? We shall be coming back – for the summers?'

'I truly hope that we shall,' replied Tengel, 'I am pleased that you would want to.'

She glared at him. 'I *love* this wonderful valley, the lake and the mountains. I love the uplands with their yellow mountain violets, and those tiny, impossibly blue flowers – you know the ones I mean? I just don't want to be forced to live here. What's more, I could happily live apart from the people in the valley – some of them anyway.'

'On that we are agreed,' smiled Tengel, hurriedly snatching a kiss before the children came in.

Silje brought out the carved casket Tengel had given her as a wedding gift. 'Because I plucked the lily before I had God's blessing,' he had said on giving it to her. It had never occurred to Silje that she could probably have carved it far more artistically, had she wished, and it was one of her most treasured possessions. Wistfully she folded the blanket and covers that the new-born Dag had been wrapped in when she found him and placed them on the pile of things that they would never leave behind. 'That's enough for now,' she said quietly. 'The little ones must prepare for bed. They are so worked up about the packing.'

'Yes, the sun is behind the mountains,' observed Tengel. 'This will never do. Where can they be?'

As the two of them stepped out into the yard to look, the three children came rushing wildly towards them round the corner of the cottage. 'Father! Mother!' they shouted. 'Come and see quickly! There's a fire!'

Silje and Tengel ran out of the yard and heard terrible screams coming from the end of the valley closest to the entrance to the ice tunnel that led under the glacier. In sharp relief against the evening clouds they saw flames flickering skyward through a thick pall of smoke.

'Oh my God!' whispered Tengel.

'It's the cottage that guards the tunnel,' cried Silje. 'We must run and help!'

'No!' All colour had drained from Tengel's face. 'Look, it's not only there. Hanna's cottage is burning too – and the Bratten's farm.' His voice rose to a shout. 'We'll never get through there, Silje. It's too late!'

'Oh no,' she groaned. 'Has Heming done this?'

'Yes, he's been captured yet again – and this time he has betrayed us all to save his cowardly skin. I'll wager he wanted revenge too – for that thrashing I gave him when he set upon you. I should have heeded my inner voice. I should have listened to you and Hanna. She was right, I *am* a fool. God, what are we going to do?'

'Hanna's house?' wailed Sol. 'My Hanna's house is burning! I must go to her!'

Tengel grabbed her and held her back. Sol sank her teeth into him, but he ignored it. This was not the time to get angry with her.

'We saw a lot of men by the ice gate,' said Dag, 'and their hats were all shiny.'

'Soldiers' helmets!' Finally Tengel's mind had begun to grasp the situation. 'Hurry! We must get away from here and we must hide. Luckily our cottage is at the top end of the valley, so they will come here last of all. But we are the ones they're after – we are the blood line of Tengel the Evil.'

'Where can we go?' asked Silje, her desperate tone indicating she was prepared for anything.

'Into the forest. There is nowhere else.' Tengel's voice was filled with anxiety. 'But I don't know how long we can hide there.'

'What about the pass?'

Tengel stopped and thought for a moment. 'Leave through the mountains, you mean? Yes! Yes, you're right. The journey will be a nightmare, but we must try. The birch forest will give us cover for the first part of the way. I'll saddle the horse, while you gather up only the most vital things – as little as possible. We will be sleeping outside, so bring some rugs and furs. Children, help your mother! We have so little time left.'

Realising the danger she found herself in, Sol stopped trying to run off. Sobbing uncontrollably, she could only cast sorrowful glances down the valley towards where Hanna's cottage was now rapidly becoming engulfed in flames.

****

They hurried to and fro, carrying out their tasks swiftly and efficiently. There was no time to stop and think – they had to hurry – and Silje was reminded of a similar occasion when they had fled from Benedikt's farm, although on this occasion there was a much greater need for urgency and the situation was far more frenzied.

'My cat!' shouted Sol. 'Has anyone seen her?'

Silje, loving animals as she did, understood the girl's sense of panic. 'Look in the empty barn. And when you find her, put her in this sack.'

Sol tore the sack from her mother's hands and raced off.

'We ought to warn the neighbours,' said Silje as she went out to Tengel with another load.

'There is no time for that.'

'But what about their livestock?'

'The soldiers will take them – they are too valuable to be left unattended.' Tengel grimaced when he saw Silje was carrying a large doll. 'Oh no! This doll's far too big to take.'

'We mustn't leave Liv's doll behind, we just can't!'

Tengel had carved the wooden doll and Silje had made clothes for it. Liv adored it.

'No, you are right, we can't,' he agreed. 'Was that the last bundle?'

'I think so. Now let us be gone. At once!'

'The book is there – so are Dag's clothes and your

wedding gift. Silje you're so fond of useless things with sentimental value – but I love you for it. Wait, you've forgotten the glazed mosaic!'

'We cannot take that as well.'

'We have to,' said Tengel and ran back inside, shouting, 'Get the children into the saddle!'

Silje hoisted up the two youngest children, thinking that she wasn't the only one fond of useless items. How would he get the mosaic onto a horse?

'Sol! Sol! Where are you?' she yelled. 'For God's sake come on!'

Sol reappeared from the barn in tears. 'I can't find her!' she cried just as Tengel emerged from the house to fasten the mosaic to the rest of the baggage.

'The cat?' he asked. 'She was behind the workshop a minute ago, hunting for mice.'

Sol rushed away again and returned a few minutes later proudly grasping the sack in front of her, just as the rest of them were setting off. A coal-black tail thrashed angily through the top of the sack, displaying to the world how unjust humans could be in disturbing a great mouse-hunt!

'Well, thank heavens for that,' Silje sighed.

Soon after they left the farmyard they were swallowed up from view by the forest of birch.

'We have too little food with us,' Silje told Tengel anxiously. 'Grimar ate the cloudberries and almost everything else. I was going to bake more bread tomorrow.'

'That can't be helped. We at least have *some* food with us, don't we?'

'Of course, but it won't last long.'

****

The Valley of the Ice People now lay beneath them under a thick pall of smoke, but this did not prevent the sounds of the raging fires and panic-filled screams from reaching them. Silje had to run in an effort to keep up with the horse and she was constantly fighting down a wave of nausea brought on by a mixture of fear for her family and pity for those left behind. Tengel drove the horse onward outpacing her, whilst the three children perched on its back had to cling on tightly. Her breathing became painful, burning in her throat and making her chest ache as she struggled to carry the belongings that they had been unable to put on the horse. So many things we've had to leave behind, she thought, so much of the past abandoned.

She felt like shouting, 'Wait, I can't keep up! I have another child to think of!' But she said nothing, knowing that each moment was precious. She could imagine no situation more desperate than the one in which they now found themselves – running uphill like this over rough ground with the threat of certain death close behind them, driven on by blind panic, fighting for the strength to go on.

Noticing how far Silje was lagging behind, Tengel eventually stopped and waited for her to catch up. As she passed an opening between the trees, Silje turned and looked back. She was wheezing badly, trying to catch her breath, and what she saw almost caused her legs to buckle beneath her. Every farmstead now stood in flames, including the chieftain's house with its beautiful woodcarvings. And there – yes! Their house as well! Tengel's childhood home was ablaze!

'Oh, Tengel!' she wailed.

'We must go on,' he said sharply. 'Hurry!'

'Do you think they are following us?'

'Maybe not yet. Who can say? Come on.'

Her rest had been short-lived. Tengel had barely waited for her to make up ground and then started off again – so he had rested, while she had not. The uphill trek became a nightmare. Occasionally she caught sight of the countryside stretching away below them in the fading light. Then suddenly she saw something that made the hairs on the nape of her neck stand on end.

'Tengel!' she called. 'Look!'

He stopped and muttered something inaudible through clenched teeth. From the direction of their cottage, and coming up the hillside behind them, three young lads were running for their lives, closely pursued by a pack of soldiers.

'Poor boys,' groaned Silje. 'Poor, dear boys! But they are leading the guards this way! We shan't be able to escape them!' She turned and half-ran, half-stumbled to reach Tengel and the horse.

'Don't look,' he said to the children as he grasped Silje's hand and urged the horse forward.

A terrible scream of anguish reached them a few moments later and they knew that the boys' attempts to flee had been in vain. Tengel glanced back to where he could see the group of soldiers huddled together in a stationary group. 'The guards are standing talking. We must keep still, we're well hidden from them here.'

The effort required to stand without moving, unable to run away, was almost unbearable, even though the soldiers were still a safe distance away. Silje's lungs ached with every breath she took as she peered between the branches of the birch trees. Fatigue was causing her vision to blur, but she could see guards and soldiers everywhere; a small herd of cattle was also being driven towards the entrance to the ice tunnel. These were probably all the animals that were left after the hard winter. There was no sign of the people of the valley and Silje shuddered violently.

'I don't know what's happened to those soldiers who were behind us,' said Tengel uneasily. 'Either they're still following us or they've gone back down. Whichever it is, we must keep going as fast as we can.'

They climbed steadily higher and as they did so their progress became slower and slower. Silje fell behind once more, suffering now from cramps in her stomach. She started to worry about the tiny life within her that she had been trying so hard to conceal; every heartbeat throbbed through her brain, her legs had lost all feeling and each breath was torture – but still Tengel pressed on relentlessly.

They had reached the edge of the forest and would now have to continue across open countryside. The midsummer twilight would not be dark enough to conceal them from any watching eyes. At that point, beside the last trees, Silje gave up. Overcome with nausea, she collapsed behind a large boulder vomiting uncontrollably, the pain in her belly more than she could bear.

Finally she got to her feet again and wiped the sweat from her face. She took a couple of deep breaths and then staggered backwards, losing her balance. Tengel was coming towards her. 'Well, now, my young woman,' his tone was worryingly calm, 'is there something you should be telling me?'

There was no strength left in her legs and her willpower was completely drained. 'Yes,' she sobbed.

He put his arm around her and helped her back to where the horse was waiting. 'Silly thing!' he said lovingly. 'Silly thing! And you were going to say nothing at all?'

'No!' she replied sniffing and wiping her nose. 'We are not in agreement.'

'No, we are not, but now is not the time to think about it. You must not fear me, dearest! Now you must have help.'

'You were walking so quickly,' she choked back another sob. 'I couldn't keep up with you.'

'I did not notice. I was fearful for the children and desperate to get away from the soldiers. Forgive me, my dearest! Sol and Dag, climb down from the horse. Mother must climb up and rest.'

They started off again, but their progress was much slower with Silje riding and the two children on foot. Silje felt guilty about this, despite knowing that she barely had strength enough to cling to the horse. Little Liv was perched behind her, small hands gripping the waistband of her skirts.

She looked down at the others. Tengel and the children were all wearing tunics and cowls that covered their shoulders. They had pulled these off their heads to let them hang down their backs, now that they were beginning to feel warm from their exertions. Both the children had grim expressions on their faces, as they trudged determinedly onward and Silje could not help wondering what they might be thinking or how much they understood. Inside its sack, the cat hissed angrily, causing Sol's grip to tighten still further.

Without thinking, Silje glanced back the way they had come. 'Tengel! They will see us! We can look down over the whole valley.'

'There is too much smoke down there.'

'But what if someone has come up above the smoke – looking for us?'

'You keep going,' he said as he stopped abruptly.

Silje turned to see what he was doing and felt a chill run through her veins. He was standing on the edge of a precipice, looking down into the valley far below, with both arms outstretched in front of him, palms forward, as though trying to bar the way to an intruder. A strange authority, an air of majesty, seemed to surround him.

Silje had rarely witnessed him practising the powers he was said to command, but she realised immediately that this was what he was doing. Then, to her horror, Sol walked over and stood beside Tengel, glancing briefly up at him before stretching out her arms just as he had done.

Silje dared not move for fear of disturbing the pair of them. Dag and Liv were also watching in wonderment, almost in veneration, and nobody could deny that Tengel and Sol, standing tall and dominant, were imposing something powerful but indefinable on their surroundings. Finally Tengel lowered his arms and released his pent-up breath. Sol followed suit and together they walked back to the others. Sol joined her brother and Tengel made his way to where Silje sat with Liv on the horse and they resumed their journey once more.

'What were you doing?' Silje asked softly after a while. 'Did you make us invisible to them?'

Despite his wry smile, Tengel's eyes had a sombre expression. 'Nothing quite so extreme – no one can do that! I tried to force all thoughts of looking up here out of their heads.'

This was very hard for her to grasp. 'A bit like reading their minds, you mean?'

'You might say something like that. Or call it hypnosis – directing their minds – something of that kind.'

'Do you think that it worked?'

'I can't say,' he replied with an awkward chuckle. 'I don't know the strength of my power, I simply did my best.'

'And Sol, did she know what she was doing?'

Tengel shuddered. 'Of that I'm certain. A mighty force was binding us to each other. We understood and sustained one another. But, Silje, I fear for that girl!'

Silje's reply was slow and deliberate. 'She has a large bundle of things hidden among the baggage.'

'I know. Hanna gave it to her.'

'Had you thought to let her keep it?'

'Had you?' he asked instantly.

'That is something *you* must decide. Have you ever wondered whether it is all Hanna's – what shall I call it? Has Sol inherited Hanna?'

'I am certain of it. I have been sure for a long time that Hanna had chosen Sol as her successor. There was a time, many years ago, when she tried to persuade me to be her successor, but I refused. Since that day she has hated me. Sol was the answer to her wishes and there are certain to be extremely valuable things in that bundle. There will be salves and remedies, otherwise forgotten and no longer used, which must not leave the protection of the family. I expect Hanna kept herself alive just long enough to find a person to pass them on to. So I do not want to take the bundle from Sol just yet.'

'No,' she said, 'you're right. Come on, children! Try to keep up!'

They began to walk faster. Although the evening light had faded, the night sky at that time of year never became completely dark. This was a blessing, for they had almost reached the mountain pass.

'Do you think you will get the horse through?' asked Silje, her voice betraying a note of doubt as she took in the threatening mass of jagged rock rearing above the crevice through which they would have to pass.

'I'll try, or else he will have to be left behind.'

'Here? Alone in this deserted valley and unable to leave? We can't do that!'

'That wasn't what I meant, Silje.'

She stared at him, aggressive and defiant. She knew what he was thinking.

'The horse will get through,' she said tersely. 'We need him, don't we?'

'True.'

'And he needs us!'

Tengel looked away, hiding the trace of a smile at her determination. It had turned her cheeks a bright crimson and he knew that she would fight to the last to save the horse. Tears welled up and he was overcome with great affection for his young wife. Then he blinked quickly and brushed the tears from his face.

****

Step by step they trudged onwards, around and over the harsh and jagged rocks, only to find themselves again and again trapped in a morass. Each time they carefully retraced their steps to find a better way forward. There was no doubt that the horse presented the greatest problem, but by this time they were all determined to get the creature over the pass. Then, in due course, came the inescapable moment when they stopped and took a final sorrowful look back towards the devastated Valley of the Ice People.

Although it was almost totally concealed by the blanket of smoke spreading along the length and breadth of the valley, they knew that their abandoned home lay hidden from view somewhere far below – a home to which they would never return!

They stood in silence for a long time. Dag tried not to let

his sobs be heard, but he understood their predicament very well. Tengel put a hand on his shoulder.

'I shall miss the valley,' said Silje surprisingly. 'It holds many good memories. We, this little family, were safe and happy there.'

Tengel nodded, 'Yes, we were.'

'So we should not hold a grudge against those children that tormented and bullied ours. They had little of which to be proud and needed a scapegoat, the way people often do. As kindred blood to Tengel the Evil, it was easy for them to pick on our little ones.'

'Yes. The poor children.'

Silje realised he didn't mean their own children. 'Tengel,' she blurted out suddenly, her voice overcome with sorrow, 'do you recall what Hanna once told us? That we were the only Ice People! We and no others!'

'I do. And now I fear we know what she meant.'

'Has nobody been spared? Oh, Tengel, it does not bear thinking about – I find it hard to catch my breath!'

In her mind's eye she saw the faces of people she knew: the children, their parents, the horrible events. She felt faint. No, she could not, *would* not allow herself to dwell on this. She straightened up and took a deep breath. 'But what about Eldrid and her husband? She at least was of the Ice People.'

'Her line dies with her.'

'Heming then?'

'Probably dead by now. To buy one's freedom is not as easy as he thought. It is clear what has happened, as I said before. He was taken prisoner again and betrayed us to save his miserable neck, showed them the way to the Valley of the Ice People: "that rat's nest of witches and sorcerers", as it is called on the outside.'

Silje watched as Sol's small hands tightly twisted the top of the sack she was holding. Between gritted teeth she repeated one word over and over in an almost silent whisper, 'Heming! That's his name. Heming! Heming!'

Dag for his part was far more pragmatic. 'So haven't we been very lucky, really?'

'You could say so, I suppose,' replied Tengel tersely. 'Now come on – we must keep going.'

'All night?'

'Yes, we have to. This is no place to rest, and the sky is light enough to travel by. It's important that we get away as far as possible, just in case they try to follow us. We shall be out on the glacier shortly and it will be dangerous. It is best that I walk in front with a stick and test the surface step by step, so that we don't fall into any ravines hidden by the snow. We must walk in line, one after the other, even the horse. It will be worse for him, because he is heavy and has four legs. We shall bind cloths round his hooves to make them bigger and spread his weight. It will be a long and perilous journey over the glacier, but there is no choice.'

Silje gave a nod. Now on foot, having put the children back on the horse, she walked silently at Tengel's side across the desert of stones that littered the sharp rocky surface of the pass. She led the horse very carefully, so that it would find the firmest footings, but the animal was nervous, continually shying and twitching, fearful of the bleak inhospitable landscape and the ground underfoot. Gradually the Valley of the Ice People, with its cloak of black smoke, faded into the distance behind them and, once they had crested the pass, it was lost entirely from their view.

Chapter 3

Unbeknown to Silje and Tengel, as they continued their dangerous journey high in the mountains, Heming the bailiff-killer was still alive. But just as Tengel had expected, Heming had indeed revealed everything he knew about the valley and how to reach it. He had even described in detail where to find the homesteads of Tengel and Hanna, as these two individuals were believed to be the most evil descendants of Tengel the Evil One. The bitter memory of the humiliation he had suffered when Tengel thrashed him so soundly and caused him to leave the valley, made it easier for him to justify his betrayal of the Ice People to himself.

The bailiff's wife and daughter had both been present at Heming's hearing and this had proved to be his salvation. The women had appealed for mercy to be shown towards this handsome young man and consequently he was discharged and banished from Trondheim, cast out of the city by the guards and soldiers. In his defence it must be said that, having betrayed his kinfolk, he was overcome with guilt and remorse; he could not forget that his father and all his family lived in the hidden valley. But surely no harm would befall them, he tried to reason to himself, because only the witches and warlocks were being sought by the authorities – weren't they? Although he mulled this over in his mind many times, he had eventually found it difficult to persuade himself that this reasoning was truly sound.

Six men had forced their way into Hanna and Grimar's tiny cottage – chosen because they were the bravest among the soldiers. Now, having carried out their orders, this party of six were making their way out of the valley again. They had been discharged ahead of their comrades, because the task they were given had been considered so dangerous. Heming had made a point of giving a special warning for all the soldiers to be especially wary of Hanna.

As they walked along the tunnel beneath the glacier, the soldiers' voices echoed eerily in the silence. 'Huh! That was easy,' declared the youngest of them. 'It was just an old woman. Child's play!' He struck his lance against the icy wall with such force that the sound reverberated deeply through the ice and along the tunnel.

His red-haired companion smirked and asked, 'Did you see how I skewered the old man?'

'Yes,' replied the oldest one among them, speaking a little uneasily. 'But the old woman was scary. She was very strange, she was. I was rooted to the spot when I first caught sight of her.'

'As was I!' chirped in another of them, so fat that the straps on his breastplate were stretched to breaking. 'She was the ugliest thing I have ever seen in my whole life.'

The conversation died away. The spine-chilling unworldly atmosphere down in that frozen burrow evoked memories that none of them wanted to relive. At last one of the men, called Willibert, broke the silence. 'She wasn't a bit afraid either,' he said. 'Did you see how she just stood there by the fire, grinning at us. Her legs could barely hold her, but she stood there just the same. Like she was waiting for us.'

'Yeah! And what about those terrible fingernails she had!' said the last member of the troop, a tall lanky youth. 'She scratched me! Ye gods! How I jumped! She looked more like a half-rotted corpse than a person! I thought they felt like talons, I did. When we grabbed her to get her outside, I had to get behind her. That's when she scratched me.'

'And me,' said another, 'just as I took hold of her arm!'

'Me too, but I just got one scratch from that claw of hers.'

Every one of the soldiers who had come into direct contact with her had found her touch, and her scratching, loathsome. As she was a witch, they knew that she had to be burned alive and they had taken her outside because the hearth in the cottage was not large enough for the job.

'Did you hear what she said when we'd managed to drag her out into the yard and get a torch to her?'

'No?'

'She mumbled, "Now they are free". You might ask yourself what she meant by that.'

'From the look on her face, you'd have thought she'd won a victory over us! Well, I suppose it could be that she was talking about the other one – the warlock. The one that we'd also got to burn? I hope they got him. Still, it's nought to do with us now.'

'Well, we've put an end to the old bat, and that's for sure.'

Silence settled on them again, the awfulness of their deeds still too fresh in their minds, and soon they emerged from the tunnel onto the open flatlands. The summer night was not dark, although the air up there had a chill to which these men from the valleys were not accustomed. Quietly, swiftly, they marched forward and it seemed that they had no more to say to each other.

The youngest of them, however, kept scratching at his arm and muttering to himself. 'Damnation!' he cursed softly. 'This itches all the time.'

Shortly afterwards the red-haired one stopped. 'Wait up! I can't walk so fast.'

'What's with you?' asked the oldest one.

'I think I've got a fever or something.'

The youngest rolled up his sleeve to examine his arm. 'Jesus and Mary!' he cried. 'Look at this!'

On his arm was a hideous suppurating boil. There was another on his underarm. On seeing this, his companions stepped back from him.

'You're pox-ridden, you bastard!'

'No, I ain't. Pox don't look like this – nor the plague neither. These are much bigger. It's – it's – I don't *know* what it is!'

As they resumed their march, the others kept a noticeable distance from him. The short tufted grass of the plain whined and whistled and hissed at their feet, as though cursing their every step.

'Wait!' yelled the red-haired man suddenly. 'I can't go on.'

'What's up with you now?'

'The fever – I'm hotter than the fires of hell. See! Look at my hands! Oh, dear God, now they're covered in these horrible sores! Wait! Wait for me! Don't run! Please, I need your help, can't you see?'

He tried to run after them, but it was too much for him. He stopped – his hands clutching at his chest. When he started off again, the others were a long way ahead, nothing but five small dots fading in the distance. The oaths he screamed after them were lost on the night air.

The pale moon rose and shone down on the red-haired soldier as he lurched and faltered onwards. He had thrown away his helmet and his lank hair was drenched with sweat from the fever and the terror he felt. A thunderous pounding reverberated inside his head. He pulled back his sleeves and found there were pustules covering his arms. When he put his hands to his face he could feel more of them. His whole body had begun to itch. He whimpered in self-pity – then screamed. 'Wait! Wait for me! Don't leave me!'

His companions could not hear him now – and, even if they had heard his cries, it is unlikely that they would have taken any notice of him. Then he almost trod on a body. Stopping and looking down, he flinched. Barely recognisable because of the hideous boils that covered it, the face of the youngest soldier stared back at him with cold, sightless eyes. The red-haired soldier gave a shriek of terror and stumbled away, his whole body racked with convulsions. He clutched at his throat and sank slowly to his knees. Then he fell forward on his face and lay motionless on the ground.

Meanwhile, the four remaining guards, driven on by fear, were rushing to get away. As they neared the edge of the flatlands, the fat one shouted out suddenly in panic. 'I'm smitten! Look! Look!' He ran frantically back and forth, trying to brush away the pustules and sores that had appeared on one of his hands. 'It's the plague!'

''Tis not,' said the oldest man. 'No plague looks like that and it doesn't come on so quick. This is different. 'Tis her doing – the old witch! She did for us with her talons and put a sickness curse on us all!'

'But it's not got me,' said Willibert. 'Can you see! My hands are clean. I hardly touched her – it'll not trouble me!'

'Me neither,' said the tall lanky youth. 'I did her no harm, you all know that. I treated her right, so I'm safe from it too.'

The oldest of them was not feeling well. He was feeling very ill in fact, but dare not tell the other three. He hardly dared admit it to himself.

'I'm safe from it,' the lanky one repeated ecstatically, chanting the words as though he were casting a spell upon himself. 'Move away,' he shouted at the fat man. 'You'll have to look out for yourself. It was you that …'

'Shut up!' screamed his companion. ' Don't speak about what we did! You're all guilty, all of you!'

'Not all of us! Not me! I'm not!'

He started to itch, but that was only natural, wasn't it? It was only a nervous reaction because he was frightened of the symptoms, wasn't it? He *had* been kind to the old woman, hadn't he? That little whack he'd given her didn't mean that much, did it?

The fat one was grovelling, moaning. 'No, don't run off, please. No, no! Help me! Help.'

His cries never reached their ears. Soon the fat one fell far behind the others and was left to die a lonely and agonising death. In fact, in the end not one of the six soldiers lived long enough to reach the settlement down in the valley below.

****

The glacier, when they reached it, was in every way as forbidding as Tengel had told them it would be. It sapped their energy and wasted their time. Silje's first impression of it, as they emerged from the pass, was one she would always recall with horror – jagged, worn and weather-beaten peaks, surrounded by a vast expanse of white that resembled a frozen river, pouring out from a great gash in the highest mountains. There was not a blade of grass to be seen nor a strip of

49

ground to walk on. Yet the whole scene before them was bathed in bleak silver light from the moon, as it climbed higher in the night sky, and this was making the millions of icy crystals on the glacier sparkle and gleam like precious gems.

Silje knew at once that she would carry the memory of that journey across the glacier with her forever. Her heart burdened with sorrow, despair and hopelessness, she staggered along behind the children, doing her best to make sure that no harm came to them.

Exhausted, Liv had soon given up; she had been half asleep as she plodded along and she finally fell in a heap, sound asleep in the cold snow. They tied her onto the horse, despite their fear for the safety of the animal. What if it broke through the crust of snow and ice or decided to bolt? What would happen to the girl then? But there was no other way. Neither of them could carry her. Tengel had his hands full leading the animal and testing the way ahead with his staff, while Silje carried her bundles and watched over the two older children.

The resilience shown by Sol and Dag was remarkable, but they were impatient. It was hard for them to understand the need for caution – they were in a hurry to get out of the bitter cold. Tengel, however, would take no risks, carefully probing the surface before every step he took.

None of them could throw off the ceaseless worry that they were being followed. They had lost count of the number of times they had turned to look behind them during the night, but every glance had revealed a reassuringly empty white expanse of the glacier, tarnished only by the blue ribbon of their own meandering tracks.

They kept going all through the first night, before finally coming down from the other side of the glacier. An inhospitable boggy plateau infested with mosquitoes and covered in gnarled and stunted trees welcomed them. For a while they followed the course of the glacier until it flowed into a wide river, but eventually, under a grey, cloudy dawn sky that hid the sun, Tengel decided that the children, above all else, needed rest.

Not wanting to be taken by surprise by any pursuing soldiers, they continued over some hillocks to a dell where, in the biting early morning wind, Silje set up camp for them all. Sharing the few blankets they had brought with them, they huddled together as close as they could to stay warm. The children were fast asleep in no time – they were beyond exhaustion. Silje cuddled them from one side and Tengel from the other.

'I will not be thanking God for our wonderful salvation if we survive this,' she whispered.

'Why so?'

'Because I have never understood those who endure some great catastrophe and then say, "God held his hand over me and saved me". What of all the others who perish? I think it is so conceited to speak in that way, as if they were somehow better than all those who did not survive. I shall say a prayer for their souls instead. It will be more honest, don't you think?'

Tengel agreed with her. 'What you say is true. Not that you have ever been conceited, Silje. You always put others first. God or no God, I am forever grateful that I have you all here. The danger has not passed, but we are alive so far – all five of us.'

'Eight,' she reminded him with a sleepy smile. 'You forgot the horse, the cat and one more, who has yet to see the light of day.'

'All eight,' he repeated, smiling at her – but his smile was tinged slightly with pain.

As the moments passed, Tengel found he dared not allow himself to sleep. He lay awake listening for any telltale sounds of pursuit, while the others slept for an hour or two. When they resumed their arduous journey, their limbs were stiff and aching and they felt cold and lost in a world they did not recognise. Almost immediately, Sol's cat ran off into a thicket. They wasted an hour trying to find it before it emerged of its own free will, loping along after them oblivious to the anxiety it had caused.

Once or twice they found themselves in difficulty because of the treacherous nature of the terrain. On one occasion they had to negotiate a steep incline, but the horse refused, at which point Tengel gave serious thought to ending its misery. However Silje and the children pleaded for the animal to be spared and as usual Tengel had given way. Nonetheless, the time and effort needed to coax it along was stressful for them all and Silje had almost changed her mind several times. Finally they all reached the bottom of the slope and gave a relieved cheer. Laughing, Sol pointed out that the horse was the only one not joining in.

With great relief Tengel set to work at once tending to the animal's minor scrapes and cuts. When he had finished Silje could see the look of contentment on his face as he stood resting his head against the horse's neck. He was obviously relieved and delighted that their old and faithful companion was still with them.

As they trudged on, the landscape began to change, and the air began to feel warmer now that the ice-laden wind from the glacier no longer tore into them. It had become quite clear that they were closer to the valley floor than the mountain peaks and, not wanting to tire the little ones, they broke their journey in the late afternoon and made camp among some birch trees growing in a narrow cleft in the valley. There were fir trees and pines dotted around them as well, while forest flowers carpeted the mossy ground underfoot.

Within minutes the children had dozed off. Tired as she was, Silje had passed the point at which she could hold her emotions in check and she began to sob unendingly. With Tengel holding her close in his arms, she shed tears for all those who lay dead in the Valley of the Ice People and for the little homestead, furnished with all their belongings, that they would never set eyes on again. She wept because of the uncertain future that they now faced and not least from sheer exhaustion. However, she could not tell Tengel that part of her was crying with relief at coming back into the outside world once more. She did not want to hurt him by letting him see that she was glad to be leaving the place of his birth.

'All my tapestries,' she sniffed. 'I left them behind. It's so hard to let go of something you've created – and now they're gone.'

'There, there,' he consoled her. 'You haven't seen what's under the horse's saddle. I tucked two of your biggest tapestries under it. I could not bear to be parted from them either.'

Heartened by this, Silje hugged him tight and eventually she fell asleep in his arms. But once again he remained awake, fearing an attack by wild animals. There would certainly be wolf, bear, lynx and wolverine in these parts. Of these, his greatest worry was an attack by a bear. He was concerned about his ability to fight off such an attack, if it came, because he was himself suffering from a wound to one of his feet. It had been caused by treading on a sharp piece of rock during the night and this he knew would make it difficult to turn and jump to avoid further injury.

He too was filled with misgivings about their future, and now they had a new worry to contend with. 'Worry' he thought was far too mild a word. Tengel looked down at his young wife and knew that he could not blame her. The blame was his. When he lay with her it was so easy to be swept away in the ecstasy of her embrace and forget that he had an obligation to her as well. She should on no account give birth again, but this time she had caught him out. He rested his hand on her belly and there was no doubt he could feel the life within her. It was already well developed – how had he been so blind to it?

If he should lose Silje, what then? The fear of it made his blood run cold. Yet she could not be expected to survive another difficult delivery. So what was he to do? In truth, he told himself, there was only one thing he could do – drive it from her! But would he have the courage to do this? He would surely lose her love if she lost the child!

Tengel was deeply troubled. He had no idea where he could find Eldrid; the place they had told him they would be going to settle was unknown to him. It lay far to the east of Tröndelag, or so he thought, Anyway it would not be right to follow them and perhaps put their future at risk. Finding he was too tired to contemplate any longer, he gently moved Silje so she would be more comfortable under her cape. Then he lay back in resignation against the trunk of a birch tree.

****

Tengel and his family continued travelling for two more nights and a further day before they came upon the first signs of human habitation. By then they and the horse were all completely exhausted and barely able to stand. They were making their way along the edge of the forest in that part of Tröndelag where Benedikt's farm lay. They dared not show themselves on the road and kept out of sight among the trees. Tengel's foot was aching; the horse had sustained injuries to three of its legs and was limping badly; the children were also fretting from hunger and fatigue. Then suddenly Silje gave a shout.

'Look! There, on the riverbank! Is that not Benedikt's farmhand – fishing for salmon?'

Indeed it was, and they all hurried over to him. The old man was taken aback when he realised who they were. He was thrilled to see how the two older children had grown, and congratulated them on the youngest member of the family. He could not hide his disappointment when Sol failed to recognise him, but he had not really expected that she would, as she had only been two years old when they had left.

'And how are things on the farm?' asked Tengel and Silje in unison.

The man looked gravely at them. ''Tis bad. Very bad.'

'Are they alive still?' Silje asked anxiously.

'Oh, yes! Yes, they're alive – all of them. I'm not workin' there no more. Y'see, I just couldn't take that old bat Abelone any longer, so I found work on another farm. I hear tell that they can't keep servants or working-hands for long at Master Benedikt's farm nowadays.'

Sol interrupted them suddenly, chuckling to herself, 'I remember you now! You used to tickle me!'

The old man's face lit up. 'Aha! So you *do* remember me, you young scallywag. Just you wait till I catch you …' He made a move towards her and Sol ran off squealing – just as in the old days.

'So Abelone is still there?' exclaimed Tengel.

The farmhand stopped chasing Sol, saying, 'That she is. And those horrible children too. They hounded out Grete and Marie as well. They now live as parish paupers, moving from farm to farm and not getting treated too well neither.'

'But that's awful,' gasped Silje. 'They're such lovely people! It shouldn't be allowed! What of Master Benedikt?'

'Aah, that kind-hearted old man. He's in jail!'

'How can that be?'

'It all happened just a while back. He weren't enjoying his life with Abelone in charge, but most of the time he could stand his ground.' The man leaned forward and whispered, 'Found friendship in the bottle – if you get my drift! But then when those rebels were reported to the authorities ...'

'Heming!' muttered Tengel through clenched teeth.

'There can be no doubt now who is the real evil spirit of the Ice People,' declared Silje under her breath.

The farmhand nodded absently. 'When the soldiers came to the farm, asking Master Benedikt questions an' all, Abelone told them bad tales about him. She just wanted rid of him – he was a nuisance to her. So there he sits, locked up in Trondheim, and everything's in a sorry old state!'

'These are terrible goings on,' exclaimed Silje. 'Tengel, we have to do something!'

'Yes, we must,' he agreed, while at the same time wondering what they would be able to achieve in their present condition. 'Have all the rebels fled?'

'I fear so. They do say that Dyre Alvson was taken. They were all given up by one of the rebels who got captured.'

Tengel cursed Heming, mumbling a long series of oaths and incantations. Silje saw his eyes gleam with fury – seldom had he been so enraged. After a moment he brought his anger under control and turned to the old man. In a few short minutes he told him all about the terrible fate that had befallen the Ice People and the farmhand stared at him aghast.

'We had thought to bide our time up on the ridge where I used to stay,' concluded Tengel, 'until we find a better, safer place.' As he spoke, he wondered whether anywhere was safe now, but said nothing of this fear.

'There's folk living there now,' said the farmhand ruefully. 'If only I knew of somewhere hereabouts.'

'I know of one other place where I used to hide,' interrupted Tengel with a deep sigh. 'It lies closer to Trondheim and is not really fit for children. But we will have to try it anyway.'

They asked him to remember them to Grete and Marie and assured him that they would return sometime to try and help, however remote their chances of success might be. With that, they sadly took their leave of the farmhand and set off again on their cheerless journey.

They travelled on in silence for a long while and, with the day half over, they stopped to rest and eat in a forest clearing. Tengel's foot was badly swollen and he ought to have been travelling on horseback to rest it, but he refused, saying that the children were in greater need. This was partly true, but it did not stop Silje from nagging him about being so obstinate – calling it stupid pride. Unsurprisingly, the atmosphere became somewhat fraught for a little while. They were all suffering from the effects of the experiences they had been through and in their different ways were worried about what the future had in store.

Late that evening they arrived at the forest hut Tengel had told them about. It was an extremely simple, A-frame shelter with two side walls leaning inwards to the ridge and a triangular wall forming each gable. The air inside was dank and musty; mildew and mould were everywhere.

'I can see that nobody has been in this place since my last visit,' said Tengel lightly. But the optimism in his tone was not completely convincing. 'At least we shall be safe here,' he added in a more subdued tone.

Suppressing a sigh of hopelessness Silje did what she could to tidy and clean. She placed dry brushwood on the earth floor for them to lie on and then got the children off to sleep. That done, it was time to look after Tengel's foot.

'It's not very pretty to look at,' she told him, 'but resting it is the best thing to do.'

Tengel asked her to find his 'things'. These 'things', she knew, were his secret potions and herbs. With them, he treated his foot as best he could before falling into a deep slumber, exhausted beyond measure from two long nights keeping watch over them all and the burden of a thousand misgivings. Outside the crude hut the horse was grazing one last time before nightfall and the cat had already set off in search of prey.

Silje found she was unable to sleep. Her thoughts went round and round unceasingly. Anxiety and stress accompanied every heartbeat. She gazed at the walls – it was impossible for this to be called a home – and considered their dwindling supply of food and how hard it would be to survive. When she finally did fall asleep, she had reached a decision.

****

Next morning Silje took stock of the food they had left then announced resolutely, 'You are all to stay here today! There is something I must do.'

Softly Tengel asked, 'And what might that be?'

'We are in difficulty – you can see that!'

'Yes, only too well.'

'Then I see only one possible solution. Do you agree that, when things are grave, we must cast aside niceties and good manners.'

'Silje! You are not about to …?'

She smiled. 'Don't worry, I am not going to sell my body, if that was what you thought! But I might sell my soul.'

He glanced quickly over to the corner – the glazed mosaic was still there.

'No, not that either,' she said, reading his thoughts. 'Trust me, Tengel, I know what I am to do. I am thinking of you and also of Benedikt and Grete and Marie. I also cannot bear to think that the children will again suffer hunger as they did last winter. The food we have will soon be gone. We have nothing to fish with. You are injured and cannot get about. I see only one way out of this, and even though it might be very uncertain, it is worth trying. I shall return as swiftly as I can. I don't know how long it will take – perhaps until evening, but it may be that I don't come back until tomorrow. Do not start to fret about me!'

Tengel did not want her to go, but faced with her determination and stubborn resolve there was little he could say to change her mind.

'Do not put yourself in harm's way, Silje!'

'I shall be careful,' she assured him. 'Nobody will concern themselves with me and they cannot know that I am kin to the Ice People.'

'But by which road will you travel? In case you are gone too long?'

She paused. 'To Trondheim. If needs be then search for me there! But allow me a few days before you do.' With that, she said goodbye to them all and left.

Silje trudged along the country road, heading north.

Her feet were swollen and blistered and she was grateful that a passing farmer let her ride on his wagon for some of the way. It also saved time on her journey.

She arrived in Trondheim in the early afternoon. Hunger – and trepidation – was making her stomach churn. How strange it felt to be there once more! Five years had gone by since she left. Now people were bustling to and fro – goods of every kind imaginable were being sold from market stalls, while in the shops and workshops that lined the streets, smiths and craftsmen worked by their braziers.

Dogs, cats and other animals kept getting in her way. How different it all was, as she walked around in a daze, almost unable to believe she was back in the city. The place held no pleasant memories for her, she reflected as she gazed about. Yes, over there was a doorway where she had slept on so many freezing nights. And she recognised another place where a man had jumped out of the shadows and attacked her. She had fought like an animal then, and quickly learnt the best places to strike a blow at any man who tried to force himself upon her. She had needed to use those skills many times after that! But at least now the sight and smell of corpses littering the street had gone. There was no plague in Trondheim any more on this summer's day – as far as she could tell.

Silje asked passers-by for directions and it was not long before she stood before the grand residence of Baron Meiden. Her heart was racing suddenly in her chest and she asked herself if she really dared go through with her audacious plan? For a brief moment she wanted to turn and run. Then the memory of the children's hungry faces came back to her – and the way they would look again if she did turn and run away – and she thought of Tengel, so worried and full of sorrow at not being able to help and protect those he loved. That morning she had seen the same dejected expression on his face as she had during the terrible food shortage the previous winter. Then the ice on the lake had been too thick for them to fish, there were no deer or wild boar to hunt, the barns were empty of grain and the sheep were all dead.

Remembering this, Silje took a last deep breath to calm herself. Unconsciously she ran her hand over the basket she carried – and knocked. When a maid opened the door, Silje introduced herself and asked to see Mistress Charlotte Meiden. The maid looked her up and down before asking the nature of her business.

'I wish only to speak with Her Grace.'

'About what?'

'It is a private matter.'

The maid gave Silje a withering, insolent look that seemed to last forever. Then in a harsh voice she ordered her to wait and slammed the door in her face. Silje endured a long, humiliating delay on the steps before at last the door opened once again.

'Come in, then!' There was still no trace of friendliness or courtesy in the maid's voice, but Silje ignored this as she stepped into a wonderful entrance hall with white painted walls, a few pieces of expensive, elegant furniture and fine wrought-iron torch-holders. She had barely time to take in more of her surroundings before a woman, about thirty years old with a long narrow face, came into the room. She was dressed in a gown of brown and gold, glittering with pearls.

She is the one! I've come to the right place, thought Silje.

The woman studied her with a haughty, questioning gaze. An older woman, wearing a gown with a starched ruff collar and a sleeveless brocade coat, came and stood behind her. This must be her mother, thought Silje and curtseyed low to both of them.

Charlotte Meiden scrutinised the young woman standing beside the door. She saw a soft, attractive face framed in brown curly hair, and although tired and showing signs of anxiety, the blue eyes had an honest gaze. She was dressed in a very old worn-out blue velvet cape and in a strange way Charlotte felt she knew her.

'What is it?' she demanded icily.

Silje was taken aback because the woman addressed her in Danish. I should have known, she thought to herself. There are so few noble Norwegian families left. Perhaps our Dag is a young Dane! But this woman has suffered – it shows in her face. And she appears to have lost all hope.

'My name is Silje Arngrimsdotter and I am a married woman from the countryside. With your permission, I beg a private audience with Your Grace.'

An educated voice, thought Charlotte Meiden, but before she could reply her mother interrupted. 'If you are here to beg then leave now – by the scullery door!'

Silje shook her head. This was becoming awkward. However, she felt that she must try to impress both these noble ladies with her determination, so she continued, 'My duty is to speak privately with the gracious Mistress. The subject of the conversation is most confidential.'

What can she mean by this? thought Charlotte. 'Are you here to deliver a message?' she asked.

Silje didn't reply, but just looked calmly back at her, waiting. Despite herself, Charlotte Meiden had become curious. 'Oh, very well! Follow me!' she said at last, and turned to lead Silje upstairs to her boudoir.

Her mother, the Countess, called after her, 'I shall accompany you, Charlotte.'

'There's no need,' replied her daughter as she leaned over the balustrade. 'It's certain to be nothing more than a message.'

If it was a message from one of those handsome young cavalrymen at the Austråt garrison, then maternal interference was the last thing she wanted. Yet why would she get a message from one of them? When had she last had an admirer? She showed Silje into her chambers and closed the door. Silje gazed at the heavy oak-panelled walls and the high ceiling of this large elegant room. Everything displayed great wealth – but happiness? There were no signs of that here.

'Can anyone hear us in here?'

'No.'

'And what if someone should listen at the door?'

'This is getting beyond secrecy,' declared Charlotte haughtily, but she nevertheless bolted the door leading to the corridor and ushered Silje into a sumptuous bedchamber where a giant four-poster bed swallowed up most of the room.

'There! Are you satisfied now?'

Silje nodded.

'Well? What is it that you have to say to me?'

They stood on either side of a marble table and Silje took a deep breath as she looked at the woman before her. 'I must tell you at once that nothing I may say is intended to cause you harm, Mistress Charlotte. This is not what I would wish. But desperation has forced this upon me.'

Charlotte Meiden frowned disdainfully. 'So you *are* here as a beggar?' she said and began to walk towards the door.

'No! No!' said Silje quickly. 'You must hear me out. This concerns you more than me.'

Charlotte turned. 'Me? Whatever do you mean?'

Silje swallowed hard and braced herself.

'Before we begin this difficult conversation we must both be sure of something. It may be that I am speaking to the wrong person.'

Silje opened her basket and placed the three pieces of fabric on the table – the shawl, the brocade blanket and the linen cloth. 'Does Your Grace recognise these things?'

At first, Charlotte stared blankly at the items. It was as though her brain had stopped working. Gently her hand touched the shawl. So many thoughts rushed through her head. Her throat felt dry. Then the blood rushed to her face, only to drain away almost at once, leaving her looking ashen. She heard her own rasping breaths when she snatched back her hand from the cloth as if it had been on fire. The room had started to spin before her eyes and she felt the unknown woman's arms supporting her, leading her towards the bed. Then everything went black.

Chapter 4

When Charlotte Meiden stirred and came to her senses again, she found she was looking straight into those blue, anxious eyes. 'You – you …' she stuttered. Then she sat up with a start, looking wildly again at the shawl and the brocade blanket. 'No, I know nothing of these things. Now be gone and take them with you before I call for help!'

'Mistress Charlotte, this is important,' pleaded Silje. 'You must hear what I have to say, because I know that you recognise them.'

The genteel lady's thin lips formed a contemptuous smile while her eyes, small and a little too close together for her to be beautiful, showed great fear. 'So you are here only to demand ransom! You want nothing more than money to buy your silence! And what is the price of this silence?'

'No!' Silje was appalled. She was not accustomed to people questioning her honour. 'I told Your Grace that I mean you no harm.'

'You seek to take advantage of another woman's misfortune – is that not harm enough? How were you able to find me?'

Charlotte had managed to get to her feet and now stood

facing Silje, her expression one of infinite distaste. But shock and alarm had left her face a pallid grey colour.

'Your crest is embroidered on the linen cloth. I have known who you are for many years, but never had cause to trouble you. Not until now. For I see no other way open to me. A hateful man once tried to steal these things, because he had learned that there were letters embroidered on them. *He* would have found out who you were and extorted money from you. But luckily my husband stopped him and your name was never made known. Many times I have thought about you, Mistress Charlotte, and how difficult everything must have been. Then when I *saw* you I was sure that it was your child. I could tell straightaway.'

The Baron's daughter fixed Silje with a questioning gaze as she lowered herself into the chair beside the table, her legs still unable to carry her.

'We have met once before,' Silje continued. 'You don't remember?'

Charlotte Meiden pursed her lips, opened them, but no sound emerged. There was a vague expression on her pear-shaped face as she tried to search her memory. Why, yes! Those innocent blue eyes? There was a long silence, then she replied hesitantly, 'Yes … Just inside the city gates – on the very night. You were carrying a little girl in your arms. You were so terribly young and looked so cold. You spoke to me.'

'Yes, I did. Please believe me, Mistress Charlotte, when I say that I have never thought badly of you. I realised that despair must have driven you to do what you did in spite of yourself. I found the little pot of milk …'

Charlotte was drowning in reawakened memories: the finality of what she had done; the freezing night; the hunger and loneliness the little mite must have suffered.

And she was too late – too weak and cowardly – too late, too late! For a long time she sat slumped in the chair, her hands resting in her lap, and tears ran unchecked down her cheeks while she sobbed uncontrollably.

'You should never have come,' she managed to say at last, still choking back her tears. 'You should not have brought all this back to me. I do not have the strength to go through it all again! To have taken the life of one's own … Oh! *Why* did you come here? No good will ever come of this!'

'I could do nothing else,' said Silje softly. 'We have done all we could to make sure that the children would be well cared for. Now they are in distress and will suffer more and more until they are so weak they die of hunger and exhaustion. Your little boy as well.'

At that moment it seemed as if everything – time, the air itself – stood still and listened while Charlotte stared blankly at the pattern on a gilded leather wall-hanging. The heavy silence seemed to last for an eternity. Finally she turned slowly and faced Silje, who was starting to worry about how unwell she looked. 'You mean – my child – is alive?'

'Of course! I happened upon him not long after I had passed you and took him with me. I could not have left him there.' Silje's voice was almost apologetic. 'It was so cold and he was crying so pitifully. You must believe me when I say that I should never have troubled you if the child had died. I could never have been that heartless.'

Slender fingers reached out in desperation to grasp Silje's arm. 'A boy?'

'A fine young boy,' smiled Silje. 'He will soon be five years old. But of course you know that. He is called Dag – Dag Christian. "Christian" after your initials on the blanket.'

The sound of Charlotte's sobbing subsided and she sniffed and snuffled breathlessly, wiping her tears. 'Oh, dear God,' she breathed. ' I can hardly believe what you are saying. Thank you – thank you for what you have done.'

In the tense silence that followed, there was a sharp knock at the door of the anteroom.

'Charlotte!' called the stern voice of the Baroness. 'Are you all right?'

The young gentlewoman looked up in sudden panic, her eyes still red with tears. 'Oh, no! That's my mother!' she whispered and ran from the bedchamber.

The door handle was rattling loudly as her mother pushed against it. 'Charlotte! Charlotte, what is going on in there.'

'Nothing at all, Mother. We are merely in conversation.'

'I see. But all this time? You sound strange – may I come in?'

'Presently, Mother dear. I shall soon come downstairs. Be good enough to wait down there.'

The woman was heard walking away, grumbling loudly as she did so. Charlotte now bolted the inner door, turned and stood resting her back against it, letting out a shuddering sigh of relief.

'Is it true,' her voice faltered, 'that my child is alive – is that true? A little boy – Dag, you say? Why did you name him "Dag"?'

'Because I found him in darkness. I sought to preserve him from all the evil forces of the night. Besides, it was the little girl who led me to him. For my part I believed him to be a "myling".'

Charlotte nodded. He would most certainly have become just such a lost soul if this woman had not …

'I would gladly have run away, but for the little girl. A

short time earlier I had come across her beside the body of her dead mother. In truth, it was she who saved the infant's life, not I. We have also taken care of her since then.'

'I remember now that I thought you looked very young to have a daughter so old,' reflected Charlotte absent-mindedly. 'Tell me, is he handsome?'

Silje gave her a wry smile. 'He takes after you, Mistress.'

Charlotte pulled a face and with great self-irony declared, 'The poor child!'

Silje's face lit up. So this distinguished lady had a sense of humour! Their eyes met for a moment, and both knew in that instant that they were kindred spirits, united by a shared secret.

'He is a *very* fine lad,' Silje told her warmly. 'He is blond, and has a thin noble face. He is good-natured, although perhaps at times a little particular and fussy. And very intelligent!'

Charlotte had been daydreaming, reflecting inwardly and a rare smile was lighting up her face. Suddenly she remembered something and stepped quickly across to where Silje stood, grasping her arm. 'You said he is in distress?'

'All our children are suffering,' Silje told her solemnly. 'There is no future for us any more, Mistress Charlotte. A few days ago we were overtaken by disaster. After that my husband injured his foot and ...' In spite of herself she could not go on and subsided into tears. Perhaps the release of the pent-up tension, the stress that had been building up all day, was to blame.

Charlotte watched her feebly, unable to help. She, who had been fussed over since birth, had no idea how to comfort others. It was, quite simply, something she had never had to do. 'Oh, there, there!' she said awkwardly. 'Sit down, please. Forgive me if I sound cold and offhand. That is not the real me, but you do understand that one must be careful with commoners, don't you? We are Danes and nobles – not always welcomed by everyone in your country. The past five years have left their mark on me too. You must believe me – I have not had one minute of happiness in all that time. Such things make one bitter and distraught.' She paused. 'How many children do you have?'

'Three,' muttered Silje, pulling herself together with a great effort. 'The boy and the girl, who are our foundlings, and a little daughter of our own. She is three years old.'

'And you are carrying another?' said Charlotte in a conspiratorial whisper.

'But how did you know? Oh, of course, it is something women always know.'

'I see it by your skin – the way the light shines through it. Now, something must be done! I must see him. Where is he?'

'South of Trondheim in a sickly hovel that was once a forester's shelter. We were hounded out of our home and are being followed. We have no food and my husband cannot walk. I could think of nothing other than to come to you, Mistress Charlotte.'

Once more Charlotte took her by the arm. Silje could smell the sweet perfume she wore.

'I am grateful that you did! You have brought me new life. Now, I will bring him here and raise him myself. Of course I must, when he is …'

Silje's expression turned to dark sorrow and despair.

'Well, he *is* my child,' Charlotte tried to say, but the words were left unspoken. 'Oh, dear,' Charlotte's mind had begun to piece things together. Softly she continued, 'Oh, dear me. This could become difficult. This could become *very* difficult.'

'Truly,' whispered Silje.

Charlotte had regained her composure. 'And clearly my father would never, never permit such a thing. You do not know him, but he would cast me into the gutter in the blink of an eye!'

'But a grandchild?' countered Silje.

'He has many grandchildren already. He barely sees them when they visit, but demands that they remain in another room and make not a sound – and those are the ones born in wedlock!'

'So you had reason to forsake the child?'

'Yes. I know I was thoughtless and a coward, but I could think of no other way. I foresaw none of the consequences. Dear Silje – may I call you "Silje"? I have to ponder on this. I shall not fail my son a second time, be sure of that. Nor shall I fail you – you who have cared for him all these years. But I must have time. I will also want to hear your story in full, that I can better know what to do.'

Charlotte seemed reinvigorated and there was a sparkle in her eye that pleased Silje.

'Your mother, then,' enquired Silje tentatively. 'Ought she to hear of this?'

Charlotte considered this for a long time. 'I do not know. In truth, I know my mother hardly at all. For the moment let us say that you will return once I have had time to contrive a plan.'

When Charlotte saw Silje's troubled expression, she put both her elbows on the table where she sat and dejectedly rested her head in her hands. 'No, that's no good. You have nowhere to go while you wait, and time is of the essence, you say?'

'It is. I shared out the last of the food this morning.'

'Oh, dear God! Thinking is beyond me! This has all been too much. I want to see him – to tell him that I regret so much what I did. Ask his forgiveness. Yet none of that is possible!'

'I, too, have little to offer,' said Silje. 'When I set off to come here it was without expectation. I was forced by circumstances alone …' She paused. 'But, Mistress Charlotte, do you know what I think? I believe your mother will understand.'

'You do?'

'Perhaps not straightaway, but if a daughter of mine had suffered as much as you, I should do all in my power to help her. Without doubt I would be shocked. Yes, and would likely rebuke her, but above all I would want to help her. I think that an older woman's advice can help to resolve our plight. Is your father at home?'

'No, he is journeying about the district and will not return for many days.' Under her breath Charlotte said, 'Thank God.' It was not meant for Silje's ears.

Silje stood waiting, saying nothing. The sounds of the street could be heard distantly, muffled by the heavy velvet drapes hanging at the tall windows. Sellers were calling out their wares and horses whinnying.

'All right,' declared Charlotte. 'I must be strong. I have been a coward for far too long. I shall go and fetch my mother – and ask for some refreshments to be brought. Has it been long since you ate last?'

'Last evening – a crust.'

'What's that you say? I shall have food sent up at once. It is better that we remain here where the servants cannot eavesdrop.' She stood contemplating for a moment or two, then. to no one in particular, asked, 'Should I deny my own son? A second time? No! No, in God's name, not this time!' Then resolutely, but more than a little fearfully, she walked over to the door.

'Perhaps you should speak privately with your mother,' suggested Silje.

'No, you must be here or my nerve will weaken. Besides, you must tell us *everything* that has taken place these past five years! I know nothing at all about you – I will go to talk to her now.'

Silje stood patiently at the window after Charlotte had left the room. She was surprised to find that her hands were shaking, although perhaps it was only to be expected. She gazed with interest at a small sewing-table standing against the wall beside the window. It was beautifully delicate, with narrow turned legs and inlaid with fine veneers. The room was perfect, exquisite in every last detail. She let her hands play across the gilded-leather tapestries, wondering instinctively how they were made, and admired the lustrous fabrics on the four-poster bed.

To think that she and Tengel could be so proud of their tiny glazed mosaic – a window for which they didn't even have a wall! And yet, perhaps its beauty meant more to them than all this excess of elegance did to Charlotte.

From outside the door Silje suddenly heard voices coming closer and she strained her ears to listen. 'Have you taken leave of your senses? Leaving a beggar alone in your room! How much do you think she will make off with?'

'Don't worry, mother.'

'What is all this nonsense anyway, Charlotte?' demanded the Baroness. 'I swear I haven't seen you so excited in many years. You are acting like a mysterious fool.'

As they entered the room, Silje curtseyed to the two ladies once more, very conscious of her shamefully tattered dress that had nothing in common with the genteel fashions they wore. 'I have told them to bring food for the three of us,' Charlotte said quickly. 'Please be seated at the table.'

They sat down. Charlotte swallowed visibly. Her face was ghostly pale except for two bright crimson spots on her cheeks. 'Mother, I have something to say that will shock you greatly, but I beg you to listen with understanding.'

'Whatever have you been doing now? And whatever is this? This shawl has been missing for ages!'

The Baroness scrutinised Silje, trying to work out whether there was some way that she could have stolen it. Was she trying to salve her guilty conscience by returning it? However such a small matter would not warrant all this fuss. Everyone knew that peasants stole like greedy magpies.

Charlotte's nervousness was plain to see. Her whole body was shivering, but her eyes still held the earlier sparkle of determination and eagerness. These past years, during which she had yearned to turn back the clock, telling herself that she would gladly have suffered the shame and indignity of keeping her child, had not been in vain.

'Well!' The Baroness was impatient. 'What do you have to say that will disturb me so?'

'Mother – can you recall how, about five years since, my demeanour was very strange?'

'How will I ever forget such a commotion? You have never shown a sign of happiness since that day.'

'Until today, Mama! Now I shall tell you what happened.'

Casting a glance towards Silje, the Baroness asked, 'And does it concern this "lady"?'

'It was she who thought it best to reveal everything to you. She believed that we needed a mother's wisdom and guidance.'

'So pray tell all!'

Charlotte drew a deep, deep breath. 'I bore a child, Mama.'

Her mother stared at her. 'Hmm! This is no time for jesting. Tell me what was so important.'

'It is true, Mama.'

'Don't be so foolish! I would have noticed something. Indeed, you were here all the time!'

'But it is the truth. Nobody realised – nobody! I chose my attire to conceal the condition. And I was uncommonly slender then. I corseted myself tightly.'

'No, Charlotte, I will not be persuaded of this – that *my daughter* … What about the chambermaid, she must have …?'

'My chambermaid was as witless as a goose. I deceived her throughout and I clothed myself.'

'Do you mean to sit there and ask me to take all this seriously, Charlotte?'

'Indeed I do!' Charlotte's eyes shone and she was very frightened. She would not let her resolve slip. Yet she was amazed that, now she was confessing all, her story was not believed! 'I gave birth to the infant in the hayloft, wrapped it in these clothes and placed it out in the forest. Later I sorely regretted what I had done and suffered one outburst of frenzy after another. I have been deeply miserable ever since. You remember that I wanted to enter the sisterhood?'

Baroness Meiden sat open-mouthed and motionless in her chair. 'I refuse to believe a single word!' she said tightly.

Charlotte got up and took the Bible from her night table. Looking her mother in the eye, she placed her hand on the book and said, 'I swear on God's name, and the resurrection of my soul, that my every word I have told you is true.'

Silje added softly, 'It is the truth, Your Grace.'

Charlotte watched as all the colour drained from her mother's face. Quickly she produced a bottle of smelling salts to revive her mother, but as the Baroness began to regain her composure, her face contorted and she burst into tears.

'You cannot mean what you say! How *could* you? What a terrible scandal! And what will father say?'

'Father need never know,' said Charlotte in an urgent tone. 'But Silje and I do need your help, Mama, because things have taken a turn for the worse.'

'Has anybody discovered that you – abandoned the infant in the forest? Why, yes, of course, this woman – the shawl! And now she demands money?'

Charlotte sighed. 'No, mother! I too thought that was the way of it, but it isn't so!'

The Baroness was unable to grasp all that was happening. Her voice was trembling. 'How *could* you leave a new-born infant, Charlotte?'

Those were the words Silje had been waiting to hear. That simple question had shown that Her Ladyship did indeed have a heart. It meant that there was still hope for them all.

'And perchance I had kept it? What then would my parents have said?'

Her mother stared at the floor. 'Yes, you are right. So it was stillborn, was it?'

'No! It was alive.'

Instantly the older woman's hand flew to her mouth and she looked suddenly very ill. 'And you left it out to die? Oh! My daughter! My daughter!' She sat staring for a long while with one hand pressed to her mouth, her eyes wide with worry. The only sounds were the faint squeaking noises she made as she tried hard to stifle her sobs and recover some peace of mind. At last she regained her composure and some dignity. 'But what part does this woman play? And what help can I give you? Only a priest can help you now – if anyone can!'

'The child is still alive, Mama,' Charlotte told her gently. 'I found out only a few minutes ago. Silje here rescued it and brought it up. It is a little boy.'

The Baroness was staring in disbelief at Silje, and after a long pause, Charlotte continued. 'But now she and her family find themselves in desperate times. She came to ask me for help.'

Complete silence returned to the room as her mother sat pondering. She kept dabbing at her cheeks, but silent tears quickly replaced those that she wiped away. Finally she asked, 'So, Charlotte, who is the father? Quite clearly you could not have been alone in this.'

'I will not speak his name!' snapped Charlotte.

Slowly and imperiously her mother stood up and when she spoke there was a commanding tone in her voice. 'His name, if you please!'

'Jeppe Marsvin!' said Charlotte at once.

'Him? But he is married!'

'I was unaware of that at the time. He proposed marriage and courted me relentlessly. I was young and foolish.'

The Baroness glared at her in fury. Then she swung back her arm and slapped her daughter viciously across the face. 'Hell's teeth!' she hissed, and unable to think of anything more potent to say, repeated it. 'Hell's teeth! I shall go and lie down now. I can take no more of this – it is all too much for me.'

Charlotte's treatment of an infant had gone beyond the bounds of appalling behaviour, and was obviously something the Baroness felt unable to punish. Her daughter's wanton disregard for her own virtue, however, was a very different matter altogether. *That* was something an outraged mother could and should deal with in a fitting manner. She spun quickly on her heel and the sound of rustling skirts accompanied her as she swept dramatically out of the room.

Charlotte, white with shock, put her hand gingerly to

her cheek, stuggling again to hold back tears. 'That was not very auspicious,' she said dejectedly.

'She needs time,' said Silje soothingly. 'This was no better or worse than you could have expected.'

****

A few minutes later the servants, arrived bringing food as they had been told to do. However, their expressions showed clearly what *they* felt about meals being taken in a bedchamber! One platter followed another until the table was close to collapse under the weight of food. Silje could scarcely believe her eyes at the sight of so many bowls and plates filled with steaming aromatic fare.

'Please, Silje, serve yourself,' said Charlotte. 'I cannot eat even the smallest morsel. I feel that my insides are tied in knots.'

'I also feel like that when I am upset,' smiled Silje staring at the table in awe. 'But I hardly have the heart to eat. If only I could take one of these platters to the children.'

'They will be well provided for soon, so eat with a clear conscience,' said Charlotte gently. 'It is no less than you deserve!'

Silje ate in silence, trying to be as refined as possible. When she had eaten her fill Charlotte said quietly, 'Tell me about the boy, please.'

Silje nodded and had just started to speak when the Baroness came back quietly into the room. Silje stopped talking, but with an absent-minded gesture Charlotte's mother sat down close by and motioned her to continue. So Silje began recounting episodes from Dag's life, telling them how he had grown, what were his likes and dislikes, trying to explain his personality. Charlotte sat bright-eyed as she took in every word; from time to time she dried a tear, but always demanded to hear more and more. Many times mother and daughter smilingly remarked, 'That's typical for a Meiden'.

When Silje had no more to tell her captivated listeners, both of them straightened in their chairs and, with great dignity, the older lady said, 'I have given some thought to this and I realise that we have a dilemma. We cannot simply remove the boy from the family that he counts as his own – and your father would *never* tolerate his presence here.'

'Mama – you do understand after all! Thank you. Oh! Thank you!' Charlotte left her seat, fell to her knees in front of her mother and rested her head in the woman's lap.

'There, there,' said the Baroness as she absently stroked her daughter's drab, fair hair. 'Do not worry about anything my dear.' Looking across at Silje, her features softened. 'I can see that Charlotte wants to see him and be close to him. I too would like to know my errant grandson. And of course there is the matter of payment for all you have done ...'

'No!' Silje exclaimed. 'I did not come here for that!'

'Forgive me,' said the Baroness humbly, taken aback by Silje's tone. 'But I have so little knowledge of it ...'

'Quite so,' said her daughter. 'We should hear all of Silje's story, not just small anecdotes about Dag – Dag? It seems so strange to call him by name. Dag Christian ...' Her words hung in the air as she stepped over to the bell-cord and rang for the table to be cleared.

When the servants had left, Silje began speaking again. She told them all the details of that dreadful night when it had all started. How events had turned her existence upside down and a new life had begun – the way she had found both the children and then seen Heming bound to the rack. She told of the wolf-man who had suddenly appeared out of nowhere and insisted she save the youth from the headsman. And finally how she had struck a bargain with this terrifying monster so that he would find them food and lodging before he vanished into the night.

'And he was true to his word,' she added tenderly. 'We were taken to a wonderful farm to meet some of the best and kindest people on this earth – a church painter by the name of Benedikt, his farmhand, and two older women, Grete and Marie. Grete loved Dag as though he were her own child. Marie looked after Sol – the little girl I had found. Master Benedikt allowed me to go with him to help paint murals in a little church – he told me that I was an artist, and I believe that is true, because I am not a good housekeeper!' She giggled with embarrassment. Then she said, 'Yet the wolf-man was always nearby. I never saw him, but if ever danger threatened he was there. It was as if he sensed it. Then one day I learnt his name. It was Tengel of the Ice People.'

'Ice People?' muttered the Baroness. 'I have heard speak of them. Are they not a band of witches and wizards – a terrible breed?'

'They are known as such,' agreed Silje, nodding. 'I cannot deny that there are those among them who know much about things best left alone.'

'And this Tengel of the Ice People,' the noblewoman persisted, 'I understood him to be a phantom – an evil spirit! I heard the name mentioned in passing – at a ball, I think, a long time ago.'

No doubt amusing idle chatter among the upper classes, nothing more, thought Silje. 'The *Evil* Tengel lived several centuries past,' she explained. 'It is said that he made a pact with the Devil and in so doing put a curse on his own kin. Down the generations some have inherited his secret powers and also his terrible features. Ah! There are so many fables that tell of the Ice People's curse. Some say they will not be free of it until they unearth the pot that Tengel the Evil buried. It is said to hold all his fearsome potions, and indicates how, one day a child of his blood will be born, gifted with knowledge and wisdom the like of which the world has never known. These myths abound and I cannot say whether they are to be believed or not. No, the man of whom I speak, this wolf-man, is not Tengel the Evil but simply one of his line.'

Both ladies sat hushed, listening to her tale. It was impossible to see whether they believed it or not. But they were certainly curious.

'One day,' continued Silje, 'a distant relative of Master Benedikt arrived at the farm. Abelone, for that was her name, was a dreadful woman who wanted the children and me gone. She was fearful that she might lose her inheritance to us. So she denounced me to the bailiff, saying that I was in league with Tengel of the Ice People and should be burned at the stake as a witch.'

'What a terrible thing to do!' cried Charlotte.

'It was. But Tengel saved us at the last moment and took us into the mountains, to the hidden Valley of the Ice People, and there we have lived these past years.'

'In the mountains? Summer *and* winter?' asked the Baroness, her expression incredulous.

'Yes. It was a hard living – but we were happy. Tengel and I were wed. I bore him a daughter, Liv is her name.'

'You are wedded to the wolf-man?'

'I am. And I have never had cause to regret it.'

'But – they say that anyone who ventures close to the dwellings of the Ice People will die!'

Silje gave a disconsolate smile. 'They are ordinary,

dispirited people. They are outcasts who want only to live untroubled by outsiders. In the summer months they send watchers far beyond the valley to keep strangers at bay. I cannot say what fate would befall anyone foolish enough to trespass.'

'And what has happened to them now?'

Silje sighed. 'Heming was taken prisoner yet again. He was of the Ice People's kin, but had also joined a band of rebels. Indeed, it was he who wanted to blackmail you, Mistress Charlotte.'

'Uh! We have heard about these brigands,' added the Baroness. 'Can anyone begin to understand why these people would want to oppose our Danish rule? Such a rabble! They do not realise what good fortune they have!'

Silje held her tongue. This was not the time or place to be drawn into a political discussion. 'Well, to save his own life, Heming first betrayed the rebels and then gave information that led the way to the Valley of the Ice People. This last week the soldiers came and laid waste to it, burning the farms and killing without mercy. They left no one alive. We only survived because we succeeded in escaping over the mountains. But now we have nothing.' Silje's audience sat staring at her speechless with amazement. 'But worse was to come. Heming involved Benedikt as well, by saying that he was one of the rebels.'

'And was he?'

'Not at all, he is just a gentle old man. But Abelone seized the chance to have him thrown in gaol here in Trondheim. She then ordered Grete and Marie off the farm to live as parish paupers. They are wonderful old souls who should not have been treated so …' Silje was fighting to hold back her tears and stay calm. 'There you have the heart of my story. For myself, I am the daughter of a blacksmith on a farm to the south of Trondheim. All my family died from the plague and I was left alone in the world.'

Leaning forward and speaking very softly Charlotte asked, 'This Tengel – wolf-man, you called him – is he a warlock?'

Silje hesitated before replying. 'Yes he is,' she said at last. 'But he uses his powers only for good.'

'Might not Da … the children … have been harmed by being close to him?'

'Harmed!' cried Silje. 'Nowhere in the whole of Norway will you find a spirit more benign! But you must understand that both he and Sol – whom we later discovered to be his niece – bear the signs of the Evil Tengel's kin. To show themselves would mean capture and death. Instantly!'

'Then you cannot live in the towns or country parishes?'

'No – and our home in the mountains is destroyed.' Once more Silje fought back the tears.

'There, there,' said the Baroness, laying a hand gently on Silje's shoulder. 'I believe I have found a way out of this dilemma – and even though I say it myself, it is an excellent idea!'

'What is it, Mother?' asked Charlotte.

'First, I must give it a little more consideration. You have asked for my help – and I shall not betray that trust. Silje, I know that it might appear to you that we nobles are uncaring and arrogant. But believe me, although we are very adept at socialising and are well educated, we are not heartless. Now, this forester's hut – is it far from Trondheim?' Silje told her the name of the place. 'It is too far for us to reach it before nightfall. But we do want to meet the boy, don't we Charlotte?'

'Yes! Oh, yes!'

'You mustn't worry, Silje dear, we shall not tell him who we are. We only want to meet him and speak to him. Tomorrow morning we will all take the carriage, but for now we must prepare you a room for the night. Charlotte and I will make arrangements. Oh, and by the way do not concern yourself with this Abelone. She is known to me from social gatherings here in Trondheim. A *terrible* social climber from the bourgeoisie! I have good friends with influence here, and while I neither want nor can do anything to assist any rebels, I will have an old painter set free from prison *and* see Abelone sent back to her house here in town. It is only right that those kind folk should be given back their home, the old women as well!'

'Mother!' said Charlotte in amazement. 'I had no idea you were so well connected.'

The older woman pressed her finger to her lips. 'Not a word! I am doing this because it has grieved me to see my daughter so unhappy all these years. I tell myself that this might be your redemption. For my own part, Charlotte, I find life in this mansion here in Trondheim so heartily boring. It has taken its toll on me and I have allowed my lesser traits to take over. This has served as a reminder of how I used to be. I have been given an opportunity to do something worthwhile. Benedikt and his family cared for my grandson when he was in need – and that must not go unrewarded!'

Baroness Meiden smiled and Silje's expression was one of sheer delight. They showed her to a small bedchamber with dark panelled walls and uneven panes of green glass in the windows. As she lay looking at the carved bedposts she was so excited she was sure she would never be able to sleep. However her last drowsy thought was, 'What can that headstrong woman be planning. There is no simple answer to all this!'

Charlotte Meiden, for her part, did not sleep at all. She had been involved in a long discussion with her mother before she went up to her rooms. Once there she fell immediately to her knees beside the bed and prayed fervently. 'Thank you!' she whispered over and over. 'Dear God, thank you! Thank you!'

She cried so much that her chest ached, as tears streamed endlessly down her face. She could still scarcely believe her good fortune after so many years of heartache. It simply was the best thing that could ever have happened to her.

Chapter 5

Had Baron Meiden been aware that his shiny new carriage was being driven southwards out of the city on muddy country roads, the ladies travelling inside would never have heard the last of it. Fortunately he was away in the northern part of Tröndelag and would not find out. It was a most elegant vehicle, but heavy and cumbersome with no springs on the chassis. Its gleaming purpose was to show wealth and position. Now it was overloaded, groaning under the weight of food and unwanted children's clothing that mother and daughter had excavated from old trunks and cupboards. Without exception they were items that otherwise would never again have seen the light of day.

Silje sat opposite the ladies and revelled in the bright summer morning, relishing the sight of the wild flowers growing along the roadside and the richness of the meadows. She was desperate to know what plans the two people on the other side of the carriage had been hatching. They had told her that they wanted to speak to Tengel first – and meet the boy of course.

'How much has the child been told?' enquired Charlotte.

Her eyes were red and puffy from a night of ceaseless tears whilst her hands twitched and fidgeted nervously in her lap.

Silje had been reflecting on how splendid these women looked in their fashionable courtly attire and how different it was to her shabby, worn-out dress. Thinking these thoughts, she smiled gently at Charlotte. 'Until a week ago Dag and Sol had no way of knowing they were not our children. But they look so different from each other that Sol had started to wonder about things. They had been called "bastards" by some of our neighbours' children, so we decided it was right for them to be told the truth.'

Silje saw Charlotte's concerned expression and hastily added, 'Well, not everything, you understand. We told Dag only that his mother was a very distinguished aristocrat who had lost him when he was small – we did not say *how* small. He wanted to know if she had searched for him, and I said that she had likely died from the plague. I told him that his father was most certainly dead. We named no one. We said we had tried, but had not been able to find you.'

Silje was feeling uncomfortable and undignified. She should have worn a bonnet or hat, she thought, to show she was a respectable married woman. It would have boosted her confidence – but it would also have been a conceit, because she hated covering her hair, not least because Tengel was so fond of it.

'How many people know that I am his mother?' wondered Charlotte.

'Only Tengel and I. There was one other – he who had found you out from the monogram "C.M." and the crest – but he never knew *why* we were searching for you. We think he is dead now. He was kin of the Ice People and his farm was one of the first to be put to the torch.' Silje's throat tightened and she felt for a moment that she would choke.

Breathing deeply she stared out of the window, blinking and swallowing hard, until she felt relaxed again.

Leaning across the carriage interior towards Silje and speaking in a gentle tone, the elderly Baroness asked, 'Is your husband dependable?' When Silje gave her a questioning glance she added hurriedly, 'As a worker, I mean.'

'Oh, yes, that he is! He enjoys working for his family. But he excels in the art of healing, something he cannot practice openly. You understand why, of course.'

'If only he could do something for my gout! But that's no doubt impossible. Those fools for healers want only to let my blood, leaving me weak and miserable.'

'My husband does not let blood. He says it is worthless.'

'He sounds like a sensible man!'

'Yes, he is – oh look! I think we have reached the place.'

Silje enjoyed referring to Tengel as 'my husband'. Whenever she spoke of him in this way it made her feel that the bond between them was even stronger and that it was there for all the world to see. She could not help thinking that the Church might have objections to holy vows being sworn before a chieftain of the Ice People – yet nonetheless she was sure there were very few marriages more sincere than theirs.

Silje directed them off the road and down an overgrown forest track. Eventually the carriage could go no further so they ordered the driver to wait. The three women then carried the baskets and the small trunk filled with food and clothes deeper into the forest. The genteel ladies, Silje noticed, lifted their skirts and stepped warily over every single blade of grass!

Then Silje stopped abruptly in her tracks and they all paused and stood on a slope looking down into the clearing where the hut had just become visible. After a moment Silje made to carry on, but the Baroness held her back with an admonishing glance: the two ladies wanted to relish and ponder the scene first.

Tengel, his back to them, was squatting in front of Dag helping him to string a small bow. Sol and Liv were seated on the grass playing with the large wooden doll, chattering all the while in shrill voices. Tengel stood up and took hold of Dag's hose leggings – they were always slipping down – and tugged them up properly. Tears welled up in the eyes of both ladies.

'What a wonderful man,' whispered the Baroness. 'If only my husband had shown such love to our children even once! For that I could have forgiven him many things. You are lucky, Silje.'

'Yes, I am,' she replied. 'And with each year I love and respect him all the more.'

Then Liv caught sight of them on the slope and jumped quickly to her feet. 'Mama!' she shrieked, and at once the three children came rushing headlong towards them – but they stopped timidly as they saw the two strangers.

The ladies stepped closer to the children. Charlotte could not take her eyes off the boy. She swallowed several times, then whispered almost inaudibly, 'He is so beautiful!'

'Well, I love all my grandchildren, no one must think otherwise,' muttered the Baroness. 'But normally nobody can call any Meiden "beautiful"! Yet here is an exception – an enchanting boy!'

'And he has the look of an intellectual,' added Charlotte still unable to turn her gaze away.

'Children, come and greet our guests,' said Silje anxious that they should not fail this baptism of fire.

She need not have worried, however. Although they

were dumbstruck by the sight of these elegantly dressed ladies, all three children came dutifully forward. The girls both curtseyed so deeply that they wobbled and nearly fell backwards onto the ground. In his turn Dag bowed so low that his blond hair brushed the grass. Seeing this Charlotte was overcome with emotion and she turned away to fumble for the handkerchief in her embroidered purse.

Her mother was studying the older of the two girls with growing disquiet. She knew at once that this was Sol, the fated one. She did indeed have an unusual countenance thought the Baroness. What eyes she had! A strikingly pretty girl – but – but …!

The other girl Liv, was the image of her mother. Without thinking, the Baroness smiled warmly and sincerely at the girls and they cautiously smiled back at her. Finally, as Tengel approached, the ladies looked up to greet him. They both gasped and instinctively took a step back. The 'wolf-man', thought Charlotte and felt herself begin to tremble; those sparkling amber eyes, the thick jet-black hair and powerful mouth – and those shoulders, so broad, so immense that they could not be human. Yet most frightening of all were his eyes – they seemed, thought Charlotte, to search into one's very soul! Little Sol's eyes were just the same – neither of them could ever have denied their lineage!

What the ladies could not have known was that Sol's unusual features were not apparent when she was born – they had developed little by little over the years. Unlike Tengel, she was not in the least frightening to look at and showed every sign of becoming a strikingly beautiful young woman. But there was no one alive who could look into her eyes for more than a moment.

Yet this man Tengel, he was very extraordinary. He was

not ugly – quite the contrary! It was rather that he seemed so – *unnatural*! To think that tiny, gentle Silje had married him and they'd had a child as well! It hardly bore thinking about! For a fleeting moment Charlotte wondered what it would be like to let this man – this *demon* – have his way with her. She would never for one second have dared, of course, but the image sent a warm feeling through her. At the same time she felt a pang of remorse and longing. She did not desire him – no, at least not like that – but the thought of him with a woman fascinated her. Anyone who could make such an impression on a blue-blooded creature like her must surely radiate incredible sensuality!

Silje had immediately thrown her arms around him. Standing on her toes pressed against him, she barely reached his chin. Although his embrace was swift, the love that shone in his eyes was something the ladies could not ignore and their hearts fluttered. Letting go of her husband, Silje announced, 'Tengel, may I present the Baroness Meiden and her daughter Charlotte!'

Unable to hide a flash of surprise, he instantly regained his poise and greeted the ladies respectfully. The Baroness, who had also been transfixed by Tengel's appearance, was the first to find words of greeting, although she had been trying without success to decide exactly how one should address this unlikely figure.

'We … have with us some things … for the children,' she stammered, casting a rueful glance down at the forsaken hut. 'And we should like to converse with you and your delightful wife. We have taken young Silje to our hearts.'

Tengel was unsure what to say – this had all come upon him so suddenly. What if they wanted to take little Dag from them? But, no! Her words did not suggest that. 'Yes, but of course,' he answered formally.

The sound of his deep, gruff voice again took the two ladies by surprise but they quickly recovered and busied themselves unpacking all the things they had brought with them. Sol gave a very womanly squeal of joy when the Baroness held a dress up in front of her to see whether it would suit or not. 'It appears to be a perfect fit,' the lady declared. 'Try it on, little one, and if it fits – then it is yours!'

Without a second thought Sol allowed her own ragged dress to fall to the ground where she stood and began wriggling and pulling impatiently at the pearly-studded gown as the Baroness helped her to fasten it. 'Merete and Inger would just love to see *this*!' Sol shouted out loudly without thinking.

Silje looked at Tengel and there was fear showing on her face. She felt a lump in her throat. Merete and Inger were just two of the children in the Valley! Oh, God! So much pain! The soothing touch of Tengel's hand comforted her a little and eased the sorrow.

Charlotte had been helping Dag to try on a pair of trousers and a jacket. She delighted at his touch, his warm flesh, and it took a superhuman effort for her to restrain herself from hugging him and holding on to him forever. While battling with these emotions Charlotte suddenly caught sight of Liv standing wide-eyed, watching whilst the other two children were being dressed in such finery. 'Here, Liv,' she said hurriedly, 'we have not forgotten you!'

'Ooh!' gasped Sol when she saw the dark green velvet ball gown Charlotte held up for Liv to see. 'I wish I was still three years old!'

Charlotte and the Baroness laughed out loud and tears of joy ran down their faces. It felt as though the Yuletide festivities had already begun. As she watched all this, Silje was growing concerned about how the children would be able to walk dressed in all their wonderful new attire. Luckily, however, there were more sensible, day-to-day clothes as well and this pleased her and the children.

'Mother,' Dag whispered when nobody was in earshot, 'that lady hugged me and said, "Forgive me." Why did she do that?'

'It might have been because she thought she had scratched you,' Silje whispered back.

Eventually the excitement subsided and the Baroness looked around the clearing. 'We should sit and have a conversation but…'

'No, there is not much here to sit upon,' smiled Tengel. Both ladies understood even better than before why Silje adored him. 'And inside the shelter is worse – mould and damp everywhere – and if you stand up straight your head hits the roof!'

'And the children must be hungry,' said Charlotte. Why was she finding it so difficult to talk easily and naturally with this man? 'Can we not take a drive in the carriage?'

'Oh, yes! A splendid idea!' agreed her mother. 'And we can talk more comfortably while we drive.'

Little Liv steadfastly refused to take off her fine new dress. She screamed loudly in protest until Charlotte told her that, as they were about to travel in a magnificent carriage, it was only fair that she and the others should be dressed for the occasion.

'I pray she won't want to sleep in it as well!' laughed Silje, watching them all walk off in their finery.

The elegant vehicle waiting for them provoked still more screams of wonder and excitement from the children. They were perched up front with the coachman, who handed out food while earnestly discussing the workings of the contraption with Dag, who was intent to learn all about it.

Silje had managed to save a piece of chicken and some wine for Tengel. This he had quickly consumed, out of sight in the shelter, while the ladies were putting things back in the trunk before they set off back to the carriage. She did not want him taking part in serious discussions on an empty stomach! Hunger never helped the mind to work well. Perhaps, with everything going on, the noble ladies had simply forgotten that her man was also hungry. Or did they think that warlocks had no need of food?

The carriage drove very slowly down the beautiful country road. The Meiden ladies had felt ill at ease to begin with, trying so hard to look anywhere other than at this terrible demon who sat so close to them. Indeed, he was so close that the air around them seemed to pulsate with his presence. However, after realising that he felt no less awkward than they did, their voices became more relaxed and normal conversation began to be exchanged.

'I would ask you to hear first what I have to say,' said the Baroness in a friendly tone. 'Charlotte and I have a suggestion to put to you, one that will enable the boy to remain with you, yet also allowing Charlotte to be close to him. While my husband lives, she will not disclose her identity to the boy. After his death we shall discuss the matter anew. We spoke about this long into the night and we are agreed – the only question that remains is whether it is acceptable to you?'

'There is one other matter,' said Tengel. 'I must be sure of one thing. You must not believe that you have been deceived in any way. Are you completely satisfied the boy is yours? What if this is but some trickery intended to cheat you – to force upon you some stranger's child for our own gain?'

'We are in no doubt that he is a Meiden,' said the

Baroness. 'Silje told us that he shared Charlotte's features. I would say that he is an exceptionally comely version of the young Charlotte. We are satisfied!'

'Very good. Then we can continue talking.'

'It so happens that Charlotte has never been happy with life in Trondheim. We own a chateau and land in the county of Akershus that was intended as dowry for Charlotte when she took a husband. A small estate cottage lies not far from the main house and this, if you accept, can be yours. In which case Charlotte will take up residence in the chateau with her domestic staff. Your duty while living in the cottage would be to take charge of all the estate's outbuildings and barns, for Charlotte has little knowledge of such matters.'

Silje and Tengel reacted with astonishment. For a long time they could only look at each other and the Baroness in an amazed silence.

'Do tell, Master Tengel, are the tales of the Ice People told throughout Norway?' asked the Baroness at last to break the silence.

Tengel had to try hard to focus his mind on the mundane question through his amazement. 'Uhm! No, I don't believe they are. As far as I know, they are only known here in Tröndelag.'

After another long silence Silje found her voice and looked directly across the carriage at Charlotte's mother. 'What about your husband, the Baron, Charlotte's father? What will he have to say about our possible agreement?'

'There is nothing he can say about the Akershus estates. They formed part of my inheritance from *my* father,' replied the Baroness.

Silje and Tengel were still trying to assimilate the enormity of what had been offered and both of them remained speechless. Looking at each other they began to smile bemusedly as though wondering whether they were dreaming.

'Well then? What do you say about the offer?'

Silje and Tengel continued to stare at each other. Her expression was urging him to accept, and when he turned again towards the ladies, they saw his frightening face had been completely transformed by a broad and generous smile. 'I would be a fool indeed to refuse an offer such as this! We are most grateful.'

Charlotte breathed a loud sigh of relief and a smile lit up her face too, as she looked expectantly at her mother. 'On the contrary, it is we who are grateful,' said the Baroness. Then after nodding once to indicate her satisfaction with the outcome, she adopted a more businesslike tone. 'It seems we have an accord! However, it is not intended that either of you shall perform servants' duties on the estate. Silje is not a person for such chores and if I may be so bold, you Tengel are above manual work. At first you will be there as estate foreman, but we will watch how things progress. There are a great many workmen who will answer to you alone and you yourself will decide when and where you need to lend a hand.'

Tengel raised both hands to cover his face for a second then, removing them again, he said, 'This is all beyond belief! Why only yesterday our future looked bleak and without hope. But today everything has changed! And all this because Silje decided that she should go to Trondheim. When she left I had no idea what she planned to do!'

'Silje is a strong woman,' said the Baroness thoughtfully.

'I have never doubted it,' agreed Tengel.

'I'm not strong at all,' Silje interrupted. 'I weep at the slightest thing.'

'Tears have nothing to do with weakness,' Tengel

assured her. 'You weep for a while, but then grit your teeth and set to once more. You refuse to give in – and your devotion to all living things, everything you see around you, gives you that strength.'

The Baroness nodded her agreement. 'That is exactly what I meant.'

On the way back towards the hut, before they left Tengel and Silje to go their separate ways, the Baroness asked Tengel for advice on curing her gout. 'Young Silje tells me that you can heal folk,' she prompted.

Hesitating, Tengel asked, 'Whereabouts is the gout? In every part of your body?'

'No, it is my shoulders that are most troublesome, and sometimes my arms. I ache badly at night and have trouble sleeping.'

He paused. 'If it is only in the shoulders then I can help you straightaway, Your Grace. It's just that ...'

'Oh! Then please do so. Please!'

'I don't really know,' he said, embarrassed. 'I would have to ask you to uncover them and that would be unseemly.'

The Baroness was in two minds about this. 'Mother, you must do it,' urged Charlotte. 'Besides, you have attended *soirées décolletées* many times!'

'Ah, but I was younger then. No longer is my complexion so youthful and attractive. And here in this cramped carriage – well, it seems almost indecent somehow!'

Silje understood how she felt. Women always reacted this way to the potent effects of Tengel's dominant masculinity. Tengel waited. He would not influence any decision. What's more he had enough to think about, as the plans this noblewoman had surprised him with tumbled around inside his head. What did he know about running a farm? Had he taken on more than he could cope with?

Yet it would be impossible for him to decline this offer. It meant his family would be safe; Sol and he would be far away from the dangers that threatened them in Tröndelag; there would be food and shelter for Silje and the little ones – and above all else they would have their own home again. These ladies had asked him many questions. What did he know about the economics of running a farm? How many people should work in a barn? How would he organise the animal husbandry. What did he know about types of crops, seasonal changes and their rotation in order to keep the earth fertile. He had given the best answers he could, but otherwise he could only hope that they were content with his inadequate insights.

Meanwhile Charlotte was trying to urge her mother to find courage and resolve. 'Is it better to lie awake and in pain at night? Or is it a simple matter to pull the sleeves of your gown and undergarment from your shoulders. We can close the carriage curtains as well to give us total privacy. '

'I can also leave if you feel uneasy, Milady,' said Silje.

'No!' said the Baroness abruptly. 'I will do it!'

Tengel nodded. 'Then you must turn your back to me. If you sit there …'

'Will there be time before we arrive?'

'Yes, there is still some distance to go.'

The curtains were drawn and the Baroness bared her pale, freckled flesh. Tengel smiled, 'Forgive me, but you need not be ashamed, Your Grace, for this is not an old person's skin. It is too soft and supple.'

She giggled with embarrassment, as flattered as a young maiden might have been. Then Tengel placed his great, strong hands on her shoulders and she let out a scream. This was not what she had expected.

'Please remain still!' Tengel's voice had an almost hypnotic cadence. 'Relax – a little more now please …'

There was silence in the carriage and Charlotte stared in disbelief.

'No! But – oh!' mumbled her mother. 'It's so – so … *warming*! So *wonderful*!'

'Yes, it is, isn't it,' said Silje. 'The warmth spreads through you like fingers of fire.'

'Yes! Yes, I have never known anything like this.' The Baroness closed her eyes in pleasure.

Tengel gently manipulated the Baroness's shoulder joints and then asked her to stretch out her arms in front of her. This proved difficult because her cramped fingers were determinedly holding her undergarment up to cover her scrawny bosom. With Charlotte's assistance, she was eventually able to hold out her hands without breaking the codes of virtuous conduct.

When he had examined the joints in her arms and knuckles thoroughly, Tengel told her, 'You do not have the bad type of gout, Your Grace. You have been sitting in draughts too much. Always wrap a light woollen shawl around your shoulders. Wear no more low-cut gowns. Make sure your bed is not in a draught and cover your shoulders while you sleep, but not with a heavy garment – that will be uncomfortable of course. You may have tensed up too often from time to time and that can cause pains in the neck and shoulders. If you take the best care of yourself, then I believe all will be well with you. I shall give you a salve to rub into the skin. I should have liked to treat you several times, but I think this will help you for a while.'

At last he lifted his hands from her, and as he did so the old lady gave a sigh of regret. 'Oh! But that was exquisite!' she declared, drawing her gown back onto her shoulders. 'Those other worthless healers! Here! You must allow me to pay you.'

A sudden darkness showed in Tengel's eyes. 'This day it is as though I am already living a dream, Your Grace. Please do not cause offence now!'

'No – I beg your pardon!' The Baroness was flustered by her own incivility. 'It was tactless and unforgivable. Might I commend you to – no, of course not. You are a wanted man, and you will be moving away from here as well. Such a pity, such a pity. But I shall be joining you too, just as soon as I am able.'

This last statement sounded a mite frivolous to Charlotte, as the Baron's wishes had not yet been taken into account and she exclaimed aloud, 'Mother, please!'

Although she felt she could not allow her mother to breach etiquette, Charlotte was smiling nonetheless. 'You must forgive Mama,' she said, turning towards Silje and Tengel. 'Could you but know the tyranny she and I have been subject to all these years, then you would understand – but see, we have arrived!'

As Tengel stepped down from the carriage, the Baroness reminded him of the salve he had promised her. 'Yes, of course. Sol, run and fetch me …' He muttered something to the girl.

She looked up at him and whispered back, 'For gout? But I have some …' Her voice tailed off in obscure mumbling. Tengel and Sol continued their discussion for quite some time before Sol gave a final nod and ran off. 'It is better that she goes,' said Tengel. 'My foot still bothers me, you understand.'

The two ladies were undoubtedly intrigued by the confidence he showed in his seven-year-old daughter where medicinal remedies were concerned, but they said nothing. When Sol returned, Tengel gave the Baroness an ointment, and as soon as they had decided what was to be done in the next few days, the carriage lumbered off, soon to disappear behind leafy hedgerows and pussy willows on its way back to Trondheim.

****

Baroness Meiden was true to her word: Benedikt was released from prison and Abelone was required to return ownership of the farm to him. Silje and her family had enough time to visit the farm before they left to journey south. The farmhand, now back in Benedikt's service again, had been sent to the forester's hut to fetch them. The old church painter had insisted on meeting them once more to thank them for all their help.

They could, however, do nothing to save Dyre Alvsson and the other rebels. All seven of them were executed in great secrecy because the authorities were determined to avoid stirring up more unrest among the peasants. They were convinced that this would happen very quickly if the fate of the people's beloved heroes become known.

They heard all this from the farmhand as he drove them to Benedikt's farm. Benedikt himself had told of the tragic demise of a rebellion that was always doomed to fail. He had watched as the men were taken to the scaffold. He explained how seeing this had caused his stomach ulcer to go bad again – omitting to add that his excessive drinking had probably started it.

As Silje climbed down from the cart and saw the dear old farm for the first time in five years, a lump came to her throat. Grete appeared first on the steps, a tiny shrunken figure dressed all in black, her arms outstretched in welcome. She wore a beaming smile and Silje could not hold back her tears any longer. Neither Benedikt nor Marie were well enough to come outside and greet them. Marie was bedridden, although for today she had been brought into the parlour to join them. Benedikt remained seated in his favourite chair, unable to get up.

'Can't hold on to my water,' he explained. 'It's something that happens to us old men sometimes.'

He had aged terribly. Now he was withered, smaller and he trembled noticeably. No longer did his voice have its brazen cheeriness and the veins on his nose and cheeks told of many hours in the company of the wine flagon. His hair had thinned too and what remained resembled a well worn yard broom.

Silje's first thought was that these poor old souls might be overwhelmed by this reunion and that it would prove too much for them; but she need not have worried because none of them could have been happier. Half the day was devoted to catching up on all the news and admiring the children. At one point Silje told them how she longed one day to see His Majesty the King.

'Alas, dear child,' sighed Benedikt. 'I fear that opportunity has passed you by. King Frederik the Second travelled to Norway last year – and I doubt he will return. It is said that he and I share the same weakness. We drink a little more than we ought. That, they say, will put him in an early grave. Nonsense, say I! A tankard of wine has never killed anybody!'

No, perhaps not *one,* thought Silje with gentle irony.

So the King had finally come to acquaint himself with Norway, she mused, whilst she was cut off in a high and hidden valley. Not that she would have had many chances of seeing him, even had she been here, but life could sometimes play some unkind tricks. Benedikt wanted so badly for them to return to the farm to live just as before, but even he could not deny that Tröndelag was a dangerous place for any kin of the Ice People. Tengel and his family would have to act as discreetly as possible before they left, so that no one would have reason to suspect them.

As if by silent consent, they made their farewells as brief and light-hearted as possible. They were all too aware that this was to be their last leave-taking of one another and none of them was prepared for great outpourings of emotion. These four old people would be forever grateful that they could now see out their lives in a home of their own and they sent heartfelt thanks to their own guardian angel, the Baroness Meiden.

As dusk fell, the farmhand drove them back to the forester's hut, where it was felt they would be safer during the last few days before they travelled south. No one spoke as the cart clattered along; the children slept and Tengel and Silje were absorbed in their own thoughts and emotions. In spite of the cautious enthusiasm he felt for a happier future, there was one thing that bothered Tengel – the unborn child. Yet there was nothing he could do about it at the moment, when they were about to undertake another hazardous journey. To inflict a miscarriage on her now would drain her strength and optimism when she needed it most of all.

He would have to be patient and wait until they had arrived before he tried to persuade her to do the right thing – and of course he would fail, he knew that already. Would it be better then to give her the powder covertly? It would be almost the same potion that Hanna had given her to bring Liv into the world – something that he would not have dared to give her in that condition – and Hanna's concoctions had always been far stronger and more mystical.

He would make sure, he decided, that she took it when

they arrived at their destination. It would appear quite natural for a woman to suffer a miscarriage after a long and arduous trip. Thinking such thoughts, Tengel sighed. He did not relish the plan. He hated the idea of deceiving her, especially as he would also have liked to have another child. But her life, he reflected, was more important than anything else – for all of them.

Chapter 6

Before long they were on their way. Just a few days before their departure, Charlotte Meiden ordered a rider to be sent ahead of them to ensure that everything was prepared and ready for their arrival. The houses at their destination had for the most part stood empty for many years, with only an elderly couple retained as caretakers. The land had always been worked, although not very efficiently, and had produced no more than a small income for the Meiden family.

All Charlotte's great many personal possessions had been packed up and loaded aboard a ship now lying in the harbour. The ship would not sail for at least a couple of weeks however and Charlotte could not afford to wait that long. It was vital that she leave before her father returned from his travels because he would undoubtedly have put a stop to the whole enterprise at once.

One woman alone, she could hear him say, cannot manage a farm and an estate of that size – never! Furthermore, was she perhaps trying to usurp his paternal authority? Was he no longer allowed to decide what was best for the women in his family? And if he ever found out about Tengel of the Ice People, wouldn't his retribution be merciless? No one belonging to such a godless family would be spared, not even Dag – and it would be better if he never heard a word about his existence either.

So they made urgent plans for their journey and after considerable discussion decided the road over the mountains would be the one to travel. Because carriageways were almost non-existent, they chose to take a small covered cart for the ladies to travel in. But no one was sure how far it would be able to go. Most probably they would all have to ride on horseback a lot of the way, because there were certain to be stretches of road that would be impassable. Among the worst of these was the valley known as Drivdalen and they agreed that the best that they could hope for was to keep the cart as long as possible.

Everyone was aware that this overland journey would be arduous and fraught with danger. As a passage by sea was not immediately available, there was no alternative but to attempt crossing the mountains of Dovre. They would, however, have a sizeable escort on this trip.

It fell to the Baroness to try to explain to her husband why their daughter had left home, taking with her various items of furniture, many horses and a not insignificant retinue of servants and maids. They were not concerned that he might follow them. The official trips throughout Tröndelag forced upon him as part of his duties were torment to a man of his great bulk. A long journey south was the last thing he would want, and besides it wasn't worth abandoning his home comforts or risking his own very important life for a mere daughter!

The journey through the lowland countryside towards Dovre was relatively uneventful. Silje and the children sat with Charlotte and her maid in the simple cart with its hooped-canvas roof. Tengel rode alongside or ahead of them depending on the type of terrain they were travelling through. They had kept their baggage to a minimum and the great sea cargo was entirely made up of Charlotte's dowry, something she would hardly have need of now.

From the outset the weather was beautiful and not one of them complained about the fact that the cart had no springs and the roads or tracks were so poor that after two days they had all been bumped and battered black and blue. It was all so exciting for everyone, except Silje, who while hiding her fears, tensed up each time the cart lurched, trying to protect the life growing inside her. Only Tengel noticed this but his face gave nothing away.

Three riders went ahead of the party and two men-at-arms brought up the rear. They had four extra horses with them, to be used when the cart could go no further, and it was not long before they were needed. They had reached the formidable and dangerous Vårstigen section of the old Pilgrim's Way leading into Drivdalen, when the driver of the cart made his apologies and told them he could go no further. Bidding them farewell, he turned his team around to make the tortuous journey back to Trondheim alone – fording deep rivers, negotiating marshes with barely enough hard surface for a single horseman and finding tracks through swamps and dark forests.

It took some time to load up the baggage and get the children and women onto horseback. Then began a nightmare journey along Vårstigen's narrow paths, at the edges of which were sheer precipices on one or sometimes both sides. There were times when the horses picked their way gingerly along between the rough rocky wall on one side of the path and a deep ravine on the other. From far below, the constant roar of the River Driva assaulted their ears and occasionally a horse and rider found themselves carefully balanced as they traversed a narrow ridge. Generally the women and children preferred to walk along the most daunting heights, leading the horses, because they had more confidence in their own legs.

The path finally began to widen, leading onto flatter ground. The air was thinner and colder now. They had met no other travellers and happily no wild animals either. As they caught their first glimpse of the snow-capped mountains in the misty distance, their only companions were a few birds of prey, circling and wheeling high above them.

Silje was unable to free herself from the anxiety that had mounted within her every second along Vårstigen. She had been riding, holding Sol in front of her, yet at the same time she had been trying to keep a watchful eye on all three children. This had tired her out completely, but she felt unable to trust the others, even though she knew they were more capable of looking after the children than she was. After all, she told herself, they were all big strong men. The beauty and majesty of the scenery that lay before them was simply lost on her. Everyone else was busy discussing the various features of the landscape, identifying the peaks by name: Snöhetta, Rondane and many others. But the words simply whirled around her head and vanished. It was as though she was seeing the world through a veil. A long time afterwards, when someone asked her about the journey, she discovered that she remembered nothing at all about the ride across the mountains.

Yet, despite herself, she realised that a great many things must have taken place. She had a vague recollection of how they finally reached Dovre's flatter, less foreboding foothills, when a halt was called and they all lay back on the grass to relax and settle their nerves. She had been so frightened of any harm coming to the children that her chin trembled and her teeth were chattering. Tengel was looking very pale, she noticed, as he sat with Liv in his arms resting his chin against her auburn hair. Tengel had always treated the children equally, but Silje knew that he loved Liv, his own daughter, beyond measure. He would never have shown this openly, but many was the time she had seen him bent over her bed as she slept, a look of wonder and disbelief on his face that *he* had fathered a child – and a such a beautiful child as well.

Charlotte sat with her arm around Dag, talking to him and trying to calm his fears. Silje stretched out a hand to Sol, who came and threw herself down on the grass beside her. She too was worn out by the frightful journey and could not even bring herself to speak – a rare occurrence at any time!

They were still sore from the aches and pains, bumps and bruises they had acquired from travelling in the cart previously. The colour had still not returned to Silje's face, but she didn't complain or show her discomfort. The servants, who sat together on the grass away from the group, were also greatly relieved that the worst part of the journey was over.

Clouds began to form above Dovre as they moved on again. Icy drizzle, whipped along by the wind, tore into their faces, making progress very unpleasant when they neared another high point of the track. The drizzle turned to slushy sleet as they approached a wayfarer's cabin at Hjerkinn, a very simple log building, but a welcome refuge nonetheless. They took a well deserved break in the cabin to rest and eat. There the storm worsened and snow blew in through the gaps in the timbers, forming small drifts here and there on the beaten earth floor.

Despite the weather, they could not afford to stay there

for too long. They needed to reach more appropriate lodgings to spend the night. As they left Hjerkinn the snow turned to rain once more, but they did not encounter any real problems until they reached the staging inn south of the Dovre Mountains.

Weary and exhausted after the day's hard long trek, they were well received by the innkeeper and made themselves comfortable. Gratefully they accepted the best meals the house could provide. Tengel kept his hood up to hide his features as much as possible, but there was a distinct twinkle in his eye, indicating to Silje that, in spite of himself, he was enjoying the benefits of travelling with the aristocracy!

It was while they were eating that the innkeeper came and alerted them to two strangers who were sitting together at one side in the dining-room. He told them he felt they had been observing Charlotte's finery with greedy eyes for too long. 'I can't throw them out, you understand,' he said, 'as long as they cause no trouble. But they are no better than highwaymen, and that's a fact. So if you'll take my advice, you'll place a guard on your belongings this night. Aye, and bar the doors of your rooms properly too!'

Charlotte was finding the mixture of odours in the room from humans and food alike too much for her, but she thanked the innkeeper politely and promised to do as he suggested. Tengel offered to sit in the corridor and guard her door, but she refused, saying that it was a duty suited to a couple of her servants. Sol watched everything and everyone wide-eyed and listened so closely you could almost see her ears flapping.

It was customary for travellers to be given a place to sleep in the large hall adjoining the dining-room, but there were a few small rooms on the floor above that were reserved for more distinguished guests. Silje found it quite comical that she and her family were now treated as such – although naturally she knew these privileges were the result of Charlotte's influence.

The Baroness would never have dreamt of sending her daughter away with just a few servants and Tengel's family. Consequently there was one man accompanying them who, with propriety and authority, supervised Charlotte's affairs. Silje had no idea what his real title was – he was probably a bursar – but she believed he was returning to Trondheim as soon as they had arrived at their destination.

This young noblewoman had been accustomed to more refined society and would never have chosen to share a table with people from the same class as Tengel and Silje. Now, in an unfamiliar world of which she knew nothing surrounded by disreputable travellers, she sought their company. This also brought her closer to Dag and with every hour that passed she became more attached to him. In her heart she longed for the day when she could look after him properly and openly as his mother.

'You say you think he is intelligent?' she asked Silje at one point.

'Very!' replied Silje. 'I noticed it from his very early days.'

'It would be a pity for such an intellect to be wasted,' mused Charlotte. 'I've been thinking something. Could I tutor him do you think? Just a few hours each week?'

Tengel and Silje looked at each other with broad grins. They both held the view that learning was the way to get the most out of life. 'Nothing could please us more,' said Silje. 'But would it not seem odd if … I mean …'

'Oh, I understand.' Charlotte interrupted. 'Of course, I meant *all* the children. Well, the two oldest for the moment anyway.'

'In which case, you do us a great service, Mistress

Charlotte,' declared Tengel warmly. 'And we shall be sure to repay you by giving you our undying loyalty.'

'Then we are agreed,' she said, smiling. She was astonished over how pleasant it could be to talk to the lower classes. But these people were different from others in so many ways, she told herself. Poor, dear Charlotte! She had so little experience of the world.

They were sitting apart from other travellers in a corner of the dining-room that had been reserved for the use of more distinguished company. They could not avoid the smells and hubbub, however, or escape the eyes of the other guests. But Tengel kept his back to them. When an opportunity arose, they questioned the innkeeper very discreetly about the Ice People. Did he know anything about them? Had he ever heard tell of them? Ice People? No, the name was completely unknown to him; and he had met most sorts – folk from the district as well as wayfarers passing through.

This was a great relief to them all. The notoriety of the Ice People had not crossed the Dovre Mountains. Even Tengel gave a satisfied sigh and eventually, as the realisation sank in, he felt himself relaxing from the pressures of the past weeks. He attracted people's attention, that was true, and the innkeeper had been wary of him at first. Now he sat in the shadows disturbing nobody. Other guests had not spotted him and he intended to be seen by as few people as possible.

Tired by the trip, it was not late when they went up to their beds. They called to Sol and Liv who were skipping and jumping around the dining-room, chatting with the guests as they went. Both girls were scolded for their behaviour but, while Liv took it hard and began to cry, Sol was unconcerned and merely looked at them with glittering mysterious eyes. No one could ever know what that girl was thinking – those shimmering eyes concealed so much.

In the middle of the night Charlotte was awoken by a dull heavy noise. She tried to wake her chambermaid but found she was sound asleep. There was someone in the room – she knew it by instinct! But the door had been bolted and barred. The window! The man – or were there two? They must have crept along the roof and prised open the shutter. Had they used a ladder, perhaps?

Charlotte opened her mouth to scream, but before she could let out even a squeak, a rough hand was pressed over her mouth and the blade of a knife gleamed threateningly in the half-light. While one man held her down, the other rifled through her belongings. The maid stayed sleeping – she must have been exhausted.

Despite the danger, Charlotte was in a rage. She knew that her servants were asleep on the other side of the door while Tengel's family was asleep at the other end of the corridor. And she was lying here, helpless. They probably intended to stick a knife into her …

But they didn't. The chambermaid stirred and, after a whispered conversation, the men tied the two women up securely. Then they continued searching, swearing softly, until they discovered Charlotte's most valuable casket. Her eyes had grown accustomed to the half-light and she could see them quite well. As she watched, one of them wiped the sweat from his brow.

'What shall we do with these old women?' whispered his companion. 'They might have seen us – best if we – er …?'

'Yes, you go. I must rest a little. Then I'll take care of them. We'll meet up at the usual place. Wait for me there. At the moment I'm not – feeling too good.'

The first man climbed out through the window, carrying

the casket with him. They had found nothing else – she had brought so few pieces of any value with her on this journey. The second man sat down heavily on the chambermaid's bed. He wiped his hands across his face and then grabbed at his stomach, groaning heavily. A moment later he got to his feet, trying to find his balance, and Charlotte watched helplessly as he lurched towards her bed, still brandishing the knife. She lay there paralysed with fear, the gag muffling her attempts to scream and the ropes biting into her skin. The pitiful sounds that she managed to utter were too weak to be heard through the door.

The man stood motionless over her in the middle of the room looking down into her face. Then he swayed unexpectedly, fell forwards onto the floor with a crash and lay still with one arm resting on her bed. Charlotte pushed his arm off the bed with her knee and it hit the floor with another loud thud – and that was how they remained until daybreak, both women dreading that the man would wake up and kill them. But he never woke again!

Charlotte had barred the door from the inside. This meant that the innkeeper, Tengel, the bursar and a host of other people were now desperately trying to enter her room through the window! Of them all, the only one to succeed in climbing the ladder they had discovered standing mysteriously beneath the window, was the 'man of authority'. He then opened the door for the others, who had returned to the corridor, still upset and worried.

'This man is dead,' announced the innkeeper. 'You were lucky there, Gracious Mistress! But where is his friend? They are not from these parts, you see. They only show themselves here now and then.'

'He is not far away,' said Sol calmly. She stood, wearing only her chemise, looking inquisitively at the dead man.

Tengel shot a worried glance in her direction. He ushered all the visitors, except Silje, from the room and he sat down on the chambermaid's bed, holding Sol by the shoulders. Charlotte and the maid sat on the other bed rubbing life back into their wrists.

'Sol,' asked Tengel, his voice menacingly soft, 'what is it you've done?'

She gazed at him innocently, 'I didn't want – they were going to be horrid to nice Mistress Charlotte. I heard what they said about her, down where they were eating.' The room was silent as they listened to her, their fears growing. 'So I put some stuff in their jug of ale – just a bit – when I was running around and talking to them. But I only took a little bit! From that tiny, tiny leather pouch Hanna gave me – you know! The black one.'

'Oh, dear God,' muttered Tengel.

At that moment the innkeeper put his head round the door. 'They've found the other one,' he told them. 'Lying dead on the ground not far from here. We have all your valuables, Gracious Mistress. They were strewn all around him. Two dead 'uns! Who'd have thought? What an uncanny thing, eh!'

'Thank you,' Charlotte muttered, her lips barely moving. 'Be sure to tell those worthy folk who found them of my gratitude.'

Tengel's face had taken on a grey pallor. 'Sol,' he said, through clenched teeth, 'you will give me Hanna's bundle now – all of it – at once!'

'But it's *mine*!' she yelled.

'Yes, that it is. But until you are grown up enough to master the healing arts, you shall not have it. Do you understand?' Although he had said 'healing arts', everyone in the room knew that he meant something entirely different.

For a brief moment Charlotte shivered violently. Nothing like this had ever happened in her life, which had been largely lacking in love and full of indifference. She could not deny the thrill she felt at being in the presence of two such extraordinarily forceful individuals as Tengel and Sol. Tengel was a good person through and through – but she was not so sure about Sol.

Charlotte did the only thing she could under the circumstances. She stretched out a hand to the girl whose eyes were brimming with tears of defiance and disappointment – but not of regret! 'I am so grateful to you, Sol my dear,' she said sincerely. 'You saved my life and that of my maid. You did what you did with good intent, but your father is right – you weren't able to measure the dose properly. I am certain he will return all your things when you are older.'

'Yes, I shall,' affirmed Tengel. 'Now we must leave these young ladies alone. Pardon the intrusion, Mistress Charlotte.'

'Entirely forgivable,' she replied with a condescending nod of the head. 'Please inform everyone that we will be leaving directly we have eaten.'

'Of course,' said Tengel. He was still shaken by what had occurred, because he *knew* that Sol was perfectly capable of judging the correct doses of Hanna's concoctions. 'It would be wise for us to leave here before the bailiff arrives to investigate the deaths. And, Mistress Charlotte, perhaps you should try to dress more simply? We do not want to attract any more of their sort.'

Charlotte nodded, indicating that she understood completely.

****

Tengel and Silje stood in awe at the approach to their new home. To their right, about seven furlongs away, they could see Charlotte Meiden's dowry, Gråstensholm. It was a large imposing granite building, complete with clock tower and flags waving in the breeze. Charlotte had left them and was now making her way there. But their house …!

'Tengel,' said Silje, lost in amazement, 'I thought her house would be a mansion and ours just a small cottage on the estate. But the Meiden house is a palace! *This* place of ours is itself a mansion! Are we truly going to live here?'

'So it seems,' he answered, his voice sounding tired.

In fact the house was not as extravagant as Silje, with her unpretentious view of life, had imagined. Gråstensholm was a fortified mansion – a tall, square, compact building but not very attractive to look at. What Silje had called 'a mansion' was a much smaller, long narrow house with outbuildings at both ends. They formed three sides of a pretty, grass-covered yard and, judging from the height of the gables, there seemed to be rooms upstairs as well. So this was to be a new, exciting enterprise for them both.

'Tengel!' said Silje full of emotion and gripping his hand. 'Oh, Tengel!'

'We shall do everything we can to look after this house properly for her,' he said solemnly.

The children stared at the house. 'Shall *we* live in that house?' asked Sol.

'Yes, and if we carry out our duties well it could be our home for many years, perhaps.'

'Then that's what we'll do, won't we Dag and Liv?' said Sol turning to the two little ones. A simple 'yes' was all they could say.

As soon as they reached the house, Silje wandered inquisitively from room to room. She was pleased to see some items of furniture were still there: beds, cupboards and one or two tables that were fixed against the walls.

'I am a good carpenter,' called Tengel, full of excitement. 'Silje! That wall – can you see? It only has a wooden shutter, but isn't it just big enough …?'

'For Benedikt's glass mosaic!' squealed Silje. 'Yes, Tengel, it's perfect! How the colours in the mosaic will sparkle with the sun shining through it. We must ask if we may put it there! Pinch my arm, Tengel, in case this is all a dream!'

They had arrived during the middle of the day and all that afternoon was spent planning, admiring and investigating every nook and cranny as well as unpacking the few things they had brought with them. It would be some time before their other belongings arrived on the ship. Later, while Silje was preparing the first evening meal in their new home, Tengel went into their bedroom alone. He stood very still, deep in thought, listening to the children rushing happily about the house. It was far bigger than anything they had ever known before, so their voices echoed from the half-empty rooms and their footsteps clattered constantly across the wooden floors.

He opened his bag of 'things', as Silje preferred to call them. Searching amongst the small jars and leather pouches, he finally found a small box and for a long time let it weigh in his hand. Now, he told himself, at the end of their journey, this would be the right time. He would just put the powder into her bowl. She would never suspect it was anything other than fatigue and the hardships of the trip that had cost the unborn child its life.

The very thought of what he was proposing made Tengel feel as though cold steel had pierced his heart. He dearly wanted another child, but did not dare let it happen. The risk was too great. If he failed to do something now, then the most likely outcome would be that Silje would die and he would be left to raise a monster – one that would grow to be as wretched as he had been during all the years he had lived alone, or maybe even worse. He, Tengel, had at least been spared the most sinister traits of his evil inheritance.

Silje would never understand why he needed to do this; he knew that. She would mourn the loss of the child and, even if she never discovered that he was responsible for … In mid-thought he paused and frowned. Without turning he sensed he was not alone in the room; somebody was watching him. And he was not overly surprised, when he swung round, to find Sol leaning against the doorframe watching him intently. There was a curious bond, a synergy, between him and his young niece, and he had never doubted that her powers were far greater than his own had ever been. Sol sensed so many things. All the secrets of the world lay hidden behind her eyes.

Without saying a word, she walked across and took the box from his hand. Just as calmly, she put it in her pocket. Tengel was left speechless. He had been caught redhanded!

The look in Sol's eyes was impossible to endure. Her intense gaze bore into his very being and he sensed her words rather than heard them. 'Like unto like. A life for a life. Would you really wish such suffering upon Silje?'

He let out a long, deep, quiet sigh and lay his hand on her head. He was tired, downcast and sorrowful. Nothing was said, but he walked across to his bed and, from the shelf above it, took down Sol's bundle and held it out to her. Her gaze did not falter as she took hold of it and offered him the box in her other hand.

'No,' he said. 'Keep it until the baby is born!'

She simply nodded, turned and left the room. Wearily, Tengel stood and watched her go. Now there could be no going back.

****

They had just finished their evening meal when a message arrived from the Lady of the Manor that she wished to speak with Tengel. He set off straightaway, walking along a small path across the fields, and his spirits were lifted by the beautiful scenery all around him. Behind the house was woodland and forest while from the front one looked down on open countryside and the church. Far off in the distance he could see an expanse of water but whether it was a lake or the inlet of a fjord was impossible to tell. It was something to be explored in due course. An exciting life lay ahead of them, of that he was sure.

Charlotte Meiden and Tengel met in one of the smaller drawing-rooms and spent a long time talking about the running of the farms and estates. To him the room seemed vast. All the proportions and dimensions of this castle, which was how he thought of it, were so huge. This house was not completely furnished either, and was barely ready to live in. Charlotte's household goods and furniture were needed and would be well suited here.

'And finally, Master Tengel,' she said formally, 'we must make sure all the papers are signed and sealed.'

He froze. Wasn't this just what he had suspected all along – it was all too good to be true! Now came the rub – but what form would it take?

He frowned slightly. 'Which papers?'

'Why, the deeds to the house of course. They will show that you have purchased the house for a certain sum, but that is a mere matter of form. Naturally you will not be expected to pay anything at all.'

Tengel had stopped breathing. He had remained standing respectfully during their discussions, despite being offered a chair, but now he slumped gratefully into it.

'You mean that the little home farm will be ours? Properly?'

'Indeed I do. I thought that was understood.'

He went quiet again. Charlotte waited, yet despite her businesslike expression there was a tiny hint that she had discovered the joy of giving and the thrill of expectation.

'Mistress Charlotte, we simply cannot accept! You have already done so much for us.'

When she spoke her words were full of passion. 'Do you know, Master Tengel, how it feels, having taken the life of a child and bitterly regretted the deed for so long. Then to have the child restored to you in good health and happy. *Do* you know how that feels, Master Tengel?'

'I do,' he said softly. 'I know well. For Silje's own sake I tried both times to take the life within her. First it was Liv – and now I love that girl more than myself. Then ...'

'The new baby?'

'Yes, but Sol stayed my hand. I understand very well what you did those five years past.'

Charlotte considered this curious man with so many facets to his character. 'You have also treated *me* with exquisite courtesy, by not informing the authorities that I had abandoned a living child.'

'That *never* came into our thoughts. To that I can swear!'

'Thank you! Thank you so much.' Charlotte paused for a moment then continued. 'Sol – is a – remarkable child, but I must tell you that I am a little afraid of her.'

'You need not be Mistress Charlotte. She would go to the grave for those who are dear to her.'

'Yes, I had already realised that.'

She began arranging the flowers in a vase that had been placed on the table a little while earlier. Tengel watched the young noblewoman from the corner of his eye and realised that he had a lot of sympathy for her. She was by no means a pretty woman and to have been so mistreated and become so embittered in her young years must have hurt her so much. Yet she remained so warm-hearted. He decided there and then that he would be a true friend to her as long as she needed him.

'But our discussion has strayed,' he said swiftly. 'I – I cannot accept such a great gift.'

'Try to see it as I do. My life has been a wasteland of nothing but anguish for these last five years. Nor is my gift entirely unselfish – I will be close to my son, and when the time comes he shall inherit Gråstensholm.'

Had Tengel not already been sitting down, he would have done so now. 'This great estate? All of it? Castle, farms, pasture and woodland too?'

'Master Tengel, let us look things in the eye. I shall never be wed, but this boy has brought meaning to my life. If God permits, then one day he will come to stay here with me. But mark well, this shall be a gift, it is not offered as barter. He will come only if *he* wishes it for himself.'

It took a little time before Tengel could find the words to say what he had been thinking. 'You are an uncommonly fine person, Mistress Charlotte,' he told her, quietly and deliberately.

'Am I?' She sounded bitter. 'If that is so, then it is because you and Silje, and your little family, have shown me how.'

When all the papers had been signed, Tengel rose to his feet and made to leave. He bowed his head formally towards the noble woman in a final gesture of gratitude that still betrayed his sense of disbelief at his good fortune.

'Is there anything else I can do?' asked Charlotte very quietly.

Tengel stopped as he was walking towards the door, turned to her and smiled. 'As if all this were not enough!' Then suddenly a thought came to him, and he said earnestly, 'There is perhaps just one thing.'

'Pray tell.'

'I could probably manage it all myself, but I need your advice and your help to ... Well, let me explain. Silje once had a dream that she would live in a house with an avenue, an allée, of linden trees leading to it. It was but a dream of course, and could never be real while we lived such a meagre life in the Valley of the Ice People. But now? Could you help me to give her this happiness? To find some small linden saplings for us?'

'With pleasure! I shall make enquiries. It ought to be easy to arrange.'

So, a fortnight later, Tengel was to be found digging deep holes on both sides of the track leading to their house. He dug only six, because they had been given that number of saplings. But he fully intended that they would get more later. As he completed his digging, Silje and the children were all gathered round watching.

'This one is for me as father of the house,' he announced with a big smile as he placed the first young tree in its hole. The children pushed the earth back round its trunk and merrily tramped it down. 'And this one is for Silje,' he said crossing over to the other side of the drive. 'Then Sol gets her tree – then Dag – then Liv. And what about the last one?' He gave Silje an enquiring stare.

'The last one is for Mistress Charlotte,' she said instantly.

Tengel chuckled. 'You're not taking anything for granted, I see.'

'No,' she smiled back at him, shivering slightly.

'For Mistress Charlotte!' he said with great ceremony.

'Because she is kind,' added Sol.

Afterwards, however, Silje became slightly concerned by Tengel's behaviour. While she and the children walked back up to the house, he stayed behind with his few small trees. He moved to each one in turn as she watched – and Silje became certain in that moment that he was reading incantations over all the saplings.

Chapter 7

It took a long time for Tengel to accept that a house and farm of such proportions really belonged to them – and that his name was written officially on the deed papers. When at last he had accepted his good fortune, he spent a whole evening quietly walking around and touching the walls. He had waited until everyone else was asleep and was overwhelmed with feelings of amazement and wonder.

'This is mine,' he said to himself running his fingers over the woodwork. He wandered out into the yard and leaned on the fence; then he walked over to the well, strolled through the empty outhouses and barns, and all the time he felt he could scarcely contain the happiness inside him. Although he had inherited and owned the tiny hillside farm in the Valley of the Ice People, it had been nothing compared with this. This was larger than anything he could ever have conceived in a dream. Now in the back of his mind he found he was beginning to think of things he could do there.

It was late when he finally went back to the bedchamber and snuggled down alongside Silje's sleeping form. He stroked her hair tenderly and pulled it back from her brow.

Thank you, dear God, for our salvation, he mused, and bless Charlotte Meiden!

It soon became apparent that the Gråstensholm estate had not been managed very well while the Meiden family were living in Trondheim and Tengel found he had a sizeable task in bringing it back to a fit state again. But this was work he enjoyed and he felt as though he was doing something worthwhile. Slowly, but surely, the estate began to get back on its feet.

Silje relented and allowed a few animals to be kept in the farmyard, on condition that she had nothing to do with slaughtering them or 'anything like that'. Tengel, smiling, promptly agreed.

****

The death of Baron Meiden came unexpectedly, as the result of an apoplectic fit following an eighteen-course dinner. Not long afterwards, the now Dowager Baroness moved down to Gråstensholm, complete with her household and belongings. This was a pleasant turn of events, welcomed by everyone, including herself. Social life started to improve, as distinguished folk came to visit from Oslo and Tönsberg and even farther afield.

Then one day a surprise awaited Tengel. The Baroness had enjoyed boasting to all and sundry about her 'astounding physician' who had cured her gout by no other means than laying his hands upon her shoulders. Unexpectedly Tengel was summoned to Akershus Castle. Full of misgivings he saddled his horse and set off.

The wife of one of the Lord Lieutenant's closest men had sent for him. She was suffering from poor health in general and had heard tell of the Baroness Meiden's wonderful healer. The couple were waiting – the woman's husband being equally curious – when a guard escorted Tengel across the bailey to their drawing room.

The woman stared wide-eyed as he entered and the young Danish aristocrat with her exclaimed, 'How can anyone look like that!'

Thinking that he may be dusty and dirty from his ride, Tengel was about to apologise, but the insolent young man continued, 'Were you born like that?'

'How?'

'Looking like – that?'

'Our face is our own,' Tengel said abruptly. 'I am sorry if mine offends you.'

The nobleman decided he ought to change the subject of conversation. 'Would you please examine my lady wife? She suffers from a variety of ailments of which she reminds me constantly.'

Tengel nodded his assent and asked him if he would kindly leave the room. 'No! Why should I? Do you plan to seduce her?'

Tengel's anger was beginning to show. 'Do I look like a seducer of women?'

'Oh, no,' laughed the man nervously, finally realising that he had gone too far. 'No, you most certainly do not!' He left the room, leaving Tengel alone with his eminent patient.

Tengel helped her as best he could, although sparing her vanity, he held back from telling her the harsh truth, which was that all her problems were the result of too much good living. He named several foodstuffs that 'her delicate and sensitive personage could not endure' with the intention of reducing her excessive intake of food. To humour her he asked her to lie down and he placed his hands on her belly, allowing the feeling of warmth to radiate through her body. I am behaving like a charlatan he told himself, but this woman needs to be influenced by suggestion to make her obey me.

Last of all he told her to take a walk along the battlements of Akershus Castle every day, because this would improve the quality of her blood. The lady was delighted with her treatment and showed her appreciation with a purse of silver coin that Tengel received with gratitude and a not-too-sullied conscience. They would need a lot of money if they were to do everything they wanted with the home farm.

As he was leaving, the woman's husband met Tengel in the anteroom. 'Well? Did you manage to cure her delusions?' he asked, with a sneer.

'It was hardly a delusion. I believe that she will start to get better.'

'If that is true perhaps, as you are here, you might be so good as to take a look at old Bröms, would you? He complains constantly about his leg.'

Tengel agreed and was taken to another part of the castle. What confronted him there was far worse. It was a marvel that the blood in the veins of the old and vastly overweight Bröms managed to move at all. It circulated at a snail's pace.

'You do understand that you may well lose this leg!' Tengel told him quite brutally. 'You must begin to walk about on it. And you are much too heavy. I shall do what I can to help you, and with your permission I shall come back once each week for more treatments.'

The old gentleman, sweating profusely and frightened, nodded and swore to follow Tengel's instructions diligently.

'Good living,' thought Tengel as he rode homewards.

'While peasants are suffering hunger and misery all around us, these people are dying from excess!' But when he arrived home again, he revelled in telling Silje about his experiences at the Castle of Akershus.

And so it began. The Lord Lieutenant's friends had been so happy with him that, before long, Tengel was receiving summonses from one noble family after another. Occasionally he travelled to see them – and he could not fail to notice that it was the women who were especially curious about him. They called him the 'Demon Physician', a title he did not care for at all. Silje had decided to call these excursions his 'glory trips'.

On his return from one such trip, Sol came into his room and told him that a little old woman had been sitting for several hours in a nearby room, patiently waiting for his help in treating her ailment. 'Tell her that I have no time for her now,' he said abruptly. 'Doesn't she know I have been very busy all day.'

'No, she doesn't – and she won't pay very well either,' retorted Sol sharply and left.

Tengel stopped what he was doing instantly. Images of his recent successes with wealthy nobles and dignitaries flashed through his mind and he was suddenly overcome with shame, Turning he hurried out to catch up with the girl.

'Thank you, Sol!' was all he said, as he hastened to see the old woman.

****

Tengel soon made it known to his growing list of aristocratic clients that he would not be able to make trips away from the farm as often as before – in fact he would travel in future only in cases of dire need and emergency. So instead they began to come to him, those highborn and wealthy people who had learned of his reputation for wonderful healing. Despite the shock that his patients felt the first time they saw his face, they all soon warmed to his sympathetic manner and their confidence in him quickly grew. Soon he was receiving patients from every class and walk of life, not just the aristocracy. However, it remained an unwritten rule in the family that words like Ice People, sorcerer or witchcraft should never be spoken in the company of the sick and suffering.

Life continued happily for them all and in the autumn Silje took her husband to one side. 'Tengel – if some fate should befall me …' she began hesitantly.

'No!' he interrupted. 'Nothing can happen to you.'

'No, no. I know,' her voice softer this time. 'But let us say that it did, then I should wish to know that my legacy is in safe hands.'

He didn't answer, but just looked at her in despair.

'Would you care for the children, Tengel? All of them?'

'You know full well that I would,' he said in a tormented, choked voice.

'But they would need a mother.'

'I can care for them myself!' he blurted out. Then, almost in an act of desperation, he reached out and threw his arms around her, pulling her tightly to him. 'You know that I should never take another wife, Silje. I was alone for thirty-three years until I met you. And after you there can be no other.'

She never doubted his sincerity. Tengel was the sort of man who would only ever belong to one woman. There and then she decided not to voice her suggestion, knowing at once that it would have been impossible from the start. Furthermore she had to admit that she was quite happy with his answer.

****

October had painted the groves of trees on the estate a burning gold that gleamed beneath azure blue skies. Returning home one day, admidst this beauty, from a rare visit to a patient – this one had been unavoidable because the person was too ill to leave their bed – Tengel was overcome with a sense of unease and he suddenly urged his horse on as fast as he dared.

From a distance he saw Sol running towards him down the approach to the farm, the long track that would one day become an allée. When he saw her expression, his blood ran cold. 'Father! Father!' she yelled. 'Hurry! Hurry please! Mama is very sick!'

This was the first time he had ever heard Sol call him 'Father' or Silje 'Mama'. Tears were streaming down her cheeks and she looked completely distraught.

'Now?' he called back. 'Do you mean she is sick right now?'

'Yes, please hurry.'

He spurred the horse on. When he reached the yard, he saw a carriage and realised that Sol had been to fetch both the midwife and an old field surgeon whom they had asked to help when Silje's time came. He jumped from the saddle and ran to the door. The midwife came onto the porch and stopped abruptly when she saw him approaching. She tried to hide some disturbingly dark red sheets in a corner and gasping, Tengel rushed past her to the bedchamber and threw open the door.

As he stood there, for the first time in his life he knew how it felt to lose consciousness. He had vague impressions and noted odd details of the scene that confronted him: the field surgeon, a wrinkled, hardened old warrior who had seen service on most of Europe's battlefields, but who had also brought children into the world; a woman, it must have been Charlotte, but he could not see her clearly; and blood,

blood everywhere! From the corner came the sound of someone's angry, abandoned, weak cries. And there on the pillow, Silje's pale and lifeless face.

There was something primitive, primeval even, about Tengel's deep, choking sobs. Suddenly he was the man-beast once more, conscious only that he might be losing his mate, his woman, his life, his one and only happiness. 'Silje!' he howled, falling to his knees at her bedside.

He took her unfeeling hand and pressed it to his cheek, letting his tears run over it. He did not look up, even when the midwife came back into the room. 'We are doing the best we can, Master Tengel,' she said softly.

He managed to find his self-control and looked up at them. 'Does she still live?' he asked breathlessly.

'We believe she does,' the old surgeon answered.

Tengel jumped to his feet. 'I shall fetch my medicaments. Keep her alive a while longer! For God's sake, keep her alive! And try to stop the bleeding.'

'We shall do all we can,' Charlotte assured him. 'But you must hurry.' It was obvious that she had infinite belief in his power to heal.

Entering the parlour, Tengel bumped into Sol. 'You can have this as well,' she said handing him her bundle. 'Hanna marked everything, so you'll know what it is.'

'Thank you, Sol. It'll help.'

In no time at all he was back where Silje lay. Although unable to stop his hands from shaking, he found what he needed to staunch the flow of blood. The strong smell of yarrow and other odours, unknown to them, pervaded the room. When the old surgeon looked more closely at Tengel's and Sol's 'remedies' he whistled quietly.

'Not what you'd expect to see every day,' he muttered. 'Don't let the witch-finders see it, else there'll be trouble!

The last time I saw anything like that I was in Paris, at the court of the French King. They belonged to a witch who had been executed.'

Tengel was barely listening, but he knew he could trust this man. They worked for a long time, swiftly and efficiently, not needing to speak. Only the unrelenting crying from the crib in the corner disturbed the silence, but no one had time to pay heed to it. Eventually they stopped the bleeding.

'We can do nothing more,' said Tengel, 'but pray that everything is not too late – and, should she wake, she must have plenty to drink. Someone boil water that I may prepare a brew of herbs to fortify her blood.'

'Should she wake …?' He realised fully in that moment the extreme danger that had been admitted and expressed in his own words. She must awaken, she must! He listened for her breathing. Yes! He could hear it. She was alive. He placed his hands on her chest, hoping to stimulate her heart with his extraordinary warmth.

Charlotte whispered, 'Will you not look to the child, Tengel?'

'Later.' A grimace of distaste clear to see distorted his features. Tengel had no desire to see the 'monster' that might have killed his beloved. 'What happened?' he muttered, not taking his eyes off Silje's face.

His answer came from Charlotte Meiden and her voice had a soft, ladylike calmness that he had not heard before. 'Sol came running to Gråstensholm. Silje had sent her to say that she thought her time was very soon. My mother took the two little ones and I sent a rider for the midwife and surgeon before I rushed down here myself. I fear that Silje wandered around for too long – but there was no time!'

'It all went so quickly,' said the old man apologetically. 'You know that your wife has already suffered difficulty in childbirth and this child was unusually big.'

'More than nine pounds, you can be sure,' asserted the midwife. Tengel gritted his teeth. Nine pounds and more was an unbelievable size, he knew. And for little Silje …

'Because the child came so quickly, your wife was badly torn,' the surgeon continued. 'I had just stepped through the door when I was called to help.'

Normally there would only be women present during childbirth, but they knew Silje's case might present problems. As a precaution Tengel had made arrangements with this experienced man, for whom he had great respect, to be on hand. He was glad he had done so.

Charlotte said softly, 'It's a boy.'

The helpless, forlorn crying continued. Everybody was busy; the surgeon was finishing off, while the midwife performed her rituals to make the room safe from evil spirits. Charlotte was washing herself.

Tengel's thoughts went back to his own mother. She had been alone and despised when she gave birth to him and then lost her own life to her injuries. It was so different for Silje – at least she was surrounded by love.

And how had he fared? Nobody had wanted to take in the feared motherless child. Finally, his maternal grandfather had been compelled to care for him – and he heard a thousand times and more how he had killed his own mother. As an act of unmitigated spite, his grandfather had named him Tengel – a reminder of the evil spectre of the Ice People. Now he felt like that small boy again; listening to the whispers about him but not grasping what they meant; not being allowed to play with the other children; being kept apart and always, always lonely; and every morning he was beaten with a birch – just in case!

Drawing a deep breath, he got to his feet and summoned the courage to face his own hateful image reflected in the newborn child, or even worse perhaps – the image of Hanna or Grimar! To gaze at the yellow or amber eyes that were the unmistakable sign of a wretched creature, affected by the evil legacy and the hidden powers that it bestowed.

From where he stood, he saw only tufts of pitch-black hair showing above the edge of the blanket. It was not a good sign. He stepped closer and looked down at the boy's bad-tempered, screaming face. It was not easy to see what he looked like. He pulled back the blanket and the swaddling in which the boy was wrapped and examined his shoulders. They were broad – but not unusually so – and well formed. Undeniably this was a large baby, but he could find no obvious signs of the baneful inheritance he feared. As far as he could tell from this shocked and angry face, the boy appeared to have inherited Tengel's basic looks, but been spared his more grotesque features.

The infant seemed to sense the closeness of a warm human hand and its cries abated. Tengel put his finger against the tiny cramped fist and the boy grasped it instantly. Who, he wondered, had been there to comfort him when he came into the world? Probably no one.

Tengel drew back the covers and picked up the swaddled bundle. The others in the room said nothing. The quiet hiccoughs and sniffs were the only sounds, as the child struggled to open his eyes. Despite everything, you are my little boy, thought Tengel. No matter what you look like and even if you are tainted, you still deserve to be cared for. You are worthy of my love, and as God is my witness, I believe you have it already!

At last the infant managed to open his eyes – two circles of heavenly blue that tried to find focus on something, blinked at the light and closed again. The crying began once more, this time sounding like the screech from a cartwheel that needed greasing. Tengel did not need to see anything more. Blue eyes and a pretty little face that, although it resembled his, did not have the demonic, wild features that made him so frightening. Everyone heard Tengel's sigh of relief.

'She's stirring,' a voice said.

Still holding the child he went and sat beside Silje. He could hardly believe his good fortune, as she murmured and turned her head.

'Silje,' he whispered. He thought of how his own poor mother had lain dying, with no one to comfort her. He would not let that happen to Silje. 'Everything has gone well, and see! Such a wonderful little boy we have. I love you both.'

Her smile was very weak. She tried to open her eyes but it was too much for her. 'All … wen' so … quick,' she mumbled. 'Couldn't tell … you.'

'You never have been good at numbers,' he smiled. 'Last time you got it wrong as well and surprised us all when we weren't ready.'

She smiled again. 'I'm s…so c…cold,' she whispered.

The infant was put back in the crib, where it immediately made its discomfort known by screaming more loudly than before. Tengel placed his hands on Silje's shoulders and the midwife brought a quilt and spread it over her. When Charlotte arrived, carrying the hot water, Tengel asked them to bring in Sol.

Whilst he warmed Silje with his hands, he told the girl what she should do. 'Take the comfrey, most of it. Then nettle and lady's-mantle. Have you found it? Good! Now take some acorn … There is none? No matter. Then some hawthorn and lots of juniper berry. Good! Now do you have everything?'

'Yes,' answered Sol.

'Very good. Mistress Charlotte will help you brew a draught from them.'

Silje was very thirsty and her tongue was sticky and swollen. When it was ready she drank the potion eagerly. Before long she felt strong enough to talk and admire her new-born child, clasping Tengel's hand in her own.

'Do you know,' she whispered, 'I haven't dared to think of any names for this child? As we have not named any child in honour of our families, would you like him to have a name from your mother's side?'

'There is no need,' he smiled. 'We have already done it without you knowing. Her name was Line.'

'Ah! And Liv is a version of that. Your father then?'

Tengel's eye's turned cold. 'His name was not spoken, neither is he worth being named after. There is *your* father? His name was Arngrim of course.'

'Yes, but I think it sounds too serious. What would you say to "Are"? After the osprey.'

'Yes, that's it! Oh, and Silje ... he shows none of the signs.'

'That's wonderful. So now you will have to plant a new tree, won't you?'

'Yes,' he chuckled, 'I'll have to do several at a time, so that you get your "allée" and not just a clump of trees at the end of the track.'

He was overjoyed – ecstatic – and silently he thanked Sol for stopping him on that fateful day from doing what he had planned. But today had been distressing. The girl was standing at his side. The strength of the bond between them was frightening. Their eyes met. 'It might have gone badly today,' he said pensively.

Sol shook her head. 'Hanna once said that both you and

Silje would come to be well known people. You are – but she is not.'

'So you knew that she was to live beyond this day?'

'Yes, because Hanna said so.'

Hanna – Sol worshipped her as a goddess. 'Why did you say nothing to me? Have you not known the anxious months Silje and I have endured?'

'Would you have believed me – or Hanna?'

Tengel had no answer. His struggles with Hanna had always been tainted by prestige. And he had never allowed himself to admit that he had great admiration and respect for the old hag.

Before long Silje developed childbed fever and they called for the field surgeon again. 'Well, you've done it this time,' the old veteran told them sharply. 'This birth was much too arduous. Without doubt your wife will never have any more children.'

'Is it certain?' asked Tengel when Charlotte – who now came to help every day – took the children out to the scullery for a bite of food.

The veteran nodded. 'You know as well as I do that such a difficult birth can have consequences. There will be no more children! It's out of the question! No matter how hard you try. However, the childbed fever is healing well.' And with that he too went out to get some food – and a well-earned tankard of *brännvin*.

Left alone, the two new parents stared at each other in silence and slowly they both began to smile. Never had a husband and wife received such depressing news with such delight!

'We shall have an orgy!' whispered Tengel.

'A whole night!' Silje whispered back.

'A whole *lifetime*,' confirmed Tengel.

****

The Dowager Baroness Meiden was in a mood to grumble. Tengel found himself the unwilling audience one day, when he visited the castle to talk about matters on the farms. Gråstensholm was not a proper castle, although Tengel and Silje always thought of it as one. It was a country mansion with estate forests and farmland, nothing more. The foundation walls were built of large, grey stone blocks that stood unusually high above ground, lending them a fortress-like appearance. However the enormous mansion which they supported was a normal half-timbered building, boasting a small tower above the entrance upon which a pennant was flown.

'Master Tengel, we really must have some gilt-leather tapestries in the dining salon. Just look at the walls – they are simply *awful*! And not a soul in all of Norway makes gilt leather, so one has to get it from the Continent. And then, of course, all their designs are so terribly *dull*! Honestly I despair; everything is so frighteningly awkward nowadays. I expect it is because I am growing old that I fret so much about everything.'

Had she been expecting Tengel to contradict her about her age, then the wait would have been a long one because he was lost in thoughts of his own. 'Would Silje be able to learn how to decorate leather?' he asked at last. 'Your Grace does know that she has artistic talent? Her fingers itch to do something other than housework – she hates it with a passion.'

The Baroness beamed. 'But of course! Silje – yes, yes indeed! Have I not always said that household chores are not for her? And how is she?'

'Better, thank you. Better with every day. She has colour in her cheeks again.'

'Good – good. And the little one?'

'He keeps her busy,' Tengel smiled. 'He'll be a fine lad.'

'Yes, your children are exceptionally fortunate, all of them. But no! I think the work of leather gilding is too heavy and dangerous for Silje – all those acids and heavy lifting it requires. No, Master Tengel, you have given me another idea. I have noticed that in many country houses it has become fashionable to hang hand-painted wall coverings. *That* is what I shall ask Silje to do! I shall find a couple of girls to keep house for you. So pointless that Silje should wear herself out with washing and cooking and the like when there are others more suited to such work. We must look after our Silje, you understand.'

'Indeed I do,' said Tengel.

'And I admit to a certain selfishness in what I am proposing,' the old lady added with a grin. 'I shall have wall coverings superior to everybody else's.'

Tengel laughed. 'How goes the children's teaching? Do they behave well?'

'Why yes! Charlotte is so happy. She says that both the children are horribly clever! They have their ways, though. Sol is restless and sometimes makes mistakes. She loses patience it seems. But they are both eager to learn.' She walked over to him and whispered conspiratorially, 'Is not young Dag just the most delightful boy?'

'Oh, yes!' smiled Tengel. 'We have never had any worries about Dag. Not like …'

The Baroness sighed. 'We must all try to understand Sol. She is so good-hearted, really she is. And she has never given *us* cause to worry.'

'No, she will remain your friend until death. Yet it is hard to guide her along the right path. She has much that torments her from within.'

'Ah! But am I not correct in saying that you also, Master Tengel, could sometimes be difficult as a child?'

'That is true.'

'So there's hope for Sol as well!' she added, giving him the sort of backhanded compliment only possible because of the mutual respect and understanding that had developed between them since he cured her gout.

Silje was thrilled when she heard the Baroness's suggestion. 'Oh, Tengel! Is it true? To paint tapestries and wall hangings? Do you believe I can do it?' Then she paused, thinking, before adding, 'Girls to help in the house? My how grand we have become! I hope they are not too young and too beautiful!'

'Silje! What must you be thinking?!' he exclaimed, grinning. 'But your jealousy flatters me.'

Tengel moved to embrace his smiling wife but at that precise moment the young Are interrupted their loving banter. They laughed at the coincidence and broke off from a caress to see what the newest member of their family required. Son of Tengel of the Ice People, Are as might have been expected, was an energetic infant with a strong will – and very powerful lungs!

****

In the event they had to wait three months for their 'orgy', by which time Silje was her old self again. Charlotte had suggested one night that the three older children be allowed to stay overnight at the castle, and they had gleefully accepted. Tengel and Silje had not objected, but had kept their reasons to themselves. So at long last they were alone in the cottage, except for an infant sleeping peacefully in the next room.

'Now, Silje!' Tengel said, his voice full of vulgar

anticipation. 'Now we can make up for all we have missed these past years.'

'No more cares, no more worries,' she replied with a high-pitched giggle, feigning horror at the resolute look in his eyes. 'Tengel – stand still just there, on the rug! I want this to be slow and pleasurable, and I have never seen you properly – you know what I mean – we have always had to do things under the covers, in secret, because of the children. Not now! Stand still and let me undress you.'

He gave a deep and happy laugh. He had hardly been able to keep a straight face. 'My old Silje is back at last.'

One after the other she slowly removed his garments, kissing every part of his body as she did so: arms, shoulders, neck, hands, torso … Tengel could not help but become aroused. A single candle burned on the table and logs crackled in the open fireplace in the corner, but there was no other light in the room.

He stood in front of her, the glow from the flickering fire highlighting the muscles of his strong body. Silje took his hands in hers and stepped back to admire his enormous shoulders and powerful chest covered in hair, a thin ribbon of which continued downwards towards his narrow hips, long thighs and straight legs. Most of his body in fact was covered in hair.

'You are truly a demon,' she whispered. 'The Green Man, a satyr of the forest who will seduce every amorous nymph.' Her eyes were teasing him. 'But that life is over now! You are mine, Tengel, the most attractive and desirable creature on earth. Be my man and my master!'

She sank to her knees in front of him and placed her hands on his hips. He caressed her hair and her forehead while his whole body trembled.

'I have never told you my second dream,' she whispered

hoarsely, letting her hands glide slowly forwards. 'Oh, how I have longed for you.'

Then, gently kissing the part of him that her hand clasped so readily, she told him what she had dreamt shortly after they had met for the second time. How she had lain naked and helpless while the soldiers wanted to desecrate her. How the 'man-beast' that had saved her in the dream was a real demon. That his long tongue had been hot against her throat and how, finally, he had fallen to his knees, licking her thighs until she awoke, burning with untamed lust.

'I shall do all those things and more,' Tengel told her quietly, his passion aroused. 'Come, my beloved, now I shall undress you! This night belongs to us and there is much we must share before the dawn.'

Chapter 8

Some years later, in 1594, a new young stable lad named Klaus came to work at Gråstensholm. Muscular and well built, he was endowed with passable good looks, but unfortunately he was not the most intellectually gifted of young men. As a result the other stable lads harried him with ribald and suggestive tales of big-bosomed serving wenches, the activities of cows on heat and other similar topics. Klaus usually responded to their taunts with silent tight-lipped smiles and for the most part kept himself to himself.

He had not been there very long when he began to notice an attractive girl, aged about eleven, who often came up to the house to play with the young master Dag, a fair-haired twelve- or thirteen-year-old with a friendly, abstracted expression. Klaus knew the girl's name was Liv, because he had heard Dag call her that. She had wavy, chestnut-brown hair and was so pretty, in fact, that he would watch her in secret admiration whenever he got the chance, marvelling at the sweetness of her charm.

He had listened to the other stable lads telling how Mistress Charlotte at the big house had shown great courage during the past winter. She had proudly declared the boy, Dag, to be her son and consequently she had lost many friends from her social circle. However those who had remained true to her had proved to be worthy friends indeed. But oh, what gossip there had been – from the scullery and servants' quarters to the finest salons. They said, although it had been a very difficult time for her, she had bravely weathered the storm. Anyway, it was rumoured that this blond boy would now inherit all Gråstensholm! How foolish this seemed; he appeared to have no interest at all in the land, preferring instead to bury his head in books.

One day, while Klaus was grooming a horse, Dag came out to the stable yard to meet Liv, who was accompanied on this particular occasion by her brother and sister. Hearing them approach, Klaus looked up in surprise. The brother was clearly the youngest, even though he was a strapping lad, already as tall as Liv. He had jet-black hair, prominent cheekbones and widely-spaced eyes that lent a quiet assurance to his expression. But this time Klaus only gave the boy and Liv the briefest of glances, because his attention was drawn immediately to the other girl, who was obviously a few year older than Liv.

Liv was very pretty, but never in his life had he seen anyone more alluring than the older girl. As he looked at her, powerful emotions began to stir deep within him. Framed by dark brown curls, her face, with its high cheekbones, sparkling green eyes and stunning cherry red lips, had an almost feline quality. As he studied her from the shadows of a stable he was seized by a fierce yearning to reach out and embrace her. But, seemingly without noticing him, she moved casually away with the others in the direction of the main courtyard, her well rounded hips swaying provocatively as she walked.

Klaus stood distractedly brushing the same spot on the horse's rump and only woke from his reverie when the animal jostled him impatiently. Suddenly he saw Liv's younger brother walking across the yard towards him. The boy bowed respectfully and asked Klaus if the horse was good-natured.

'Yes, he is,' replied the stable lad. 'Do you want to ride it?'

The boy was very keen to try a ride, so Klaus quickly lifted him up onto the animal and began walking him round the stable yard. 'What's your name, then?'

'I'm called Are and I'm seven, nearly eight years old.'

'So is this just a visit to Gråstensholm?'

'Yes. Dag is giving a Saint Hans feast for all the children hereabouts because it's Midsummer. Dag is my brother.'

'Is he?' Klaus was bewildered and couldn't quite understand this. 'Was they your sisters with you, then?'

'Yes. Liv and Sol.'

The stable lad's heart began to pound. 'Sol – is she the bigger one?'

'Yes, and Liv is the little one.'

'How old's Sol then?'

'She's fourteen.'

Klaus's heart sank. He could have sworn she was at least sixteen.

'Here come the Eikeby children,' said Are, his attention elsewhere. He was an innocent child, who saw nothing unusual in Klaus's questions. 'They are coming to the feast too. Poor things! Folk say they get beaten every day – lots of times.'

'Of course. Don't all children get beaten?'

'Not us. We don't get beaten.'

Klaus was astonished. 'But that is dangerous! How else is original sin to be driven out?'

'What's that, then?'

'You go to church, don't you?'

'Yeah, but it's very boring, so I sit and count the stars painted up in the roof. Sometimes I watch the priest's beard jiggle up and down. I never listen to him 'cos he's so angry and shouting at us all the time.'

'But every child *must* be beaten! To drive out the Devil – don't you know?'

'What devil?'

'The one who lives inside us all!' exclaimed Klaus.

Are considered this. 'Why do you drive him out if he just jumps back in again?'

Klaus asked, 'Are you *never* beaten?' He simply could not believe this.

'Oh, yes! When I set fire to the grass once. And when I shut the girls in the sheep shed. Ooh, they screamed lots and lots!' He grinned at the memory. 'But it wasn't any devil that did it – it was me! All by myself! No, father doesn't hold with birching 'cos he thinks children have to feel wanted. He wasn't wanted when he was little, so he said.'

All this was beyond Klaus. 'Where d'you live then?'

Are pointed to the cottage that was his home.

'There?' said the stable lad. 'But that's where the famous healer, Tengel, lives, isn't it?'

'Yeah. He's my father and Silje Arngrimsdotter is my mother. Have you heard of her?'

'No-o,' said Klaus hesitantly. He was still trying to work out the family connection between Dag and Mistress Charlotte. He hadn't been blessed with Are's intellect.

'But you've heard of Master Arngrim, haven't you?' asked Are.

'Yes, he paints pictures on walls.'

'Well then, that's my mother, that is. You see she couldn't

go by her own name 'cos women can't do painting and such things. So nobody, except the ones who made her a Master of her craft, knows that Master Arngrim is my mother. She paints tapestries and wall hangings on cloth, but she also paints straight onto the walls. She likes doing the cloth ones best 'cos then she can stay at home. Lots of people want them – and they say she's clever.'

Klaus wasn't really paying attention to all this. He was still churning through his own thoughts. 'So Master Tengel is Dag's father?'

'Yes.'

'And the Mistress Charlotte is his mother?'

'No, it's … No, this is what happened: Dag is only my foster brother. He is not blood kin at all. Mother and Father took him in when he was very small, so we've always been brothers.'

Klaus nodded; things were becoming clearer.

'And Sol is not my sister either.'

'Is she not?' The stable boy's interest was rekindled.

'No, she's really my cousin. Her parents died of the plague. Sol can do magic – but you mustn't tell!'

Klaus smiled. That was something he did *not* believe. By this time, they had walked twice round the yard, so he stopped and helped the young boy down from the horse.

Charlotte Meiden had been watching them from the window, where she stood while waiting for the food to be laid out ready for the feast. In the background she heard Dag talking with his 'sisters' and on the lawns she could now see that the other children had begun to gather. She was remembering the day last winter when she had summoned every ounce of courage she possessed in order to explain to the boy who she was. Obviously she had sought permission from Tengel and Silje and they had both readily agreed that he was old enough to hear the truth.

'Dag,' she had said in a soft voice that trembled slightly, 'have you never wondered who your real mother is?'

His clear, intelligent eyes settled on her. 'No, I didn't need to wonder. It's you, isn't it?'

She was so startled a shudder ran through her. 'Who told you this?'

'No one at all. I simply knew it. I have known it for a long time.'

Charlotte remained transfixed. 'Does it make you unhappy?'

Slowly and deliberately he said, 'No. We all call you our fairy godmother.'

These thoughts were going round in her head as she stood at the window. Yes, it was true that she and her mother had done a lot for them, pulling them out of humiliating poverty to a life of which their goodness and character were worthy. Charlotte's own siblings had openly reproached them. They were unable to comprehend how she and her mother could mix with people of such low standing, who were probably just tricksters intent on taking everything from them

But the family did not know Silje and Tengel, Charlotte reflected, or the unbreakable bond that joined them to her. None of them would understand the richness that this had brought both to her mother's life and her own. Charlotte had been shaken by the events surrounding Are's birth, witnessing how Silje had almost died. But she hoped that in a small way she had begun to make amends for her unforgivable behaviour when Dag was born. She had undoubtedly played a small part in Silje's survival, quickly summoning help and running over to the house. But of course it was Tengel who had done most to save the situation.

Never had she or her mother regretted anything they had done for Silje and Tengel. They were the best friends anybody could wish to have, and because they too had now become well known and respected, nobody was embarrassed at being acquainted with them. Charlotte and her mother, however, had *never* been ashamed of them.

Dag had moved into the 'Big House' on his twelfth birthday. Are had stayed with him for the first few days, so that he would not feel lonely in his new surroundings, but in fact Dag had felt at home from the beginning. He knew Charlotte and her mother very well and was quite pleased to think that he would one day be master of the estate. Also, with his 'siblings' living close by, he knew he would never want for company. After some thought he decided to call his mothers 'Mama Silje' and 'Mama Charlotte', while the Dowager Baroness would be Grand-mama.

Charlotte watched through the window as Sol came outside to fetch her little brother. Are was completely different in looks and personality from his brother and sisters – everyone considered them all to be siblings, even though only Liv and Are were truly brother and sister. The young lad had a quiet strength, and seemed at one with the earth; and although he was probably the least gifted of them all as far as schooling was concerned, he more than made up for this with his gentle humour and passion for the world around him. Are had no doubt where his future lay – he would become a farmer and take care of the home farm, or Linden Allée as it was now called. He would do it on his own and he would do it properly! Mother and father had made a clumsy attempt to play at farming and already he didn't think much of it.

Linden Allée – Charlotte could see it from her window. All the trees had been planted and had grown well, each of them now taller than the man who planted them. She had known for a long time that one of them was named for her. There was one for her mother as well, planted at the same time as Are's on the other side of the allée. None of the other trees had been given names – yet.

Sol, she could see, was now standing in the yard talking to the stable lad. Charlotte did not think this was wise. Sol was so unthinking. She had obviously forgotten the advances that had already been made to her by young lads from some of the other farms, and how angered she had been by their vulgar suggestions. Tengel had been in such a fury that even Charlotte had been scared of him on that occasion. She realised then that he could be a dangerous man if anyone threatened those closest to him.

No, thought Charlotte, Sol ought not to be passing time with that strong well built stable boy – she was much too attractive and precocious! Yet what could anyone do? Silje had told her that for as long as she could remember, Sol had always been drawn to stable lads, carriage drivers and other simple muscular men. And there she was now admiring the lad's physique, watching his muscles ripple beneath his linen singlet. Charlotte could see that Sol clearly enjoyed toying with him, causing him to blush and turn away whenever her green eyes transfixed him.

Klaus for his part dared not look directly at her. All his instincts were telling him to be very wary. In the first place, he reminded himself, he was a stable hand and she was from a fine family; secondly she was but fourteen years old. Thirdly her physical presence so overpowered and aroused him that he found it difficult to breathe. Aware that he was unable to conceal this entirely, he stole a quick glance down at himself and turned hurriedly away in embarrassment.

Sol's eyes were sparkling green and gold as she smiled at

Klaus. 'Thank you for letting my little brother ride,' she said sweetly. 'Come, Are, the feasting is about to start.' She turned and walked away, feeling wondrously elated. Knowing Klaus would be watching, she exaggerated the swaying of her hips as she went up the steps into the house.

I will have to speak to Silje about this, thought Charlotte with a worried frown. Sweet young Sol – she could be so tender and kind-hearted and took such good care of the little ones – but wouldn't she burn herself out unless somebody stopped her in time? She never did anything by halves, Charlotte reflected. It was as if she was living and doing everything too fast.

****

The following day Silje received a visitor. The wife from one of the neighbouring farms had surprised her in the little 'studio' she had set up at home. Silje would not usually have let people see what she was working on, but the servant girls must have been busy elsewhere, because the woman, Beate, had marched straight in, unannounced.

Beate was a middle-aged woman who was only too pleased to share her woes and complain about life in general, but when she saw what Silje was occupying herself with she became uncommonly agitated. For a full fifteen minutes she held forth with many repetitions of 'Oh, dear' and 'Alas' about such a terrible waste of time.

'I can't see why you want to do all this rubbish, Fru Silje,' she declared waving a dismissive hand in the direction of the soon-to-be-finished tapestry. 'Wherever do you find the time to do your household chores?'

'We have help with those.'

'My husband would *never* tolerate such a thing as this!

Ungodly doings is what it is, all of it. Lord save me from such foolishness! It's a woman's *duty* to keep house and be respectful to her husband and give him comfort, so it is! And what's more, Fru Silje, you should be wearing a hat – proper sinful not to …' Silje chuckled and tried to concentrate on her painting. 'And my husband says there is nothing worse than a lazy, useless wife.' Beate's whining droned on and on. 'You wouldn't believe how hard I work from the moment I get up 'till evening, and still he complains!'

Silje interrupted the flow – she couldn't help herself. 'My husband never complains,' she said.

The woman stared at her. 'Then there must be something wrong with him! It's a man's rightful duty to chastise his woman and his children. That's how it is and that's how it always will be. All else would be unthinkable!'

'Are you saying that you are content with your life?' asked Silje.

'Content? Of course I'm content! I have a man and he lets me live under his roof. Any woman would be grateful for that.'

'Really?' Silje was feeling argumentative now. 'Even if he beats you?'

The previous week Beate had arrived with her face black and blue as a result of what she called her husband's chastisement. 'Any man who does not beat his wife is not the master of his house. You should know that, Fru Silje.'

Silje put down her brushes. 'No! That is something I do *not* know! Tengel has never hit me and what is more he has never had cause to do so. We can speak to one another about anything we wish, and that is more important than trying to show who is the most powerful.'

At this point Beate realised the conversation was heading into deep water and she was about to sink, so she changed the subject. 'Anyway what is all this you're doing? Wasting time, I'm sure, messing up good expensive cloth with fancy colours!'

'It's just something I'm doing to pass the time. I'm going to hang it in the bedchamber,' Silje lied, not wanting it to be widely known who she was. 'Have you finished all your chores already, Beate? My, you have done well!'

Having just boasted how much hard work she did from morning to night, Beate perhaps began to see that she wasn't so industrious after all. She left not long after that, leaving Silje alone in her studio to carry on with her painting; but the mood had deserted Silje and her head filled with thoughts about the ups and downs of the married couples they knew.

At first she did not realise that she had a second visitor that day. Charlotte stood in the doorway for a while watching her as she sat painting her designs on a great expanse of stretched canvas. Silje had her back to Charlotte, and was mumbling angrily through gritted teeth while making sweeping strokes with her brushes.

Artistic temperament! thought Charlotte. She couldn't have known that it was Martin Luther, and particularly his declaration that *man* was the superior being in the natural order of things, that had provoked Silje's rage. Charlotte never ceased to be amazed at how young Silje looked, even though she must by now be about thirty years old. There could be no question she was genuinely talented – every design was unique and her motifs varied with each canvas – and it came as no surprise that her work was in demand.

Yet nothing she produced would ever be as fine as the first tapestry she had painted for Gråstensholm. It depicted Charlotte's journey from Trondheim over Vårstigen and

Dovre, down through Gudbrandsdalen, showing the wayfarers' lodges and everything as she and Silje had remembered it. It was a glorious wall hanging that caught everyone's attention.

Charlotte cast a glance around for Liv, but she was not there. Liv, having inherited her mother's imagination, was also blessed with artistic talent, although as yet she was too young to help with any painting. In spite of this she happily amused herself in the studio while Silje worked, making things on her own, cleaning brushes and painting her own small scenes of simple landscapes, never failing to include gleaming rays of sunshine. There was obviously a lot of sunlight and brilliance in Liv's own world.

It was a pity that their son, Are, had not been the artistic one, thought Charlotte. A girl could do so little. Just like Silje, she would have to hide her light under a bushel, working unseen without either recognition or praise. Of course she did not think for one moment that Silje cared for fame – but one never knew.

Choosing her moment, Charlotte stepped fully into the room and quietly announced her arrival. 'Aha! I see Master Arngrim is finding inspiration today?'

Silje turned. One cheek was painted vermilion and a black smudge marked her forehead.

'Charlotte! I didn't hear you come in. Yes, isn't it awful that I have to call myself "Master" Arngrim? Tengel likes to tease me about it. Sometimes he says, "I slept with a master last night!" You cannot imagine how I had to fight to be acknowledged by the other members of the Guild and become articled. Some of the old men sniffed at the idea. "Whoever heard of a woman who could paint?" one of them said. And another, "We'll be a laughing stock." But after a lot of demeaning comments they allowed me to take my articles – and I was admitted straightaway – on the condition that I didn't reveal that I was a woman, of course. It was some consolation to hear one of the judges say that while most of the Guild were craftsmen, *I* was an artist. Yet even then there were those who refused to believe that I had completed my master's qualification on my own! Now it's time for a break.'

It was during the previous winter that they had ceased using titles to address each other. In fact so much had changed between them since Dag had moved up to the big house. In general they were all more relaxed and at ease with each other. There was, above everything else, a greater sense of family.

'Thank you by the way for the children's revels yesterday,' said Silje as she put away her palette. 'They couldn't stop talking about them last evening and carried on again this morning. It must have been very successful.'

'Yes, it was. I had invited twenty children from the estate and some others from farms round about. I do feel so sorry for the children at harvest festivals and the like. They have to be dressed up in their finery and aren't allowed to *move* from their parents' side. Then they must stay still and silent while the pastor drones on and after that they're hardly allowed to show themselves! No, I wanted Dag to have a proper feast just for the children. What's more it's good for him to become known to them now that he will be the landowner. I think it was terribly successful.'

'Did they all get on well together from the very start?' asked Silje.

'Well, once they had shaken off their shyness, they did. They were everywhere; playing hide-and-seek in the salons; boys fighting and then making up and the girls admiring my dolls' house. And do you know, I think I was the happiest of them all! You see I am inspired by the lovely atmosphere in your home – it is so unlike any other. And I thank God that Dag's path and yours crossed that night long ago. No one else but you could have coped and still had such strength, kindness and tact. Imagine! Mother and I might still be sitting all alone and bitter up in Trondheim if you hadn't come into our lives. Mother is so awfully happy now, and my goodness how she spoils the boy!'

Charlotte came over to the canvas. The years had not brought her beauty, but she glowed with an inner loveliness. This, Silje knew, came from her devotion to Dag.

'What is that, just there?' she asked. 'I like it – but what is it supposed to be?'

'Oh, it's an allegory – it symbolises springtime,' replied Silje, somewhat embarrassed. She picked up a small bell and its ring was answered by the appearance of a maid who was neither young nor pretty. Silje asked for refreshments to be served in the parlour, and they sat down to fruit juice and slices of bread spread with dripping.

'Do you know how happy you are looking, Silje?' said Charlotte affectionately. 'It absolutely shines out of you.'

Silje laughed. 'These years since Are was born have been perfect. Tengel and I have been able to do the things we wanted and I have not had to trouble myself with unbearable housework. And the children are growing up well.'

Noticing a change in her expression, Charlotte asked, 'Do you miss having Dag here?'

'Heavens, no! Dag is fine and I see him a lot,' Silje assured her. 'No, *he's* not the one I worry over.'

'Well, that's why I came to talk to you. I am concerned about Sol.'

'Who could not be? Is there something in particular on your mind?'

'Yes, but I don't know how to tell you – yet I feel I ought to, for her sake.'

'Indeed you must! We work like beasts in the field to keep her on a straight and narrow path.'

Charlotte bit her bottom lip. 'Yesterday I saw her speak to our new stable lad – and she beguiled him completely. She was precocious, womanly and enticing far beyond her years. The boy was completely enchanted.'

Silje closed her eyes. 'And now ... *that* as well.'

'Is there more then?' Charlotte asked cautiously.

'She experiments. She takes Hanna's bag of things and goes off into the forest, where she can be alone. She mixes up dangerous ointments and the other children say she can do magic. Tengel has told her not to do it many times and she always promises to stop, but after a while she's off again. You see she and Tengel belong to two different groups of their evil ancestor's kin. Tengel has only the good in him but Sol takes after Hanna and wants to preserve the evil side. Sometimes I think she is proud to be ...' she lowered her voice to an almost inaudible whisper, 'a witch!'

'You mustn't say such a word!' said Charlotte.

'But she *is*,' said Silje wearily. 'It's something that none of us can deny – not you, not Tengel nor me. Not even Sol herself can deny it! All we can do is to try and help her and hope that she is a *good* ... what-I-just-said.'

Charlotte shook her head. 'The girl is becoming a woman, and you remember how hard it was for us at that age. It will pass as she gets older, mark my words.'

'I pray it does. Whatever happens, we must make sure that she doesn't keep company with frivolous men. Thank you for warning me. Now tell me how things are with "our" son Dag.'

Charlotte's excitement was obvious. 'I have great plans

for him, I just have to tell you! He has a sharp intellect, and even though running the estate itself does not really appeal to him, it is of no consequence. A good steward can do that job. I have pondered long and hard about whether he should study? Or be presented at Court? Or become a soldier? He could have rank – perhaps, one day, Field Marshal Dag Christian Meiden.'

'That last idea, a soldier, I do not like,' said Silje hastily. 'He is a gentle thoughtful boy. Wouldn't his intelligence be wasted there?'

Charlotte laughed. 'Were it not that you looked so serious, I would swear you were being discourteous. Well, who can say? He will be blessed with so many opportunities. Look! There's Tengel – and on horseback! Silje, my dear, I declare you are still in love with that man!'

Silje tried with little success to hide the happy sparkle in her eyes and the blushes that coloured her cheeks.

'Yes I really am,' she readily agreed, grinning with embarrassment. 'More and more with each year that passes. I sometimes wonder if he hasn't secretly entranced me – if he didn't put a proper spell on me that first time we met. They know how to do that, Charlotte, I promise you. Old Hanna once tried to make me take a love potion, so that I might ensnare Tengel. I refused it of course.'

'I do not think he would have needed one from you.'

'No. He became like a fever running through my veins from the first moment I saw him. Even if I did think he was hideous, I was still completely fascinated by him. He even forced his way into my dreams – but what's that he's doing? Has he dismounted in the allée?'

'He's walking over to one of the linden trees. He's touching its leaves and looking at it closely. Now he's coming this way.'

Shortly afterwards, Tengel stood in the doorway. He still looks unbelievably youthful, Charlotte thought to herself. He had very few grey hairs, despite his 45 years or more, although he had let his beard grow at last. It was sparse – two narrow bands from the corners of his mouth to his chin, where they joined a thin black beard, giving him a distinctly Mongolian appearance.

As soon as he saw them, his dour expression faded and his face lit up. 'Are you two sitting, gossiping? I hope it's all about me.' His broad smile revealed strong white teeth.

'Not directly,' replied Silje. 'Do you want a pot of ale?'

'Please.'

He crossed the floor with a confident stride, like a lion patrolling its realm. Charlotte understood Silje's adoration of him. Once accustomed to his unusual appearance, it was easy for anybody to see his good qualities – and there were many.

'How is it with your mother?' he asked Charlotte, his voice oddly tense.

'She is well, I think. She feels a little tired and rests a good deal.'

He nodded. 'I think I shall go and see her now. The ale will wait.'

There and then, he turned and hastily left the room. The two women exchanged questioning glances and then, through the windows, they watched Tengel as he stopped in the allée and approached one of the lindens.

'That is mother's tree,' said Charlotte, uneasily.

'Yes it is. Good heavens, Charlotte, you don't think that he …? No, it's not possible!'

'You know him better than I do.'

'I remember when he planted them,' she told Charlotte, tight-lipped. 'How he went from one tree to the next, and seemed to mumble a spell over each one.'

Looking concerned, Charlotte got to her feet. 'I shall go up to mother as well,' she said in a tight voice and hurried from the room.

Chapter 9

The Dowager Baroness Meiden received Tengel a short time later in her fine apartment on the second floor of the castle. She was wearing her dressing-gown, but under it he could see she was still in her nightdress. Her cheeks were bright crimson and they contrasted suspiciously with her otherwise languid complexion.

'Well, Master Tengel,' she smiled without getting up from her chair, 'to what do I owe this honour?'

'Your Grace,' he replied in a reserved but friendly voice, 'you know that you can call upon me whenever you feel unwell.'

Aristocratic eyebrows were raised. 'But I ...'

'We cannot afford to lose you, Baroness.'

The softness of the words helped her to relax. 'Are you always able to see through me? How do you know?'

'The important thing is that I *do* know. If it is something delicate that you find difficult to mention, just say so, and I shall try to find out in other ways where you have discomfort.'

'I am sure you can help me, Master Tengel, but it is not something of which one usually speaks.'

'You can trust my discretion completely. Although you

are among those most trusted and closest to me, have I ever related to you embarrassing details from my visits to other wealthy patients?'

'No, you have not, but ...'

After some discussion it emerged that she had a deep ache in the small of her back and experienced intense pain whenever she visited the 'unmentionable' little room of the house.

Tengel nodded sympathetically. 'It is a small closet built out from this wall, is it not? And is it open beneath, right to the ground, so the wind blows through it?'

'Yes,' admitted the Baroness, mortified at discussing the matter. 'It is terribly cold there in the winter.'

'Hmm! You have allowed yourself to get too cold and the trouble has spread up into your body. Do you have a fever?'

'Just for a few days, yes. But I am a little better today.'

Tengel doubted this last statement. She gave every appearance of having risen from her bed for no other reason than to receive him. He opened his coffer, a far grander article than the little bundle he used to carry and a sign of how well he was doing as *medicus* to the gentry. From it he produced a tiny bag.

Handing it to her he said, 'Drink an infusion of this today. Tomorrow I shall return with a better preparation. And I must speak to Sol as well, because in matters concerning Your Grace I want to be sure that we only do the very best we can for you.'

'Thank you, Master Tengel. Your words warm my heart.'

'And stay away from the little 'bay window'! There are – other means?'

'Indeed there are. And you want me to remain abed, do you not?'

'Yes, without question.'

At that moment Charlotte came rushing in. 'Mama! Are you unwell?'

'My dear Charlotte, why do you come dashing in so? No, it is nothing too serious – a slight fever, nothing more. Herr Tengel has given me medicine,' and, without pausing, she blithely carried on, changing the subject instantly to the rose garden she planned to develop outside the salon window.

****

Left on her own, Silje had been sitting deep in thought. Although she was mostly concerned for Sol, there was something else bothering her as well. Beate, always one to whine, had sat with her not long ago and complained bitterly about the agonies of married life.

'You know how it is, Fru Silje, I'm sure. In bed, I mean. He has his rights and we poor women can do no more than suffer and put up with them.'

Silje had stared at her, wide-eyed. '*Suffer*? Do you mean that it hurts you?'

'No – not hurt. But we do suffer it, you must agree. Here he comes, the disgusting pig, at least once each fourteen-nights wanting his, well – you *know* – and soon as he's finished gruntin' and puffin' he rolls off and sleeps.'

Feeling that she had shrunk to the size of an ant, Silje asked timidly, 'But – does he not caress you first? And afterwards? Does he not tell you he likes you? And don't you say the same things to him? Do you not play together? Aren't you happy when he comes to you?'

Beate stared, disbelieving. 'Do you think I am a whore? A shameless slut? What would the world be coming to? If a wife took an interest in such nonsense, well! I never thought, Fru Silje, that I should hear the like from your lips, never!'

Silje had smiled and tried to interject a word of explanation, but Beate had not wished to be interrupted.

'Ah! But of course, now I see – you spoke in jest. It is the duty of a wife to obey her man and bring babes into the world. Why else should anyone do it? Besides, what would the church have to say about the kind of lechery that you spoke of just now.'

Silje had been dumbfounded. She had been so disturbed by what Beate had said that she went at once to look for Tengel. It was one of those rare moments when he had no patients to attend, and he was mending a dry-stone wall in one of the pastures.

After telling him what Beate had said, she asked shyly, 'Have I been ungodly, Tengel? Have I done shameful things? Have I brought disgrace upon you?'

'Dear Silje,' he answered, dismayed, 'what on earth can you mean?' Very gently he put his hands on her shoulders and looked steadfastly into her eyes. 'Don't you see that is the difference between our wedded life and theirs? Our unending love for one another – our honesty – and our trust in each other. Whenever I am alone and think of you, a lump comes to my throat. My heart warms because you are who you are and you must never change. Never become prim and boring like Beate – and doubtless a good many other womenfolk. Promise me that you will always show me that you like it when I come to you!'

Slowly her face began to light up again and they embraced warmly right there in the field by the stone wall.

'Don't you realise how empty their lives are, Silje?' he asked softly. 'What do you think their men would have given for a wife like mine?'

'Or their wives for a man like mine,' she retorted with a broad, joyful grin. 'We are so fortunate, Tengel!'

Yes, they were fortunate, but as she sat contemplating those events, she could not escape the feeling that something was starting to go badly wrong. Dismally Silje mulled over and over whether or not she should talk to Sol – or should she explain it all to Tengel and leave it to him? Annoyance showed on her face. She didn't want to tackle any new problems. She was content to remain wrapped in her cloak of serenity, sitting in seclusion in her studio with her art. They had enjoyed many good years and the children were all growing well now. The hard years were behind them. Her days of bringing up a very young family were over. She didn't want any more turmoil!

Having remained there for a while, steeped in self-pity, she suddenly sat up with a start. What was she thinking of? Sol, her beloved foster-daughter, was in need of help and guidance and all she could do was moan about how it might affect her comfortable life!

How long, she wondered, had she hidden behind her own self-importance? Did she really know how her children were doing? Now that they had maids in the house, did she rely on them too much? She rose early and came straight down to her studio and began painting. Although she ate meals with the family and spent the evenings with them, what about the rest of the day? Was she living in the ecstasy fuelled by her own enthusiasm and inspiration?

Dag was no longer with them – his move had been surprisingly painless. She was relieved that she had taken it all so well. The occasional pang of regret she had felt had been quickly stifled; besides, he lived not far away. She saw him almost every day, when he came to pass the time with Liv and whenever she herself paid a visit to Gråstensholm.

Yet was it right for her to let him think she didn't miss him? Perhaps he felt hurt that he was no longer wanted? Liv was the one she spent most time with, because she was so often in the studio. What about little Are though? Just seven years old. Sometimes he would come to her for help with his leggings when they wouldn't stay up, or some other small worry. She would talk to him while sorting out his problems, but could she honestly say that it wasn't simply idle chatter and that her mind was not elsewhere?

It was not often she saw Sol. A strong wilful girl, she obviously considered herself grown up now and felt she could take care of herself. But, she thought, Good God! What have I ever really done for Sol? Nothing!

Tengel was seldom at home. He was just as passionate about his work as she was about her own. Even when he was at home, there were so many people seeking his help that the family kept a respectful distance. The estate management work had, with the Baroness's full approval, been divided up among others. He had more than enough to do caring for the sick and suffering – and whenever he had free time, Silje wanted to spend every moment with him. The children took second place.

The children took second place! What a terrible truth – what an awful thing to admit to oneself! Silje flushed hot and then turned icy cold and rushed out to find Sol. She came across Are sitting in the large bay window in the vestibule, studying his books. She went over and put her arms around him from behind.

'It's lovely to see you, Are,' she whispered. 'It's *always* lovely to see you. Do you know where Sol is?'

'Out in the forest, I think,' he lisped. His new front teeth were just breaking through. 'Or else she's helping up at the big house.'

'At the big house? Helping with what?'

'She asked Father this morning if she could help with the first haymaking and he said, "Yes." But I don't think it's started yet.'

Haymaking? Wanting to be close to the new stable lad, more likely! Oh, dear, thought Silje, I must have been sleeping!

****

As Are had said, haymaking had not yet begun. It was still a few days away. When Silje walked out into the yard, she saw Sol wandering back from the direction of the woods, her little bundle over her shoulder and the black cat close on her heels. Silje walked to meet her, telling herself not to be sharp-tongued and not let her anxiety and anger show – not to yell, 'Where have you been? What have you done?'

'Hello Sol,' she said, as calmly as she could. 'I would like to talk to you.'

There was an unmistakable look of aggressive defiance in those wonderful green eyes. She is magnificent, thought Silje, and so mature. *Nobody* would think she was only fourteen summers. 'Shall we sit here on the storeroom steps?'

Sol nodded, and followed her across to the worn old timbers, where they sat down side by side. Silje was silent for a while, because she was finding it painfully hard to begin.

'Sol – I – have just been doing a bit of soul searching,' she said at last. 'I've come to realise that I have let you all down horribly! All for the sake of my painting.'

Sol looked surprised – and she was somewhat relieved to find that this conversation was about Silje and not her. 'I don't understand,' she said, frowning.

'Well it's true! I see you all so seldom. I have been so selfish, Sol, just thinking of myself. I'm awfully ashamed.'

'But that's not how we think at all,' exclaimed Sol. 'Don't you think I remember life in the Valley of the Ice People? If only you knew how often Dag and I have spoken about how harried you looked and how you always worried that we should lack nothing – how much you hated all the chores. No, you never said anything, never complained, but I well remember when you threw a mop across the room – and the time you got into a rage and threw pots and sieves and anything you could get hold of, so that we all had to run out of the way. Many times you cried in silence because our clothes were falling apart with age and you had to sew them over and over. You were always tired, tired, tired. No, Silje, we children are all happy to know that you are contented.'

'Yet I truly feel I haven't done enough for you,' protested Silje in a subdued voice.

'But surely it's the duty of the older ones among us to look after the younger ones, is it not?' replied Sol. 'And we shall, each in turn, be happy to take the burden from you. You've always, always shown us you loved us and now you always have the time to listen to us too. You didn't have the time for that in the Valley – or when we first came here. You had to struggle and toil, carrying us until your back was crooked, your hair awry and your eyes worried and helpless.'

Silje interrupted her in utter amazement. 'Are you saying that you are all content with the way things are? While it's true I *am* very happy now, and I do love you all dearly, I was worried that I was too bound up in my work.'

'Don't be,' smiled Sol. 'There's no need.'

She is so sure of herself, thought Silje, but that probably goes with being beautiful. She didn't consider her own confident personality which, although it was less forceful than Sol's, was probably more worthy.

'Sol – I ...' Silje began speaking hesitantly again then stopped. The girl was giving her an inquiring look. Oh, my! This was so difficult! 'I – must talk to you about certain things. We've always been able to talk with each other, haven't we?' She swallowed hard and continued, 'You are so very pretty, Sol and dangerous men may be drawn to you.'

'That sounds nice.'

'Sol!' said Silje, shocked. 'Dear child, you do not know what happens when men ...'

Clearly, Sol was amused by the conversation. 'Have you forgotten I was in the room when Are was born? Do you think I don't know how he came from the love that you and Tengel share? Dearest Silje, I know *all* about that! Besides, you were not so old yourself when you fell in love with Tengel, were you?'

Silje felt she was losing control of the conversation; it was taking them down the wrong path. 'I was sixteen years when I met him,' she said, blushing, 'and I was bewitched – spellbound.'

'I understand how that must have been. I have always dreamt I would meet a man like Tengel. But you need not worry for my sake. Remember how I chased young Galle out into the snow last winter when he tried to pester me! I am strong, Silje, and I can defend myself!'

'I believe you can,' said Silje, somewhat taken aback by Sol's brazen precociousness, 'but only as long as you have no interest in the man. The danger for you is that you are drawn to big, strong, simple and unreliable men who know neither common sense nor courtesy. You have *always* been attracted to such men, so be on your guard, little one! It is so easy to – to ... get carried away in the heat of the moment!' Her voice tailed off in a embarrassed whisper.

'I promise I shall be careful,' Sol assured her, a little too easily. 'And if I do have an – accident, it's nothing to be concerned about. There are things that can be done.'

'Sol!' shrieked Silje.

'Don't forget that Hanna passed on great knowledge and wise words to me.'

'Yes! Hanna. Of course.' Silje was exasperated. 'I've heard that you go into the forest and experiment.'

Sol placed her hand lightly on the small bundle at her side. 'Yes, I do. I must if I am to learn more.'

Silje was in turmoil but, not wanting to lose the girl's confidence, she dared not show how she felt. Mustering all her calm, she asked, 'But isn't that dangerous?'

'Don't worry! I have everything under control.'

'I am not so sure. Is there not a folk tale about a sorcerer's young apprentice? He tried to perform his magic before he was ready and it became his master instead.'

'It will not happen to me,' answered Sol confidently. 'Hanna said that I had the talent to be her equal.'

Hardly the ideal person to look up to, thought Silje. But she was aware that Hanna was sacred to Sol and said nothing.

The eyes of this young, bewitching lass had now taken on a fanatical glow that contrasted so strangely with the beauty of that summer's day. 'If I found the man responsible for the killing of all the Ice People,' said Sol quietly, 'and Hanna with them, I should ...'

'Hanna was very, very old,' Silje said. 'I sometimes think she kept herself alive only to instruct someone such as you.'

'It's true, she told me so. She had tried with Tengel, but he was unwilling. She was overjoyed when I came to her. That man – his name was Heming, was it not?'

'Heming, the bailiff-killer. Yes. He was a badly flawed man, Sol. He hurt us all greatly, but he is surely long dead.' She put her hand on Sol's. 'I beg you, little friend, to take care in everything you do! We live in unfortunate times, and anyone with your legacy is very, very insecure. There are special tribunals for such things. There now! I have given vent to my feelings. Let's go and find Are and find something nice to eat. I think there is still some honeycomb left in the kitchen.'

'Where is Liv?'

'At the castle with Dag, as usual.'

'Can I go and fetch her?' Sol asked, far too eagerly.

'Later, Sol, later,' replied Silje with the distinct feeling that everything she had said had been no more than water off a duck's back.

****

In Gråstensholm's church the verger was watching the congregation from his privileged position at the side of the chancel. From where he sat, he could observe everyone secretly without being seen. What a disgusting rabble, he thought, disdainfully. Did these pitiful little women and their slow-witted farmers believe that they could attain a state of glory? That honour was reserved for those who were called to the service of Our Lord and no others. People like himself.

The skin of his scrawny, yellowing and fanatical face was stretched across his cheekbones so tightly that his canine teeth were exposed and his cold metal-grey eyes protruded from his skull. They wandered over the congregation. Wasn't that lecherous peasant from Nerhaug staring down the cleavage of his neighbour's wife? Fornication – fornication everywhere! Such behaviour must be punished. Anyone could see that the lewd wretch was now enjoying an unbridled vision of the woman's well rounded form.

The verger unthinkingly dried the saliva from the corners of his mouth. He knew the Nerhaug peasant wanted nothing more than to push his hand down her bosom and feel the soft, white flesh – squeezing those large breasts – and what about her? The licentious woman. Was she not sitting there twisting and turning her voluptuous body to tempt and seduce those poor simple peasants? Punish them, Oh Lord, punish them. Let them burn in the fires of hell; smite them down; let the vestments fall from the woman where she sits, so her shamefulness is laid bare for all to see! This whore!

Whore! Whore! Whore! The servant of the church could almost taste the contemptuous word in his mouth as he rolled it round his tongue, over and over again. Oh, that Nerhaug farmer is probably licking his lips with lust; craving to touch and hold those swollen breasts, burying himself in their excess. Then crazed with desire, he would force her down onto the church floor, rolling over and over, tearing the clothes from her body and plunge himself into sin!

Suddenly the verger sat up straight and crossed one leg tightly over the other, resting his hands in his lap. Anxiously he now listened to the voice of the pastor, and was relieved that he would not be called on to assist for some time. He could not stand up comfortably at that moment. Satan had made his presence felt to him again, but he would be strong!

His glance drifted across to the benches where the more distinguished members of the congregation were sitting. There was the Baroness Meiden with her revolting daughter – and her vile spawn, conceived and born in sin! Though why anyone would choose to lie with the scrawny ugly woman was beyond him! This 'mistress' dared to sit here in the purity of his and God's church – preferably in that order – next to her bastard son! And the pastor was prepared to tolerate it! But everyone knew he was weak and undisciplined. The parishioners called him mild and forgiving. Ha! He was a coward! He rarely spoke of the holy wrath of God! Judgement! Hell, the pit of evil! Would he never learn? Was it any wonder that immorality was rife in the parish?

Aha! The verger's eyes narrowed and shone with triumph. The folk from Linden Allée. The wife and the two youngest children, as usual! And where was the man of the family – that very image of the Devil himself? Nowhere to be seen – not in church. Not once had he attended. This would have to be reported. He couldn't see the eldest daughter either. She had never set foot in the church.

The verger had seen her once or twice, here and there – noticed the enticing, swaying body, the green eyes and feline looks. That black cat followed her everywhere too. What was one to make of that? Never at church, a black cat, green eyes and shameless behaviour that attracted the young boys, innocent as they were, and tempted them along the path of ungodliness. It would be plenty to build a case on. More than enough!

Hadn't they recently declared an old hunchbacked woman to be a witch because she went around muttering to herself? This girl showed far more convincing signs. Was it not his duty as a holy, God-fearing man to go into the forest of thorns and vigorously drive out Satan from her body the next time he met her? For there could be no doubt that it was she who commanded Satan to visit him. Pity the young man that didn't have his self-control or the Grace of Heaven.

And what about Herr Tengel? There was talk of miraculous deeds – of him treating cases that the healers could not cure. Where did these miracles come from? Not from the church, of that he was certain.

The verger daydreamed happily. At long last he had

something to bring before the Courts of Inquisition! True, they were not known by that name here in Norway, but the principle was the same. Witchcraft and sorcery had their own tribunals in this district and tomorrow he fully intended to ride to Akershus and present his evidence.

He would find honour and praise on earth – folk would know he was somebody special. He would be rewarded with yet one more star in the firmament to add to all those he undoubtedly had already. He would definitely be assured of a place close the throne of Our Lord. What joy! To denounce two callous heathens who would spit on the name of God. Was it not written that it pleased the Lord to drive out every trace of Satan's disciples and their work here on earth? His life was indeed most joyous and blest!

****

A few days later, three worthy gentlemen looked the verger up and down as if he reminded them of a small insect, but nothing could hide the interest that showed in their glances. They stood in the middle of a cold stone-walled hall in Oslo, close to Akershus Castle, and their voices echoed in the large cavernous space.

'What you are saying is very grave,' said the Principal Judge, an elderly, alarmingly austere man. 'But Herr Tengel's name is not entirely unknown to us. It would be putting it mildly to say that we have been after him for a long time. But his star burns bright among those with power – and folk in general. We must tread very carefully for he is well connected and is protected by people in high places. Much too high! But were we able to produce evidence …'

A younger man with dark thinning hair and eyes that burned with the passion of a true holy zealot implored,

'Let me go, Your Honour! Let me inquire into the matter and find the evidence we need!'

'Yes,' said the third man, 'let our young novice here, Master Johan, have the opportunity to show what he is capable of.'

The Principal Judge, the 'Inquisitor', who wielded power over both church and state in these particular matters, but also sat as a secular judge, weighed up his youngest and most eager colleague with a glance.

'How old are you, Master Johan?'

'I am in my thirty-fifth year, Judge.'

'Good enough. Then you have certainly reached an age where you are able to determine things correctly. You know the signs to look for. Find out whether this girl is a witch and Herr Tengel is a sorcerer; or worse still – a warlock! We shall be pleased to see what evidence you can discover.'

'But remember,' added the second man, 'to take great care! We must not tread on the toes of those who have the ear of His Majesty! Herr Tengel is not just anyone!'

The Principal Judge nodded. 'Strong evidence is required, but if we find it, if all is as this man here has told us, then Herr Tengel is something very special. Ah, to sit in judgement on a warlock …' His voice tailed off as he too began contemplating the realisation of a dream.

'When may I leave?' asked Master Johan, fired with intense enthusiasm for his mission.

'At once! And take no more than one week! You will, of course, permit no one to know who you are or what business you are about! We cannot be too careful when we perform the work of God.'

The Inquisitor turned to the verger. When he spoke, his tone was aloof and harsh. 'As for you, my good man, take this coin for your trouble! And go in peace!'

Chapter 10

'Mother,' shouted Liv from outside the front of Linden Allée. 'A poor starving man begs lodgings for a few days. He is passing through and hasn't got the strength to go on. He must have a chance to rest. Highwaymen have taken all he owned.'

Silje came out quickly onto the doorstep, her expression concerned. As soon as she was satisfied that her daughter was all right, she scrutinised the stranger and her heart warmed at once to the unfortunate man in a simple cape who stood before her.

'Oh! Dear me! Come inside,' she said, helping him up the steps. 'You must have journeyed far?'

'Yes, from Sogn, over the mountain. I was on my way to Akershus when I was waylaid a few days ago. Allow me to introduce myself. My name is Master Johan and I am a scribe by profession.'

Much against his will, Master Johan – whose ascetic looks naturally suggested he was the starving victim of vile highway robbers – was put to bed and then the maids took him some food. From his bed he looked round the beautiful low-ceilinged attic room and was baffled by all the pictures on the walls. He regretted now that he had presented himself as being in poor health, as he was unable to observe much from his bed.

She was a good woman, the mistress of the house. Of humble birth perhaps, but radiating warmth from her lively eyes. She seemed so happy! Johan had rarely known happy people in the circles in which he moved. Of course there was the fanatical joy brought on when they had captured a great many witches in one day or triumphed over the evil within themselves – but suddenly he found he was beginning to doubt that this was the only true happiness.

Taking a deep breath Master Johan sought reassurance for his many years of faith in the words of Peder Palladius. 'Witches shall now reap their reward. In the brightness of this sacred day they can survive no longer. The shame of the world is upon them – banish them from this world! It is no less than they deserve. In Denmark they are hunted like wolves and once more in the city of Malmö a pack of them are to be burned. On the island of Als they recently burned fifty-two women as witches, as each one denounced her sister and they followed each other to the other world ...'

These sweet thoughts were suddenly interrupted by the sight of a small boy standing in the doorway of his room.

'Good day, young man,' said Master Johan. 'What is your name?'

'Are Tengelsson, sir. I'm seven years old, nearly eight. Are you sick?'

'Not very.'

'You will soon get some help. But father is not at home and Sol is in the forest doing magic.'

Master Johan sat up with a start. 'Sol – is that your sister?'

'Yes.'

'You say she does magic?'

'Of course.' The boy came closer. 'She can cure you from anything at all – just by mixing her powder. And she can make things disappear. And tell what's happening in another place.'

'That's clever,' said Johan, his heart racing. 'I should like to meet her.'

Someone called from downstairs and the boy was gone but Master Johan could barely contain his excitement. This was almost too easy. Yet he still needed evidence and could do nothing lying in a bed pretending to be exhausted. The next moment the door was pushed back and Johan gasped. A man the size of a giant swept into the room with his cloak flapping in his wake. To Johan, lying flat on his back, it was unnerving to see this grotesque spectre appear, like some spirit of the underworld. Almost as wide as the door through which he entered, he had yellow eyes which glared harshly at him from a demonic face and Johan very nearly screamed out to his heavenly father for protection.

'Are you hurt?' said the figure in a hard, grating voice.

So this was Herr Tengel! The demon who was able to cure the most persistent of ills. He seemed tired, however, his sunken eyes dry from lack of sleep. He should be lying here, not I, thought Johan. 'N…no, I am not hurt,' replied Johan, stuttering with fear. 'Just very fatigued. But I am well cared for.'

'Let me look at you,' said Tengel pulling back the quilt.

Master Johan curled into a ball. 'No, no. That is not necessary. There is nothing amiss.'

He was greatly worried that Tengel would find the papers he had hidden in a small leather pouch on his belt. He had written down all the things he must identify to show he was among witches and sorcerers, but it was not usual to be so thorough. If a cow had ceased to give milk it was enough that the wife of a neighbour be accused of putting a spell on it. If a man broke his arm then it would be because a woman in the neighbourhood (one he didn't like) had willed it or given him the evil eye.

It was also common for women they had already imprisoned as witches to give the names of others, many others, when they were tortured. These other women would be taken in and questioned before being put to the supreme test – for example in the ducking pond. If a woman was thrown into the pond, it soon became clear if she was a witch or not – if she floated to the surface she was a witch and was burned. If she sank and drowned then she was innocent. It was so simple and easy to understand!

Truly, our Master Johan considered himself to be a knight in the service of the Kingdom of Heaven, saving the world from these messengers of evil in the name of the Lord God. Unfortunately such simplistic measures were out of the question in this case. Woe betide them if they took the gentry's most respected miracle worker without proper evidence of witchcraft and sorcery!

'As you will,' said Tengel, throwing back the cover. He assumed the man in the bed was shy.

'I – I feel better already,' said Johan quickly. 'Perhaps I can get up tomorrow?'

Tengel peered into his face, assessing him. He had the feeling that all was not as it seemed. Master Johan saw the sceptical scowl and became even more afraid. I must leave here as soon as possible, he thought, before this creature kills me. He could easily do so, if he wished.

Tengel studied the man a moment longer, then turned on his heel and went out of the room, closing the door quietly behind him. Left alone, Master Johan breathed a deep sigh of relief and before long fell into a fitful doze.

****

He surfaced only gradually from his slumber some time later and at first did not remember where he was. Then he was suddenly wide awake. It was dark outside and somebody stood beside his bed, candle in hand.

'You are a bear,' said a laughing and happy-sounding female voice that reverberated through his skinny torso like shining pearls falling from a broken necklace.

'What's that?' asked Master Johan in a dazed voice.

What, he could see now, was a young girl gave her joyful laugh once more and sat down on the edge of his bed without the slightest trace of shame or modesty! But she could not be very old, he thought. And what self assurance she had.

'In folklore there is a tale,' she continued in that beguiling voice, 'I wonder if you have heard it? By day you are a bear, but by night you are a handsome prince. You lie in the same bed as the princess, although they don't say that in the story. But of course *I* know what they did together! Anyway the princess wanted to see what he looked like, so she went into the room carrying a candle. Some wax fell on him and he woke up very, very angry. Were *you* angry?'

Fascinated by this confused concoction of myth and reality, Master Johan stuttered and without thinking said, 'No – no – not at all. Allow me to present myself. I am …'

'I know who you are. You are Master Johan. But I don't know why you are lying here. There is nothing wrong with you.'

In the darkness the embarrassed Johan said, 'I was simply fatigued when I arrived. I am well now.'

His eyes had gradually adjusted to the dim light in the room and he was able dimly to see the girl's face. She was almost unbearably beautiful to look upon, with sparkling eyes and an amused smile. Johan wondered how she could have known that there was nothing the matter with him. It was not possible for her to have examined him whilst he slept – or was it?

Almost as if she was reading his thoughts, she said, 'Do you know, I only have to touch your skin with my hand and I can tell whether you are sick or not from the pulse that vibrates against it. I can also tell from the smell of a person – Tengel can too.'

'Are you the one they call "Sol", Mistress? The young lad who came to me earlier spoke the name.'

'Yes, but you need not call me "Mistress". It's foolish, because I'm not a grown woman yet, am I? Tengel is my uncle, but he and Silje have looked after me and Dag – he lives at Gråstensholm now – ever since we were small. Not even our real parents could have given us more love than they have. Sometimes they tell me off because I'm not as well behaved as Dag, but I know it's because they care about me and don't want me to take the wrong path in life. I can be a bit wild sometimes and I mostly just do as I please.'

Johan lifted himself up on one elbow. Now was the time to begin his inquiry – she was offering him the perfect opportunity!

'How strange it sounds – what you said about the power of your hands. How did it happen?'

She answered willingly. 'It is because I belong to a people that are born with the gift.'

Johan decided to play all his cards at once. 'I can tell you that there is something unusual about one of my arms. It has no feeling from the elbow to the wrist. Inside the skin, if you know what I mean.'

What he had said was a lie, but it was one of the most

important tests. A real witch would have a place somewhere on her body that was completely without feeling, put there by Satan himself. This young girl would quickly fall into his trap, now he had tempted her to reveal something they might share in common.

Sol however showed nothing other than a friendly interest. 'That's strange! Do you mean that you can feel nothing at all?'

'No, nothing.'

Without giving him any warning, she pinched his arm very hard, so hard in fact that Johan only just managed to prevent himself from crying out in pain. 'Could you feel that?' she asked.

'No, I felt nothing,' he lied.

'Do you know, you're not really ugly,' she declared solemnly. 'In fact, you're quite handsome – if you didn't have your hair so short and your lips so tightly pressed together. Not as handsome as Klaus, mind. He works up at the big house and I think I'm a little bit in love with him. Have you ever been in love? I'm not completely sure that I am really. Well, have you?'

'Are you not too young to be falling in love?' asked Johan, trying to control the conversation. Besides, he didn't think that this Klaus person sounded very pleasant.

'I shall soon be fifteen.'

Oh, God! he thought. She is but a child! Such a beguiling combination of innocence and arrogance. With an effort he turned his thoughts back to the matter at hand. 'Your brother told me that you can make magic – make things disappear.'

Sol laughed. 'Ha! Are? You can make him believe anything at all. Hold the candle and I'll show you.' She took an oatcake from the table and showed it to him openly. Then she closed her hand and distracted him by keeping up her endless chatter. A moment later – hey presto – the cake was gone! Johan felt an icy chill of dread run through him. This was sorcery unlike anything he had ever seen!

Then, immediately, the giggling laughter started again. 'Now let me show you how I did it,' said Sol, 'but I'll do it slowly this time. It's the oldest trick of the fairground jugglers.' As she performed the 'magic' again very slowly, Johan's face turned crimson with embarrassment, seeing how he had been fooled. It was so easy! Not witchcraft at all!

A small voice in the back of his mind was begging the forgiveness of his superiors for having felt such compassion. It had never happened to him before in all his witch-hunts. More often than not, he would have felt great satisfaction at the faintest hint of suspicion directed at a woman and, with much feasting, he and his associates would later celebrate the triumph together. Even now he could feel the warm glow of delight in his heart that he always experienced when the fateful words of judgement were uttered which sent the guilty to torture – or to the stake. It was the honourable delight of knowing justice had been done. His thin lips tightened even more. In the fight against evil there was no room for weakness!

The pretty young wife with the sympathetic eyes came in and scolded the girl severely before begging his pardon for the intrusion and leading the girl away. He fell back onto the bed. The room had suddenly become empty and dreary. 'You're quite handsome.' No one had ever before dared speak such words to the much-feared assistant to the Inquisition. It made him feel warm all over – almost as warm as standing watching a witch burn!

****

The following morning Master Johan insisted on getting up from his bed. Pretending to be suffering from aching limbs and sore joints, he stumbled outside into the back yard. There an unexpected sight met him. The yard was filled with people from every walk of life. Some were dressed in neat, albeit simple clothes, but most of them were hopelessly poor and wearing nothing better than rags. One or two well dressed people, however, stood out from the throng. Hearing a noise, he turned as Silje came out of the door behind him.

'What has happened?' he asked, shocked by what he saw.

'Happened? How do you mean?'

'Well – all these people!'

'Oh, *them*! It is the same every day. They have come to my husband for help.'

'But I understood him to be a physician to the gentry!'

'No, they number but a few of his patients. His real work lies in safeguarding folk like these.'

'Surely he cannot have time to see all these?'

'He tries, Master Johan,' said Silje, wearily. 'He does all he can to help them and it causes me to worry greatly for him. He tires himself so.'

Johan remembered Tengel's drawn face and the eyes that seemed so raw-rimmed and tired. 'But is he not a well placed *medicus*, who is much sought after? What does he need these people for? They will never make him rich!'

'Tengel never asks for anything from them. Yet still they bring what they can – an egg, a wicker basket, some kindling from the forest. They all want to pay something, you understand. It allows them to keep the little dignity they have left.'

For the first time, Johan was seeing a world he had never known existed. Nonetheless, he did not have time for this – he was determined to seek out the Devil's trickery, and the demands of the Court of Inquisition called to him.

'Fru Silje, I should very much like to join your husband at Mass tomorrow,' he said slyly, 'if he does not object.'

Silje gave a brief, sad smile. 'You are welcome to join us but my husband will not accompany us, I fear.'

Aha! Johan was incisive. 'Why not?'

'It may be difficult for you to understand, but I would like him to live for many years yet. His work healing so many people saps his strength and he weakens every time he lays his healing hands upon people. He takes it badly whenever he fails – for that does happen from time to time. He must also make sure that his store of herbs is kept full, something that is not easy in winter, of course. So on the night before the Sabbath I order him to his bed. He sleeps like a log all through the Sunday – missing Mass and everything! I think it is better that he regains the strength to minister to these unfortunates than to sit in church, fast asleep.'

'But the Word of God? If he does not receive the Word he will be beyond the redemption of the church!'

'I hardly think so. And there is another reason why Tengel does not worship in church. Once when we lived in the north of the country, he would gladly have been a part of the congregation, but he was stopped from attending Mass because folk said that he belonged to the Evil One himself. All because of his unfortunate appearance – something that he cannot be held to account for! That hurt him, Master Johan! I believe that Tengel is afraid of being excluded again. Still, he and Sol have their own form of Mass. They make their way out into the forests and fields and commune with God on their own. They do not think of the priesthood as a special mouthpiece – at times they can even be quite disruptive.'

'I've never heard the like! The girl does not go to church either, you say?'

'No, she has a difficult temperament. We prefer to keep her here, away from places where people gather.'

'Are you saying that she is possessed? Has some evil spirit taken her?'

'Sol? No,' laughed Silje. 'She is but a strong-willed young lady who speaks her mind and does what she chooses. Her comments would cause a disturbance during the service.'

Silje said a silent prayer asking for forgiveness. She had spoken the truth about Tengel and she knew well that he had a close spiritual connection to his God. But Sol was another matter. They could say nothing about her beliefs, other than that ten wild stallions would never be enough to drag her into church. That was Hanna's influence, with her Devil worship and scorn for the men of the cloth. Not for one minute did Silje think that Sol went out into the forest to pray to God! Oh, no! Many times she had tried to talk to her, tried to bring her up with a belief in Christ, but on every occasion it had been as if Sol had drawn a veil over her senses – she had simply refused to listen.

Whenever Silje's thoughts went in these directions, Hanna's words came back to haunt her again and again. 'Sol will not pass on our true inheritance! You, girl! You are the one who will pass on the heritage of the first Great Tengel.'

Sol, our beloved little girl, thought Silje sadly, what will become of you? Have we failed you? Should we have punished you harder? No! Both she and Tengel knew how dangerous that could be. Besides none of the children had deserved or been given as many beatings as Sol. But that had been a long time ago. They had stopped because Sol's revenge had always been too frightening – something precious to them had always been destroyed under mysterious circumstances. It had been her way of sending little warnings and Tengel always knew how she had done it. However, he had no power over her since he had allowed the evil side of his craft to lie dormant for so long. What was more, he did not want to start using such methods again.

Any criticism from them would send Sol into angry tantrums. 'If I were to decide for myself, then I should do things as I wish,' she had once said. 'I would care nothing for the tastes and wants of folk. It is only because of my fondness for you that I try to behave as everyone else. I am doing my best – so don't find fault!'

Faced with such an argument they had capitulated. They understood only too well that she was suffering an inner turmoil and was not like the others. From then on they tried instead to guide her by showing her all the love they could. Sending her away would be unthinkable. She was safe and well cared for here – but among strangers she might be tormented, and who could tell what she would do then?

There had been times when Silje had thought back to the moment when Tengel had first set eyes on Sol – and how he had felt then that her life should not necessarily be saved. In her heart Silje sometimes wondered if he hadn't been right. But nevertheless they loved the girl. She could be so wonderfully considerate and loving and had always looked after the younger ones perfectly, even though, with that devilish glint in her eye, she had been known to lead them into mischief. However, she was certainly not the first nor the last child in the world to have got herself and others into trouble! In fact because of this they probably showed her somewhat greater affection, in the strange way parents always do with any child who creates more trouble and sadness.

Charlotte had wanted Sol to be a courtier, but that had been out of the question. What a scandal there would have been! Charlotte was blissfully unaware of some of the other facets of Sol's personality, yet perhaps she was right. Perhaps Sol was just going through a time of change and there was still hope that she could grow out of it.

As these thoughts chased each other through Silje's mind, she heard the stranger's voice, as if in a fog, addressing her.

'I believe I shall take a short walk,' he was saying. 'To get some strength back into my legs.'

'Yes, do that,' replied Silje warmly. 'We shall eat one hour before noon.'

Before he left the house, Master Johan had seen Sol disappear into the trees at the edge of the forest carrying her cat in her arms. Stepping out into the yard, he made his way through the crowd and set off after her. Suddenly he heard a soft 'Pssst' and, turning round, he saw the Verger standing beside him, trying to conceal his face under the hood of a great cape.

'Good day, Master Johan,' the yellowish wraith-like figure whispered in a hoarse voice. 'I wanted only to make it known that I am here close by should you need my help.'

This immediately angered Johan. He most certainly neither wanted nor needed anyone's help. 'Be so kind as to *not* creep around here looking like a thief from a band of roving outlaws! Good God, man! Are you intent on ruining everything? Be on your way! Leave – at once!'

Being a member of the Court of Inquisition had advantages, one of which was the unquestioning respect and obedience given to the office he held. A moment later, suitably chastised, the servant of the Church had disappeared from the yard and Johan prowled quietly among the sparse trees at the edge of the forest, shaded by the dappled green of the early summer foliage. He had made a circuitous approach, so that no one would suspect that he was following the girl – but he was on her trail.

'For God – against Satan!' This was his war cry and, as he made his way through the trees with the velvety moss underfoot, he repeated it over and over silently to himself. It strengthened the resolve of those in the service of righteousness. Not that Johan needed it. He was so steeped in his fanatical beliefs that he could pick out a disciple of the Devil in his sleep – without concerning himself overmuch about proving their guilt or innocence. *He* always knew best! 'For God – against Satan!'

He searched for a long time before he found her. At first he heard the tender bubbly voice and then caught sight of Sol kneeling in one of the pastures at the edge of a stream beside a cloth spread out on the ground. She was talking to the cat that was sitting obediently opposite her.

On the cloth, which he now could see was the one that had been tied around her bundle, lay a variety of strange objects, all laid out in a distinct pattern. Johan's heart quickened its beat – there could be no doubt what the girl was doing. It was sorcery!

Suddenly without turning round she called to him, 'Come out, Master Johan. Come and see what I'm doing!' Crestfallen that she had so easily discovered his presence, he rose from the bushes and went down to where she sat.

It was a wonderful day. Dog roses bloomed in the hedgerows surrounding the field and buttercups vied for a place with a variety of deep blue midsummer flowers that littered the pastures. This girl, Master Johan realised suddenly, had come into his austere life like a revelation. The colour in her cheeks, the fine soft curve of her lips and those bewitching eyes! Amber or green? It was impossible to say because the colour changed almost continually. Her features were framed in curls of darkest brown, almost black hair that cascaded down over the white blouse she wore and her figure was far more shapely than that of any other fourteen year old he had ever seen. Looking at her, Master Johan felt his eyes becoming irritated by an unfamiliar prickly sensation. Could it be caused by tears? No, how ridiculous! He had long ago forgotten what tears were.

The cat had been gauging the worth of the man, staring at him intently with its dispassionate green eyes. Then abruptly it lost interest and turned away.

'Look here. Look what I've done,' said Sol with a confidence that overwhelmed him. 'I have laid out a healing supplication for you, so that you'll be well again and not have any more pain. Everything looks fine, I think, but you suffer discomfort in your soul, Master Johan. And soon it will be worse!'

'I would rather not know what will happen to me in the future, thank you!' he said sharply. Petty illusions, he said to himself, and to think you would try to fool *me* like that! Without more ado, Sol gathered up all her strange mummified objects. Some were so old that they gave no clue as to what they might once have been.

'I'm sorry,' she mumbled. 'I was just interested in you and what your future held. Still, it's probably best not to see too much. There was *one* sign that I did not like – and I want only what is best for you.'

'It was kind of you to think of me,' he said brusquely. Still unable to take his eyes off her he leaned towards her.

'You do know, don't you that you ought not to be practising these sorts of things?'

'Asch! This is nothing! Only a game, a mere bagatelle,' replied Sol dismissively. 'Anyway, I must go. I have to give "my brother, the Baron" a message from Silje. Oh, and we aren't allowed to call Mistress Charlotte "Mistress" any longer.' She giggled again. 'Only because she is Dag's *mother*! But perhaps you knew that already?'

Oh, yes! Johan knew that all right. The verger had left nothing out of his report. 'Sin! Sin everywhere!' the obnoxious little man had said, as his eyes shone with delight and his tongue flicked back and forth like a snake's over his thin bloodless lips. Johan shuddered for a moment. This was a man who shared his values – he was a man of virtue – Johan must be of one accord with him.

The girl said farewell and ran off, sprightly as any dancer, with her cat chasing at her heels. All the intricate questions he had been composing suddenly seemed unimportant and worthless and they sank back into the recesses of his mind. For a while he stood pondering all that had been said, before he finally started walking back towards Linden Allée.

Still lost in thought, he took out his paper and stick of charcoal from their secret pouch. He had noted down in every detail all the things he needed answers to, according to the Principal Judge's wishes. Emblazoned with many whorls and flourishes, the questions stared back at him from the paper. There were lots of them, all pedantically numbered and all eternally ingenious.

He read through the lists. He had the answer to one of the most crucial questions, 'Are there any signs indicating the practice of witchcraft?' On the piece of paper with the girl's name on it, he had no choice but to write 'Yes' beside the question. He had one piece of paper for each of them, because it was exceedingly important that he always make a distinction between a witch and a wizard – or sorcerer!

At that moment Master Johan reflected on the unquestioning trust that had been vested in him and his heart swelled with pride. Feeling the responsibility keenly, he raised the stick of charcoal. Then after a moment he lowered it again without writing anything.

Irritated, he realised that he had forgotten to secure any evidence for the Court. Something, he could not say what, had twisted his train of thought and he had forgotten. How easy it would have been for him to pick up one of those old objects and pocket it. Even though he might not be able to decide what they were, he felt sure he would find all the most frightening items among them. Bats' wings; the fingers of hanged criminals; the bones of new-born babes and much else besides. To think he had missed such an opportunity – it might not present itself again.

Better to wait before answering that question then. Having hidden the paper in its pouch, he set off again. But now, for some unknown reason, every determined stride he took suddenly seemed lighter.

Chapter 11

After taking her leave of Master Johan, Sol hurried through the forest towards Gråstensholm, her thoughts rushing wildly hither and thither as only a happy adolescent's thoughts can. When she emerged into the open fields she followed the stone wall that ran along the side of the horses' paddock. In the pasture there were birch trees that had always held a special place in her heart; standing widely spaced apart with their straight white trunks etched with splashes of black, they were now proudly displaying their elegant pale green shimmering foliage in profusion.

This was where the children would come on fine spring days to pick blue anemones and the pretty white wood anemones that bloomed after them. The whole pasture was a field of blue that then turned to white, and Sol loved it so. She could imagine the cries of her siblings echoing around the birches, calling to her that they had found some special flowers, more colourful or taller than the others.

Now it was summer and it was the turn of the grasses to reign supreme. She watched as a stallion galloped across the adjoining field, its hooves thundering over the ground. He was a magnificent sight to see; a chestnut with a flaxen mane and a long, bushy, flowing tail. Unsuccessfully, Sol tried running to keep up with him, although she was glad that there was a wall between them. When she gave up, breathless and laughing, the horse whinnied in triumph.

At last Sol could see where he was heading. The new stable lad had just come into the paddock leading a filly. The new stable lad! What luck, she thought, and climbed up onto the top of the wall. 'Hello !' she shouted happily.

Klaus looked towards her, blushing bright pink. 'It's best you leave here, Mistress – and quick too!'

'Is it dangerous to sit here, then?'

'No, not dangerous, but – in Jesu's name, be swift! Go 'way!'

Sol remained seated. The stallion had reached the filly and the young female horse was pulling at the rope Klaus was holding, trying to get away. The stallion was beating his hooves on the ground and giving a deep-throated whinny, so Klaus let the filly loose and climbed over the wall. Then he walked up to where Sol was sitting and lifted her down.

What a pleasant sensation it was to feel his hands encircle her waist! Sol wanted the moment to last longer.

'I was told I had to help him,' Klaus muttered. 'But it doesn't look like he needs helping. Please, you must go now, Mistress. Please.'

'Help him with what?'

At that very moment an answer from Klaus became unnecessary. Sol stared in fascination at what was unfolding before her. Never had she seen anything like this; they did almost no farming at Linden Allée, because Silje always grew too attached to the animals and therefore could not bear to be parted from them. Whenever things 'like that' took place in the barn or stables the children were kept away.

Had it been Silje standing here now in the company of a man, confronted with this, she would have died of shame. Sol, however, was not like Silje. As she watched the two horses moving together, a joyous smile spread slowly across her face, its brilliance only matched by the sun after which she was named.

'That's grand,' she said somewhat breathlessly. 'Just watching them makes me feel funny inside – all tingly and itchy. Do you feel it too?'

Klaus didn't know where to look, but he was charged to look after the animals, so he kept his bright red face turned towards them. However it would be an untruth of massive proportions to say that he was not affected by what was going on. Sol moved slightly, rubbing her thighs together. She was looking at the young, handsome but slightly backward Klaus in a new light and let her curious and thoughtful gaze wander over him. She took an almost imperceptible step in his direction and let her arm brush against his shirt. The sensation made her shudder and she took a deep, slow breath.

When she turned her attention to the horses once more, her voice caught in her throat. 'It looks so beautiful,' she whispered. Then after a long moment she glanced round again at Klaus. 'And just look at the filly's half-closed eyes – don't you think she's enjoying it?'

Klaus stared back at Sol; seeing her welcoming smile and uninhibited interest in the horses, he grinned slightly, taking care not to offend her. Then feeling more confident, he laughed aloud, though softly in case he worried or disturbed the animals. She laughed back at him, just as quietly and respectfully, and in that instant they became simply two innocent young people, completely at one with nature, joyful to have caught a glimpse of a new and enticing world.

Before long the horses finished coupling and the stallion stood down. 'Will there be a foal from that?' asked Sol who had never been slow in understanding the world around her.

Klaus could do no more than nod his head vigorously. His pale blue eyes shone and the excitement he also felt could not be disguised. Sol acted as though she was intoxicated and in a mad moment wondered what it would be like to change places with the filly. Unthinking, she voiced her thoughts out loud.

'Mistress Sol!' said Klaus, aghast and at a loss for words. However, he too was panting slightly and he wondered suddenly whether he should tell her about the heifer that … But no! Nothing had come of it. Even though he knew many lads who had done it, he had not dared – despite being alone so much and in great need of comfort. Still it was a long time ago and he had almost forgotten the stupid idea until now. Yet he felt he wanted to tell her about it, if only to show her that he understood her feelings.

'Ha!' said Sol, unaware of his horrible secret. 'I've never understood why a person can't say whatever they want to. So long as they do not bring harm or sorrow to another, it matters not. I'm not causing you harm now, am I?'

Although Klaus was somewhat witless, his plain common sense was not lacking and he answered at once, 'No, Miss, not at all! And I think what you say is right, but one such as me can't be heard saying those sorts of things!'

'What stupidity! People are stupid, aren't they, Klaus?'

'Yes 'um,' he replied, giving her a shy, awkward glance.

At that moment Sol was experiencing a tingle of excitement unlike anything she had ever felt before. The skin on her breasts grew taut, as though an icy chill had swept over them, and the throbbing she sensed in other parts of her body was almost more than she could bear.

Klaus stood motionless, both hands gripping the bleached poles across the field entrance. He was in torment. He knew very well that if he did not withstand temptation right now, a terrible punishment would befall him afterwards. She is but a child, he told himself, his thoughts racing. What's more, she's one of fine birth. Stay away, Klaus, stay well away! Please God, guide me now!

A stifled gasp came from between his tightly pressed lips. 'Mistress – the foreman will soon be here to find out how things have gone. Best that you ...'

'Yes, I'm going. I should be up at the big house. Do you like it here at Gråstensholm?' She had been gently amused to see the discomfort the young lad was suffering and was trying instead to make him feel more relaxed.

'Yes, very much. But I'm soon to move on.'

'Move on?' echoed Sol. This was not to her liking at all. 'Where to?'

'The Baroness has found a very fine position for me, with the procurator's stables. She recommended me because I am so good with horses.'

Sol cursed deep inside – something she was strictly forbidden from doing. Neither of them knew that this was a ploy to separate the two of them. She had developed far too much of an interest in this simple young stable hand. The pair of them represented a dangerous combination – the morally irresponsible Sol and the lowly man of the earth Klaus.

'When do you leave?'

'Tuesday.'

Tuesday? That didn't leave her much time. Sol was no longer in any doubt about what she wanted, having now discovered the power she wielded over the male sex. In truth it had completely intoxicated her and she could hardly wait to go further. Well might he try to resist and strive against her – frightened and downtrodden as one of the lower classes would be – and show concern for her youth. But she had ways and means.

'Shall you be working in the stables all the time until then?' she asked lightly. 'Here I mean.'

'No. On Monday I must take the cows to new grazing up on the ridge.'

'On your own?'

'Course.'

Perfect, thought Sol, but she simply said, 'I've got to get on now. Thanks for your company.' With a laugh, she scooped up the cat – he had been stalking a beetle through the grass – and ran off.

Klaus watched her go, but his longing for her would not subside. Aroused as he was by watching the horses and by Sol's closeness, he walked over to the edge of the forest to find a private place. Wrapping his arms around a birch, he closed his eyes and imagined vividly what it would be like to hold her in his arms. Soon his breathing began to come in short gasps and he clung more tightly to the tree. Before long his legs turned weak, unable to support his weight any longer, and he sank slowly to the ground.

****

'Silje, would you consider painting Dag?' wondered Charlotte aloud. She was in Silje's studio, which was really only a re-modelled milking parlour, but it served its new purpose equally well.

'A portrait you mean?' Silje sounded doubtful. 'I don't know that I *dare* – I've never tried.'

Charlotte smiled, teasing her. 'I've heard a rumour that there's a certain church painting! They say you painted

Tengel from memory, after only seeing him once. They also say it was a perfect likeness!'

'Oh, dearest Charlotte,' chuckled Silje, hands covering her face. 'Don't remind me of that, please! Tengel has never forgiven me for portraying him as a demon. But it's an appealing thought – painting the boy, I mean!'

'It's worth trying at least. If it is a success then you could paint all the children one after the other. They are all so beautiful. I shall pay for the materials.'

'No, I won't allow it! We are shamefully rich, Tengel and I, thanks to the help you gave us in the beginning.'

'How could we not have helped? By the way, the stable boy leaves us on Tuesday.'

'Oh, thank the Lord for that! One less worry, at least! Thank you for averting that danger! Who knows what might have happened? Well *everyone* knows of course! But it's certainly taken a weight off me.'

'I'm sure it has. Now, you must tell me – who is that peculiar man you've taken into your home?'

'Master Johan? He's pleasant enough.'

'Hmmm. I'm not so sure about that. I don't like the way he keeps asking questions. He has been questioning mother and me about Tengel – and Sol!'

'Is that so? That's strange, because Tengel is also suspicious of Master Johan.'

'Really? Mother says that he seemed to want to hear disapproving things about Tengel. But he came a cropper there because mother is Tengel's greatest admirer.'

Silje smiled. 'Your mother is wonderful, Charlotte. Is she feeling any better?'

'Yes, she is well again – and full of gratitude.'

Silje looked up from her work. 'Her linden tree is also healthy again, I've noticed,' she said slowly.

'Did you look at it? That day?'

'Yes. The leaves were dried out, almost withered. Now they are all green once more.'

Silje shivered violently. She was thinking of something that she had heard a long time ago – a near-forgotten memory about how the Kverne people, an ancient warrior tribe who lived far away to the north, were said to be skilled in magic. Among them lived wise men, able to draw a sickness out of a person and dispatch it into a particular tree. Somewhere, she did not know where exactly, there *was* such a tree. It was ancient and diseased, so people said, covered in grizzly knurled outgrowths and it spelt danger to anyone who came near to it; for any person touching it would surely suffer all its ailments.

The linden trees in Tengel's avenue had reminded her of the story, except there were no diseases in them and no pain attached to them. It was as if… No – she couldn't find a way of describing precisely what had occurred. Yet she still couldn't help trying to work out how these things possibly related to each other.

Suppose, as Tengel maintained, his evil namesake really did have nothing to do with Satan. At all times Tengel insisted that there was no such being as the Prince of Darkness. So was it possible that the first Tengel had belonged to a different race of people? A Kverne perhaps? Silje knew that the Kverne came largely from the land of the Finns. But Finns did not look like Tengel or Hanna or Grimar, although it was said there were many among them who practised the magic crafts. Could it be that the Evil Tengel had journeyed with the Kverne on their travels westward towards Norway, but had himself come from a land even further to the east – a land of legend and terror about which she knew nothing?

Oh well, it was just guesswork, she told herself. Tengel himself had said that there was no reason to believe that his forefathers had not come from Norway. And according to the stories, the Kverne were people of small stature, while Tengel was huge. Neither did they have coal-black hair. But they did have high cheek-bones, just like him, and short noses. She realised she was going round in ever-decreasing circles again so, with an effort she pulled herself out of her reverie.

'I wish Tengel hadn't done what he did with the trees,' she confided a little fearfully. 'I have started to examine all of them and it makes me quite anxious.'

'Are they now all well?' asked Charlotte softly.

'Oh, yes! All very healthy, every one of them.'

****

A day or two later a courier was sent from Akershus Castle to Linden Allée again, with a message asking Tengel to attend urgently on an ailing client there. This still happened from time to time and he always did his best to accommodate them without leaving the local poor to suffer. But equally he always made it clear that he would not allow himself to be generally at the beck and call of the aristocratic residents of the castle.

However, there was a great deal of frenetic activity when he arrived this time and he noticed radical changes were taking place before he even entered the main buildings. An Italian-style bastion, consisting of stone-dressed earthworks rising above the outer wall, was under construction and once inside he was struck by the prevailing sense of urgency. He was informed that a party of visitors had arrived from Denmark during the night and one of their number had fallen ill during the journey.

As he was led hastily through the darkened passageways, poorly lit with torches fixed to the walls at infrequent strategic points, Tengel allowed himself a wry smile. Silje's wish to see a real king had been fulfilled – not once, but twice in fact. He had brought her to Akershus three years earlier when a ceremony was held to honour King Kristian IV. Silje had been a little disappointed and the event had been something of an anticlimax for her because she had been so full of anticipation. The king was just a fourteen-year-old boy, albeit dressed up in his finery. But otherwise he looked quite plain. They had not been permitted to attend the ceremony itself but had watched from outside when the boy-king appeared to receive the acclaim of his people.

'What had you been expecting?' Tengel had laughed, 'A fairy-tale king with a crown and sceptre of gold?'

Silje's first sight of a king had been a far grander occasion. The year was 1589 and Norway unexpectedly became the place for the marriage between the Scottish King James VI – who also became James I of England – and Anna, the sister of Kristian IV, King of Denmark and Norway. The ship that was taking Anna to Scotland was wrecked on the coast of Norway, so the impatient groom came post-haste to meet her in Oslo. *That* had been a wedding to remember! Silje, who had nagged and nagged to be allowed to go to Oslo, saw the procession first hand at close quarters and talked about nothing else for six months afterwards. But that was five years previously, and since then her wild excitement had abated.

As Tengel proceeded through the castle, a couple speaking Danish came towards him from the other end of the passage. Tengel braced himself for the usual scream. But there wasn't one – instead the lady gave a sigh and fainted on the spot. Tengel was annoyed. 'Please do not make the usual comments about "meeting Lucifer himself" – I am so tired of them,' he told the woman's companion as he attended to the lady and helped her to her feet.

The man, who seemed to be of noble birth, said arrogantly, 'You can hardly expect anything else, my man! The very least one can ask is that you warn people in advance. No doubt you are the demon doctor that the Lord Lieutenant boasts of?'

'No doubt I am! I believe the lady has recovered. My patient awaits me.' Bowing summarily Tengel hurried away.

A footman had come to meet him. 'This way if you please, Herr Tengel. Aha! I see you and Jacob Ulfeld have crossed paths? Yes, he might well be a little touchy, for the lady with him was not his wife. Not because I believe he has a shadowy story to hide, you understand, but just being seen in the company of the Mistress Marsvin could harm his reputation.'

Tengel turned to look back at the pair, as they were about to disappear round a bend in the passageway. Ulfeld turned at the same instant and their eyes met across the long dark space between them. Marsvin? Where had he heard that name before? Of course – Jeppe Marsvin, Dag's real father. Perhaps Dag was related to that lady he had tried to help. Yes, Tengel concluded, he most probably was.

Silje had told him the name of Dag's father because she had not wanted to keep secrets from him. He had kept her confidence and never mentioned the name to another living soul. In spite of that, he had often entertained grim thoughts about the swine – a married man who had pleasured himself with the good-natured Miss Charlotte for just one night and then left, never to concern himself about her again. Had he not understood how alone and in need of affection she had been? Or had he believed that, by showing her some pity, he had bestowed a great gift upon her? Perhaps he had expected some gratitude for his noble act?

Tengel was becoming agitated thinking about this aristocratic lout and almost trod on the heels of the footman. He made his apologies and quietened his enraged senses. But still he could not get the man out of his mind.

Jacob Ulfeld, unbeknown to Tengel at that moment, was a strong royalist and minister-confidant of King Kristian IV. This was Tengel's first encounter with the Ulfeld family and, although it was not a name he had heard before, something about the name itself continued to intrigue him. Some sixth sense told him that the seemingly chance meeting in the castle passageway had more than a surface significance. But neither he, nor the noble minister himself, could imagine at that moment just how closely entwined their descendants would one day become.

****

His patient, when he reached him, was a friendly old Danish baron, who tolerated Tengel's slightly rough-handed treatment of his worn-out body without complaint. There was precious little Tengel could do except give him something to ease his pain, for which the old fellow was very thankful. But, as always, Tengel nevertheless did his best for him.

Two young ne'er-do-wells and a somewhat faded dandy, each clasping a goblet of wine, had chosen to sit close by and pass comment while Tengel examined his patient. This had annoyed Tengel, who had asked them to show some respect for the sick man. Amid much laughter and demanding loudly to know what a 'quack doctor from the Norwegian provinces could come up with', they took their drinks and went into the adjoining chamber. There they continued their conversation so loudly that Tengel heard everything that was said.

To his astonishment he soon realised that the debauched dandy was the very same Jeppe Marsvin who had been the focus of his anger for so long. Tengel felt his head was about to explode when he heard the man brag about a little conquest he had newly made with a Norwegian girl, here at the castle, whom he would be seeing later that evening in his chamber. 'A pretty little strumpet,' he shouted at one point, 'not a day over sixteen and most surely with her maidenhood intact! But not for much longer, eh?'

All three laughed raucously. 'Aha, Marsvin,' said one of the youngsters. 'Are you indulging in a slight distraction while your wife is not with you?'

'I *always* indulge in distractions!' replied Marsvin gloating, and this provoked a new outburst of laughter.

Tengel was beside himself with fury. As soon as he had finished taking care of the kind old gentleman, he went through to where the others were sitting. Leaning on the table he asked that one of them stay close to the old Baron in case he needed anything. The two youngsters assured him that they would. However none of them noticed Tengel slip some powder into Jeppe Marsvin's goblet.

That is the reason why the well practised seducer was heard to scream a panic-stricken 'No!' in the presence of the young girl he had planned to deflower, when she visited his room later that evening. In the event no seduction could be attempted and for the rest of the evening Jeppe Marsvin was to be found in the 'privy' beside the guest lodgings suffering from very loose bowels.

In fact the severity of his condition forced him to spend most of his visit to Norway confined in that tiny room. Everyone at Akershus soon heard the story of the hapless seduction scene and Herr Marsvin quickly became the subject of much ridicule and scorn. The stories rapidly spread throughout Denmark, and it is said that from then on he kept himself to himself, spending his days sulking at home and his evenings sitting moodily in the company of his wife.

He never found out that the cause of his downfall was the tryst he had with Charlotte Meiden thirteen years earlier. He had completely forgotten Charlotte by that time and Tengel had no desire to involve him in their ordered, settled lives at Gråstensholm and Linden Allée. Charlotte had no such wish either. She knew nothing about her past lover's pitiful visit to Akershus at the time, but several months later Tengel told her what had happened when he met Jeppe Marsvin and she had laughed, hard and hearty, with more than a touch of malicious pleasure. Perhaps, more importantly, she was pleased and grateful that Tengel had shown how much he believed in her.

Dag, to the exclusion of much else, filled Charlotte's life and she was so concerned for his well being that at times the youth found it awkward. When this happened, Grand-mama, the Dowager Baroness, would come to the rescue like the wise old lady she was. She would order him to spend time at Linden Allée and rejuvenate, and Charlotte would understand and promise not to stifle him again when he returned.

However Dag enjoyed life at the mansion very much. Everybody had been worried that the move from Linden Allée to Gråstensholm would cause him problems, but everything had in fact gone without a hitch. Besides it wasn't a bad thing to be the only child, spoiled and well cared-for, no longer having to share with others, as he had done previously. The absolute perfection to detail that was demanded at Gråstensholm suited his pedantic personality. Nothing was allowed to be out of place, unlike at Linden Allée, where a spot of dirt here and there or a forgotten item of clothing left on a chair was not considered important.

Of course he missed having somebody to whisper to in the darkness of the evenings before falling asleep and it was sometimes lonely wandering around the salons, chambers and corridors of Gråstensholm. But he would always have his foster family close by – and he had Liv. She visited him almost every day when she and Are came to Charlotte for their lessons. He enjoyed the way she could follow his train of thought as they quietly played chess or other board games. Because he was younger, Are on the other hand, much preferred being in the stables or barns.

'I am to travel to Copenhagen and study at the university,' Dag told Liv one day as they strolled to and fro along the picture gallery.

'You are leaving? Now?'

'No. When I am older. I think I shall be a professor or an auctioneer or something like that.'

Not long before this, there had been an auction on a farm in the district and Dag had been greatly impressed by the auctioneer's glib banter and the banging of the gavel. Liv said nothing; she thought it sad that he was going away.

Dag continued, 'And Mama Charlotte says that she will introduce me to some aristocratic lady, maybe one at Court, to whom I may be wedded.' Liv remained silent. 'And she is going to find a wealthy merchant, or some such, for you because you are so pretty. She says it will be more difficult with Sol, but I don't know why. Sol is pretty enough, don't you think?'

'Yes, very, very pretty. Ugh! I don't want to be wed anyway – that's all stupid.'

'I think so too,' said Dag. He patted the wall of the picture gallery with his hand. 'Mama Silje is to paint me. Did you know? Then I shall have my likeness hanging with this long line of ugly boring old fellows.' They looked up at the age-darkened portraits and laughed at the idea, as they went along the row making impolite comments about each one.

Then Dag turned serious again. 'I shall come back and settle down here later, of course. Because all of you are here and this will be mine – the estate and everything. You know that, don't you?'

'That's good. I'm glad you're coming back, so I'll have someone to play with.'

'You don't *play* when you're grown up! You should know that!'

'No, of course you don't. You're right. I'm just being silly.'

They gazed out through the tall narrow windows of the gallery. 'Look, there's that funny Master Johan – down in our yard,' said Liv. 'Can you see? He's walking back and forth with his hands behind his back.'

'He does look restless,' replied Dag. 'Like a broody hen. Now he's staring at the woods. How long do you think he's going to stay here, then?'

'He did say he's leaving soon. That's good because we're not allowed to fight or argue at all while he's here. And all he does is ask lots and lots of questions. He's a bit funny, isn't he?'

'Yes, he's more than a bit funny. Shall we play a trick on him? Let's get a mirror and dazzle his eyes!'

'Yes! Good idea!'

The only mirror they could find was one that went from floor to ceiling, so they gave up the idea and carried on wandering through the castle. Finally they reached the top of the tower. It was not a very grand tower, only a small square one with a spire above the main entrance. Liv and Dag liked to stand there, leaning on the windowsills – which were always covered in pigeon droppings – and gaze out over the countryside.

From their vantage point everything appeared so tiny. They couldn't see all of Linden Allée from this side of the building, just the last few trees of the avenue, the church, the lake and the country road.

'Look! Look! Over there!' exclaimed Liv. 'Can you see what's coming from behind the woods?'

'Ooh! What on *earth* can it be?' wondered Dag.

'So *you* can see it too!' Liv felt reassured. 'Sometimes I think I see things that other people can't. Whatever that is, it looks gruesome.'

Dag smiled. 'Don't get carried away by the things Tengel and Sol say! What you see are everyday things, but you see them in a different way from other people. You have a rich imagination, and you can see ghosts everywhere, even in broad daylight. Tengel says it is a gift you have from Silje, not from him.'

'I know you are right,' she told him. She was a little disappointed at this, because she had always wanted to believe she shared the qualities of the other two. There was always the lurking temptation for her to make things up – melodramatic and dark stories that no one believed.

Dag was staring intently down the road. 'Can't you see that it's a procession of some kind?'

'Yes, but why are they all walking like that?'

They could not take their eyes off the gloomy cortège. It was the blackest thing they had ever seen, mostly men in huge black hooded cloaks mounted on black horses. The breeze ruffled their cloaks and gave them the appearance of bats' wings. Behind the horses, a large body of men marched with ponderous, solemn steps. They were all making their way towards the church. There was a cart pulled by a team of dark-grey horses and the children could clearly see some people tied up inside it. Then followed a crowd of peasants, all dressed in dark clothes, looking very drab and sombre. They all seemed like small dolls from where Dag and Liv were watching.

'You're right, it is a very ghostly sight,' Dag agreed, without realising that his voice had become a whisper. 'Like a cortège from a hundred years ago – except that it isn't!' Dag was always so precise; so all-knowing.

'What do you think they've done?' Liv whispered back.

'Hmm, could be anything at all. Murder, stealing, heresy – I couldn't say. They are probably going to be hanged.'

'There's a woman there too.'

'Probably a witch, then.'

'Don't say that!' Liv took a deep breath and reached for his hand.

Dag knew what was running through her mind. He was having similar thoughts. So they stood there, hand in hand, watching the macabre procession. The day was gripped by utter silence, disturbed only by the squeaking of the cartwheels. No voices could be heard through the heavy mantel of doom that surrounded the procession – emphasising the determination of the righteous and the resignation of the captives.

Softly Liv said, 'In some ways, Dag, we had a good life in the Valley of the Ice People, didn't we?'

'Yes, but grown-ups are evil, Liv,' he said incisively. 'All of them. And I believe we are living in a time of evil.'

Chapter 12

Master Johan was suffering great pangs of dissatisfaction. Above all else he was ill at ease, because he felt he was getting nowhere. Yes, he had found masses of things at Linden Allée that were out of the ordinary, that much was true. But still he hadn't uncovered anything that was really worth putting in his notes. He lacked evidence that would conclusively condemn a witch or a sorcerer of high standing. Of course, he had seen one or two suspicious items and appropriated them too, but somehow he had then misplaced them most carelessly.

He had not yet written a single word to complement his fine list of questions that were so cleverly compiled and full of intrigue. These people he was investigating were such friendly folk, living together so harmoniously! The two small children were so polite and well brought up. Always happy and contented, they could never do enough for him.

The parents, too, were special. Never had he known such empathy, such a sense of belonging between two human beings; they were always so considerate of each other. He had tried hard to find a weak point in this family home because he regarded such harmony with grave suspicion –

but without success. It must be an apparition – or his imagination playing tricks. There was no doubt that Fru Silje was a God-fearing woman and as honest as the day was long. So it was unthinkable that she would be associated with one of Lucifer's sorcerers. What of the old Baroness? Had she not been very irritated by his careful, but pointed, questions? When he had asked her whether or not Herr Tengel might be in danger, because of his special ability to so wondrously heal the sick, she had scoffed at him.

'Herr Tengel?' she had exclaimed in a shocked voice. 'If he were ever to be accused of practising the black arts – well then there would truly be no justice in this world of ours! He is worth more than a hundred of those pompous old men who sit on that holier-than-thou Inquisition!'

Master Johan recalled that he'd had the good grace to blush when she said that. So the only weakness would seem to be the foster daughter, Sol. That was where he would find the answers. Of that he was sure. But he was in no great haste.

Once again, in his mind's eye, he saw her eager vibrant face before him. It radiated such unbounded confidence and openness, and deep inside himself he was well aware that he was pursuing her – but not for anything related to the courts. Young Sol's appetite for life was tremendous, as though she wanted to experience everything before it was too late. He would have to look after her and see that she did not fall prey to evil men who desired only her youthful beauty. Naturally he was above such things, being first and foremost wedded to the righteous service of the inquisitorial court. All he wanted to do was …

As he pondered this thought, he felt a sudden pounding in the pit of his stomach again. This dark realisation told him that his inner self had slithered back into torment. It was most vital that he now pull himself together and focus fully on his duties: dig deep, explore, analyse the human mind – and denounce!

He wondered where Sol would be at that moment. She had already left the house but had not been down to her place beside the stream – he had checked. She had been gone a long time now and the cat was still here. That was unusual. Would she be long?

Sol, in fact, had gone far away from the farm, and now sat in the shimmering heat of that summer's day, waiting beside a small half-ruined hut, halfway up the ridge. She had brought bread-cakes and wine that lay in a basket on the grass at her feet. The wine had been laced with Mother Hanna's best aphrodisiacs – herbs of love, leaves and bark from secret plants, dried mushrooms. Although Sol was positive that these would not be required, she thought it best to be doubly sure. After all, she only had this one day, this one moment.

Then at last she heard footfalls approaching from further up the ridge. Gathering her basket onto her arm she stood up and, with her heart pounding, began to walk homewards very slowly. He caught up with her in no time – it would have been impossible for him not to at the speed she was walking. As though hearing his footsteps for the first time she turned and appeared scared.

'Oh, it's you!' she said with a sigh of relief. 'You frightened me.'

The expression on Klaus's manly face was a statement of uncertainty and betrayed more than a trace of shyness. 'I didn't mean to.'

'Oh, of course! You were going to drive the cattle up to the ridge today. But wasn't that on Monday?'

'This is Monday.'

'Is it?' Sol took time to ponder this. 'So it is! Well I've been for a walk through the woods to collect herbs that my father will need for medicaments.' This was not a complete lie – she did have two pitiful stalks in her basket. 'I was about to look for a place to eat my food. Will you join me? Surely you are hungry too?'

Klaus's heart had been racing since he first glimpsed the girl on the path in front of him and he was only now beginning to steady himself. But his confusion was also simultaneously starting to mount once more. 'Yes, I am quite hungry – but is it seemly to stop here?' he asked doubtfully.

Sol frowned slightly. Dear God, she's beautiful, he thought. He was helpless; he felt abandoned to his fate with no one to guide him. Desire rose within him again, although he dearly wished it would subside. He must not forget who she was. Fourteen years, fourteen years old, he mumbled quietly to himself as if repeating a spell. Fourteen years – and who knows what uproar there would be from amongst the landed gentry!

'Why would it not be seemly?' she asked with surprise. 'Come on! Behind that knoll it will be sunny and peaceful. And I have a flask of wine …'

She had picked out the spot earlier in the day. It was secluded and could not be seen from the path, which in any event was rarely used. Neither would any casual passer-by hear any sound unless of course one was to scream for help – something Sol did not plan to do.

Without further resistance, Klaus gave in. He felt suddenly overwhelmed by a wonderful light-headed dizziness. Most all he wished to continue gazing endlessly into her bright sparkling eyes, which now seemed to be a deep shade of amber, absorbing the radiance of the sun itself. And a swig or two of wine couldn't do any harm, could it? Some food as well. Yes, he did feel hungry after his long and laborious trek.

Half an hour later the pair were stretched out in the tall sun-kissed grass behind the bank of earth, listening to a lark trilling high above the fields that lay like a quilt all around and below them. Klaus had been telling how solitary his life was and of the companionship he found working with the animals. He said he had never been with a girl – not properly anyway. The occasional kiss on the cheek perhaps, and clumsy hands groping the bodies of giggling reluctant servant girls. But nothing more. He had never dared try to go further.

Sol had persuaded him to talk about himself, coaxing him to satisfy her curiosity. Upon hearing how inexperienced he was, she smiled like a contented kitten. As he spoke, she lay gazing into his eyes, her soft fingertips lightly stroking his cheek and neck. She had run her hand down the opening of his shirt, fingers dancing across his chest, tickling the few hairs of which he was so proud. Once or twice he let out a little yelp, a mixture of pleasure and pain.

Sol was profoundly curious about this adult side of life, what happened between a man and a woman, because she knew so little about it. She had worked some things out for herself, of course: how babies were made; how men functioned and why they were needed; that it would hurt the first time, something she decided she would gladly endure.

The sight of the horses that day they had been together had sparked her growing desire and led her into repeated imaginings of what it might be like. She wanted desperately to ask him to display his manhood for her, but perhaps he would be too shy. She knew it would not be as large as the stallion's, but it was the focus of her curiosity.

The wine they were drinking had begun to have an effect. Alone it would have eased Klaus's inhibitions, but mixed subtly with Sol's secret spices, it served to kindle a raging fire within him that demanded urgently to be snuffed out. She was the only one who could do it – it would not be enough this time to go behind the barn or hide in his room. This time it had to be real.

He felt dizzy and faint – somewhere deep inside a voice rumbled on, repeating 'Fourteen years – punished – punish' but the words no longer held any meaning for him.

Gently he allowed his fingers to touch the hem of her skirt and as he was doing so he grinned foolishly, his cheeks on fire. At once Sol moved closer and he felt her hip pushing against him. Without hesitating he took hold of it in a fierce grip. Her eyes were bright, strangely aglow – with her moist lips half open and almost without breathing, she waited expectantly. She did not care that he reeked of the smell of stables and animals. It gave him that earthy untamed quality that Sol found so attractive.

With a deep trembling intake of breath, Klaus lifted himself up on one elbow and began brushing his hand across her breasts. She did not shy away or slap his hand like the other stupid girls did. He pushed his hand inside her blouse and fondled her. As he did so, this lonely boy saw in her expression an understanding and compassion that he had never known before. A mist seemed to cover his eyes and his pulse pounded in his ears. He gripped her breast with such force that she would still carry the marks from his fingers two weeks afterwards.

His mind was in turmoil – vaguely he realised that her knees were raised and that he had not lifted them. But then the uncontrollable urge overwhelmed him and all he heard was a groan, a feral cry that might have come from him.

Without realising what had happened, his hand was seeking out the secret place he so urgently wanted to touch while he gazed at Sol's aroused, glowing features beneath him. She shuddered – one long, exquisite shiver running down the whole the length of her body. Then for a brief moment things went awry, as Klaus, fearing that she might change her mind, fumbled clumsily, catching himself in his clothing. In the end his trembling fingers were so inept that she had to help him.

When his manhood was finally exposed, the only recollection he would have was of her dazed voice, 'Oh, God! It's so wonderful – I can stand it no more. I shall die! Oh, God! I am dying!'

At the age of fourteen Sol had seduced her first lover.

****

With a blissful smile Sol wandered back home. The newly sober Klaus had been racked with guilt. He would surely have given his life to undo what he had done. To Sol he had looked somewhat pathetic as he sat bemoaning his fate. She succeeded in calming him, assuring him that no one would ever know about what had taken place. He could leave Gråstensholm and take up his duties at the procurator's stables in the knowledge that he would soon forget all about her.

'Never!' he told her. 'Never! But if I am found out it will mean the gallows!'

'If *you* say nothing, no one will find out. I have no interest in letting others know, of that you can be sure.'

He nodded, said a hasty farewell and ran off through the trees as if the Evil One himself were at his heels.

So that was one more experience, another encounter,

thought Sol, as she sauntered along in the sunshine. Not bad – not bad at all – even if it all seemed to be over before it had really started. Yet somehow she knew that there had to be something more, something better than merely the down-to-earth domination that Klaus had recently consummated. She had been in too much of a rush as well and ought to have played and coaxed and teased a lot more. But Klaus was so ignorant and so inexperienced. She imagined there was a wide variety of things in which she could delight and, with different men, such meetings would undoubtedly prove very pleasant indeed! The future seemed to be irresistibly attractive.

The trees thinned as she reached the edge of the forest and she suddenly saw a figure standing against a tree with his back to her, quite clearly spying on Linden Allée. Without making a sound, she moved closer. 'I'm coming to get you!' she shouted in deep voice as she clawed at his back.

The man cackled hysterically and spun round. Sol laughed and this seemed to upset him still more, as if she was ridiculing his dignity.

'Are you trying to frighten old folk out of their wits, you young hussy?' he yelled at her.

'Folk always make fools of themselves when they think no one's looking,' said Sol. 'Anyway, I know who you are. You're the verger, aren't you?'

'You know nothing of the sort. You, who never set foot in a church.' The verger sneered at her unpleasantly as he brushed off the pine needles, sap and bark from his coat. 'But you just wait! Your time will soon come!'

'To go to church?' mocked Sol. 'I don't think so.' She was supremely calm and confident and still filled with the assurance of the passion she had just experienced.

'No, just the opposite. And it is usual to address a man

of the church with respect, by his title. Have you no manners?'

'I see no reason to show respect to a snake in the grass. And be careful what you say about manners. It is not right to spy on other people.'

The man shut his eyes. His fists were clenched in rage but he could not return Sol's glare. Master Johan's delays were a thorn in his side and he wanted something done now, right now!

'I know what I know,' he mumbled, his eyes flitting to and fro until they finally settled on the girl's narrow waist and proud breasts. 'I know full well what you are. You and your demon father will soon see! Judgement now awaits both of you!' (Oh! What enticing hips she has!) 'The stake, you hussy!' You shall burn! For now it is my turn to do what must be done. There will be no more weakness and grovelling.'

Indignantly, with frantic movements of his hands, he brushed off his hood. If he had known Sol a little better, he would have chosen his words with more care. He had threatened those close to her, the only people in the world about whom she cared. In her view, this gave her the right to act in self-defence and at once her expression changed.

She smiled softly and her eyes, half-closed, glowed alarmingly. She rummaged in her basket until her hand touched the item she wanted: a small thorn from a rose bush that was fixed to a twig and easily concealed in her hand. 'Here, let me help you. There are so many needles on the back of your neck,' she said considerately. 'There, that's better. Oh! Forgive me, did that one stick into you?'

'Yes, it did,' he whined, aggrieved, but unable to take his eyes off her cleavage, which was so close to him. 'Leave it! I'll manage by myself!'

He felt the saliva begin to dribble from the corners of his mouth and his voice took on a different tone. He thrust his sallow face into Sol's and she drew back from him in disgust as his bad breath hit her. But he continued to move closer and whispered ingratiatingly, 'You see, my dear, I am an important person, second only to the clergy. It is within my power to save you from the stake if you co-operate.'

Sol looked at him with loathing and pushed away his hands as he tried to touch and fondle her.

'I can teach you all of life's little secrets,' he said soothingly, his eyes protruding from their sockets. 'Would you like to see what a man – a real man – looks like, my dear? I can show you, if you come to my home this evening. Or better yet, here! Now!'

'Take your hands off me!' screamed Sol angrily. 'Go to hell, you horrible old pig! Don't you dare touch me with your repulsive fingers!'

She tore herself from his grasp and started to run away although she was not in the least afraid of the despicable old creature. Nonetheless her conscience reminded her that she should not have cursed out loud. The church's manservant stayed where he was, feeling for all the world as though somebody had doused him in cold water.

'I am leaving now!' he cried indignantly. 'And tomorrow is the day that judgement awaits you! I know that you are both servants of the Devil! Whore! Harlot! Do you think I don't know that you consort with Satan himself? That is the way with all witches. I would not even want to touch you with a long stick, you – you …' He struggled without success to find a final word, but his voice faded and died away as he walked towards the road.

Sol laughed aloud, full of contempt and set off for home across the meadow. On the small rise where it was possible to stand and look out across the countryside, she stopped and watched the verger jump over a ditch and carry on down the road in the direction of the church. What a wretched figure, she thought.

'Sol!'

The sound of her name broke her reverie and she turned to see Tengel hurrying towards her. 'Where have you been all the day, girl? Silje has been fretting after you.'

Sol couldn't help thinking that he also looked worried but she smiled. 'Oh, I've been walking out and about. I thought to collect herbs, but not much came of it. I took food and had a good day – a wonderful day.'

'But you must tell us when you go so far, little friend. We knew nothing.'

'You know that I enjoy being by myself – doing what pleases me. But forgive me, for I was thoughtless.'

Tengel regarded her pensively. 'What has happened, Sol? You look so strange. Disturbed, yet at the same time pleased with yourself! And I do not like that gleam in your eye either. Who was that man I saw run along the edge of the forest a little while ago?'

Sol turned her attention back to the surrounding farms and took a few steps down from the rise, so they could not be seen from the house. Tengel followed her. 'He was an evil man, Tengel. He said he wanted to seize you and me and imprison us for being in league with the Devil.'

Tengel's face lost all colour. 'Good God! Is that really true, Sol? Well, I am not surprised – what with my healing powers and your carelessness. But who would want us so badly? Who was it? Master Johan?'

'No, the verger from the church.'

'Oh, him. He is a repulsive man, consumed with double morals. For that reason alone he will surely be dangerous.'

Sol looked every bit the innocent, as she added, 'He said something very strange, Tengel. Something I didn't understand. I should be nice to him and co-operate? Then he would let me go free. Then he grabbed at me with his nasty, bony hands. Why did he do that, Tengel?'

Her foster father had taken a deep breath that he now let out explosively.

'Whaaaat?' he yelled, barely managing to form the word. 'What did he do? Did he do anything more?'

'No,' replied Sol, unconcerned. 'I told him he was ugly and stupid and went on my way.'

It took a while for Tengel to gather his thoughts. 'Dear God, what are we to do?' he whispered. 'What are we to do, Sol? We are in trouble, you and I. Will we have to move on again – leave Linden Allée, that we have all grown to love so dearly?'

'Do not worry,' Sol said lightly. 'He will not get far.'

Tengel's face slowly changed colour again – to a grey pallor. 'Sol!' he whispered. 'What have you done?'

She shrugged her shoulders. 'I was thinking of Silje, my siblings and you – all of us.'

He took hold of her and shook her violently. 'What have you done, Sol?' he shouted, almost choking on the words. 'Answer me! Was it – one of Hanna's thorns of death? Do you have one of them?'

'Ouch! You're hurting me!'

He released his hold on her and she straightened her blouse around her shoulders. 'Yes, I do have one.'

Tengel drew breath, a great rasping sound. 'Run after him! Now, at once! Run, and curse you to hell!'

Never before had he spoken so harshly to her, but he was out of his mind with fear and despair. Sol looked calmly down across the open countryside to where the verger could be seen far away, approaching the tree-lined path leading up to the church.

'It's too late.' Her speech was slightly slurred, as though she was in a trance.

Tengel followed her gaze. The verger could be seen swaying strangely, grasping first one of the birch trees and then the next as he strove to reach the churchyard wall. Then he fell heavily – and lay still.

'Oh, Jesus Christ!'

As he uttered those words, Tengel buried his face in his hands and sank to the ground, his legs unable any longer to support him.

'He might have killed us,' said Sol innocently. 'Then what would have happened to Silje? And Liv – and Are? He was an evil man, Tengel.'

His only reply was a moaning sound. Sol waited. Finally he asked, 'Was that why you looked so ... *pleased*?'

'No, no. It was simply an idle thought that crossed my mind.'

'What?'

'Don't worry. It was nothing.'

Tengel was unable to move. He felt defeated, crushed by an invisible force.

'Nobody saw him come from over here,' she said as though she was talking about some childish mischief. 'We will be quite safe. Come on, let's go home!'

It was then that Tengel woke from his stupor. At long last, after years of suppressing the power of his extraordinary craft, he allowed it to feed on the anger and sorrow that had overwhelmed him. He rose slowly to his feet.

'Sol!'

The word was uttered fiercely, a single threatening monotone and she turned immediately to look at him. The sight that met her eyes sapped all her willpower. It was Tengel who stood before her, but not the Tengel she knew. What she saw was a spirit from the depths with its lips drawn back exposing its fangs. Its nose flared and its eyes dazzled her.

'Give me the basket.' His voice was no more than a whisper.

She hugged it closer to her, determined to resist him to the last. 'No! These are my own special things. Hanna willed them to me alone and she taught me which herbs to harvest and how I should use them. She would be displeased if …'

Sol stopped talking. A strange feeling was stealing over her and a grey mist engulfed them, making everything invisible except Tengel's frightful face and those eyes. His hand reached out, compelling her to release the basket. This was a force greater than anything Sol had ever experienced. She had always believed that her powers were superior to Tengel's – now she realised she had been mistaken. Her body was swaying to and fro and, feeling herself gripped by this unfamiliar terror, she meekly handed over the basket.

'This is not everything,' said Tengel without even glancing at its contents. Even his voice was different – it was harsh and unpleasant – the sound of an inhuman creature. 'You will surely have a hoard of things, most probably the greater part, at home. I am to have it all – you will not be allowed to hide anything from me.'

Sol nodded timidly, her will broken.

'I know what you are thinking,' said Tengel as he thrust his almost unrecognisable face still closer to her. 'You think that you will be able to gather new substances. If you do then I shall kill you – as you know that I can. You are a dangerous person, Sol, and I must protect the world from you. You also know that you do not have the power to take my life, because I can sense your innermost thoughts.'

She could tell this was true. All her self-confidence and rebelliousness had begun to drain away and tears filled her eyes.

'I did it for the best, Father,' she sobbed. 'I thought only to save you all from a wicked person.'

Tengel's fury abated and his face regained its human features. He placed the basket on the ground and stretched out his arms to her. Sol threw herself into his embrace sobbing passionately. 'Don't do that any more, Father,' she begged. 'Please don't do that again! I could not endure it. It was so horrible!'

Tengel was also close to tears as he held her and slowly stroked her hair. 'Sol, Sol, my beloved but star-crossed child, what are we to do with you? I want so badly that Silje shall be proud of you and take you to her heart. Do not forget that you are *my* niece and I feel about you as I do for any close family. You have always been like my own child. But Silje had no need to care for you. She did that out of kindness and love. I do not want you to disappoint her.'

Sol was still sobbing violently. Over and over again she called him 'Father', something she always did when she was very upset. 'I tried hard to be good, Father. Really I did. I wanted so much to do those things that are right and proper. But it is more fun – more satisfying – to be nasty.'

'I know, my little one. It is the curse of our bloodline.'

'If you take Hanna's treasures from me then you have taken my life as well.'

'Your life? No, far from it. But …' Tengel fell silent. At long last he realised what he ought to have done so many years before. He held her at arm's length and looked into the illusory innocence of her tear-filled eyes. 'Sol, I have been a fool! Of course there is an answer here!'

'What are you thinking ?'

He felt inspired and the warm glow returned to his eyes. 'You know that I am tired, almost worn out from the work I do to help those unfortunates who come to me every day seeking solace. There are times when I worry how long I can go on. Yet you have too little to occupy you, is that not true? We have maids to help in the house and Charlotte has no more she can teach you – so now you have too much time to spend engrossed in your own dangerous pastimes.'

'Yes, that is true,' she conceded.

'Sol, would you like to help me? There is no doubt that you are young, but I know that you can – even though you may not have the same gift of healing in the hands that I do. But there is much that you can do better than I – for you are able to mix powders and potions as well as any witch.'

Sol had begun to smile. 'May I? Really?'

'And use your power in the service of good? Nothing would mean more to me!'

Her exuberance was making her dizzy. 'Oh, there is so much I can do! I shall use my herbs. And if it is better for anyone to leave this life, then I'll see to that as well.'

'No!' shouted Tengel desperately. 'You are to *save* life, not snuff it out.'

'I do not understand why that should be,' she said intolerantly. 'If people become a burden to themselves and others then surely it is best they should die?'

He turned and walked away from her. 'Forget everything, Sol! Forget it! It will not work.'

She ran after him, hands pressed together in supplication. 'No, Tengel, please! I promise, I swear! By all that I hold dear, I swear I shall not end a life, I promise! I shall do everything I can to save them – but please let me work in my own fashion.'

Tengel sighed. 'I see no other way. I cannot hand you over to the authorities, even though that would be the proper thing to do. I could never do that. But you must give me all your deadly medicaments!'

She hesitated, obviously struggling with her deepest and most powerful instincts. He waited, but she still did not indicate her assent.

'All of them, Sol! You are still only a child and cannot yet measure the strength of your powers. I shall return them when you are – let us say – twenty years.'

'But that is more than five years away!'

'It must be this way. It is the only way I can protect you.'

With a sigh so deep that it might have come from the depths of the earth itself, she capitulated. 'Very well – as you wish.'

They began to walk toward the house and suddenly Tengel gave a chuckle. 'Besides you can assist in another way if you are to be my little helper. It can be awkward sometimes when some of the more noble ladies seek my help.'

'How?'

'Well, a patient looks up to her physician – and often, very often, women find they have undesirable feelings for him – a mix of admiration and passion. Perhaps it is a need to be dominated. It can be quite irksome.'

Sol burst into a fit of sniggering. 'Do you mean that they fall in love with you?'

'Something like that,' he answered wavering. 'So it would very helpful if you could be with me to attend them in their bedchambers and boudoirs. That would allay their interest.'

The girl was outrageously amused by this – Tengel less so. He used to dread going to visit some patients, remembering the searching glances from a sickbed, the night-gowns that 'accidentally' slid down and small delicate hands that inched their way up his arms.

'Do they arouse you?' wondered Sol.

Tengel frowned. 'Arouse? That is not a word I had thought to hear from you, Sol!' he reprimanded her. 'I most certainly do not get aroused. I simply feel embarrassed on their behalf and angry because they make my work harder. I have to be very tactful to get out of the situations without hurting their feelings. I just do not have the time or the energy to waste on them.'

'My poor Father,' said Sol, her voice soothing as she took hold of his hand. 'I shall protect you from these persistent women. But I can well understand! You probably look quite attractive to them, despite your ugly features.'

Only Sol would ever have spoken to him in such a fashion. But he knew she was right. One of these women who had too little to do and who filled her days with dreams had told him plainly, 'Herr Tengel, you exude the sensuality of a wild animal searching for a mate. And the demonic quality that you have makes you very dangerous! Forbidden, therefore, on two counts – and as you know, forbidden fruit …'

On that occasion Tengel had felt only disgust and revulsion. It had been difficult for him to carry on being polite.

'Does Silje know about this?' asked Sol thoughtfully.

'No. I would not want her to worry – and besides, it would never cross my mind to be unfaithful. However, it will be good to have you with me – it gladdens my heart.'

'And mine,' she replied.

'Sol, I know that you have been engrossed in something else today. I could sense just then – as soon as we met – a feeling so strong that you could barely contain it.'

She grinned. 'Yes, but it was nothing bad, Tengel. It was a feeling of happiness. I don't wish to say anything more about it.'

Tengel gave her a sidelong glance, but Sol's smile remained inscrutable. He shook his head in bafflement and walked on, still conjecturing about the mystery. After a while he gave up. Never in his wildest dreams would he have guessed what she had really been up to. In his eyes Sol was still just a child.

Chapter 13

By taking an extreme course of action, Sol had freed them from the threat posed by the verger. But the real danger, in the form of Master Johan, still remained. His presence in the house had prompted differing reactions among members of the family, but no general consenus on him had been reached.

Silje and the children were far too good-natured to believe that anyone whose only intent was evil could worm his way into their home. Despite seeing evidence to the contrary on so many occasions, they continued to believe that folk were good-hearted. Tengel and Silje had taught their children to show consideration to others – it was their most important message. Also they should always be guided and bound together by love.

Tengel, and to a lesser degree Sol, however, had grave reservations about the guest living under their roof. In their own ways they remained watchful and took note of his movements and moods. They were still ready to help him, but nevertheless both remained wary and on their guard.

Master Johan, for his part, was accustomed to sitting in vast halls and consigning his victims, innocent and guilty alike, to perish on the rack, be burnt at the stake and suffer the most terrible instruments of torture. He was definitely not accustomed to walking back and forth all through the forest as he found himself doing one day. In fact Master Johan felt really ill this time.

He was almost certain he was going to die and as he returned from his forest meanderings, having spent half the day searching for Sol, young Are looked at him inquisitively.

'Did you really walk across the mountains from Sogn?' the boy asked in his clear youthful voice. 'You've only walked up the little slope beyond the house and your breathing already sounds like an old bellows.'

Master Johan could not think what to say. He was deeply offended that anybody should cast doubt on the integrity of a man of justice in this way. He considered himself to be an instrument of God – His angel of wrath.

As it happened, Silje came to his rescue. 'You should show respect to your elders, Are! When will you learn? And you have to understand that Master Johan is so exhausted from his long trek without food that it will be many days before he is well again. Was it beautiful in the forest today, Master Johan?'

'What? Oh, yes, of course!'

If the truth be known, he had not seen anything of the forest. He had been searching constantly for Sol and had become more and more incensed as the day wore on. As soon as he had discovered that she was not in her usual place by the stream, he had begun wandering aimlessly back and forth across the open farmland, before suddenly rushing headlong into the trees again, searching wildly and charging hither and thither like an enraged bull. She would soon see who was master! The little strumpet would tremble and suffer. He would order one of his most exquisite and ingenious tortures and she would regret ever hiding from him.

'There they are,' shouted a happy Silje suddenly, interrupting his thoughts. 'Tengel and Sol are together!'

Master Johan had felt his tense shoulders relax. He had suddenly realised how bright and wonderful the day was – he hadn't really noticed it until that moment!

****

Some time later he lay in bed once more – this time with a serious illness on his chest. His shrill hoarse coughing echoed again and again through the attic yet, in spite of his misfortune, he had to concede that he was very comfortable.

The main reason for his agreeable state was the attention he was receiving from a reformed, kind-hearted Sol, who was now providing the best of all care. She served him reinvigorating broths – almost certain to be witches' brews and he would report them as such – and made sure his bedding was kept neat and cool. When her small nimble fingers plumped up his pillows or slid under his back to straighten the sheets, they warmed his worn, contrite, abstemious body.

His gaze followed her every move – what she did and where she stood. He noted each and every indication that might reveal she was a worshipper of the Devil. Naturally it was for this reason alone that he could not take his eyes off her, he told himself. He must not forget to write down everything he saw: the yellowy green, cat-like eyes; the seductive curves that had developed too early; her hips, her breasts, the waist that was so impossibly small that he wondered whether his own hands might encircle it.

On that day she had forgotten to straighten his pillows.

Master Johan opened his mouth to call her back, but stopped himself just before the words were uttered. What was he thinking of? He was the Inquisition's Grand Master in waiting! He had heard of the sudden death of the pedantic verger. Terrible skin sores they had said, and his heart had failed. Well, these things happened. Johan certainly would not mourn his passing, the ignorant peasant!

As he lay there, he felt his own arm. Looking at it more closely, he could see that it had more flesh on it than before. And he could feel that his face, too, had grown plump. They prepared good food in this house and Johan thought he ought not to deny his emaciated body, especially while he was so poorly. They forced it upon him as well, so it was not his fault. The court would not blame it on him, most assuredly not! How could one say "no" and hurt the feelings of such caring folk? But it would have to stop, now, at once! He couldn't go back looking like a fatted swine! He would stop – forthwith!

But first he would just finish off that bread cake and the large lump of cheese. They shouldn't be left alone in the bowl. That would be so uncivilised! He must make the sacrifice. The bread tasted good, helped on its way with a mug of ale. Aaaah! Delicious! A swift prayer to the Lord, of course, for gluttony.

Tengel came into the attic again. Now here was a sorcerer, God be my witness – no, as Satan is my witness, I meant to say. Forgive me, Lord, forgive me! All these unorthodox medicaments. And those hands that touched Master Johan's scrawny chest – they warmed so exquisitely. Oh no! He was using the wrong expressions again! There was nothing godly about sorcery! He was reluctant to admit it, but he was afraid of this demon. What was he doing? Was he not going to lay his hands upon him today? No! He's sitting down to talk.

Johan felt disappointed at not being treated as usual, but obviously said nothing. Tengel looked thoughtfully at him, his frightful countenance mellowed by those sympathetic eyes.

'How are you feeling today?' he asked gently. 'I think you are looking better.' Reluctantly Johan had to concede that he did indeed feel better. 'All right, if that's true, I think you should get up this afternoon. Rest well again tomorrow, then you will be able to continue your long-delayed journey to Akershus the following day.'

Master Johan nodded, unsure if he was as relieved about this as he ought to have been. The week he had been assigned had ended a couple of days earlier, but if he presented his sudden illness as a reason – it was of course life-threatening – he would probably be spared the wrath of the Principal Judge. He needed to mortify his flesh on the final day, so that he appeared suitably famished and worn when standing before the powerful ones.

He would deliver an excellent report. He would write everything down as he travelled, so that nobody here would see it. My, my! There was so much here that he would condemn. Every question on his list was answered with 'yes'!

Yet even better than that, he had discovered one more witch! Fru Silje! She painted images on cloth! Godly and sinful images one after the other! She was – a woman! Had anyone ever heard of such a thing before? Everybody knew that no woman was able to paint. But *she* could! The pictures were so alive: the figures seemed as though they were about to walk into the room. Her tapestry paintings were better than those of many men – and that could not be tolerated! It must be Satan's work – yes, Satan's evil! That's what it was!

There was also the little girl, of whom he saw almost nothing. Liv was her name, and she had *ginger* hair. Hair of that colour was one of the signs that the Inquisitors usually found suspicious. Many a witch had been brought down because if it. And the girl had so much knowledge! She knew exactly where Sogn was located, she spoke Latin and could calculate numbers that even he could not fathom – and that was not all …

Master Johan broke off from his thoughts, feeling suddenly very dizzy. He was surrounded by the Devil's evil wherever he turned! He had become ensnared in a witch's coven. The worst ones of course were Tengel and Sol. Those two would have to be annihilated as swiftly as possible. Indeed this whole family would have to be destroyed to prevent their wickedness from defiling the earth.

Then why, despite his success, did he feel so depressed? He must have overeaten. His stomach was reacting to too much rich and fatty food – the bread-cake and the cheese. He was so confused and his head seemed to be spinning. Never before had he been treated with such friendship, kindness and care as in this house!

Yet it must be a delusion – Satan's delusion! He knew very well that the bread had not caused his annoyance, yet he directed all his anger at it. All these strange thoughts tumbled around in his head as he tried to concentrate on what Tengel was saying.

'Has Sol's behaviour been as you would expect?'

Behaviour? What sort of behaviour did he mean? No, he must be imagining things, he could mean nothing special by it!

'Yes! Her behaviour has been quite excellent, thank you!'

Tengel laughed. 'You see, Master Johan – and I feel I can tell you this because you have become a friend to this household – we have been worried about the child. But it seems we need not have been.'

'Really?'

Tengel had decided to take a big chance. The damage had already been done, because this man knew far too much about them and, if he had decided to denounce them then their situation would be hopeless. It had not crossed Tengel's mind to harm the man. To render him harmless, he would depend on confidence and loyalty alone.

'Why, yes. We were concerned that she had inherited an affliction. But she has become the finest and cleverest little helper I could wish for. She is wonderful with all my patients.'

Did she care for others as well? Johan was seized by an unjustified pang of envy at the thought and struggled to dismiss it from his mind.

'Also, of course, we were afraid of the curse,' continued Tengel earnestly. 'In fact very afraid.'

Master Johan almost jumped out of the bed in his agitation. 'The curse?'

'Yes. Both Sol and I have been born with it. Liv and Are might have been, but they were spared. I have had a hard life, Master Johan. Longing to be as others are, while carrying this burden! My childhood years were so gruelling that I am loath to describe them to you. Only one who had suffered them would be able to comprehend. Many was the time when I thought of ending the accursed existence of the life I had, but as you know too well, Master Johan, it is a sin against God to take one's life. That was when I met Silje. She has brought me so much gladness. I am certainly the happiest man in the whole of Norway, Master Johan, for the day always dawns brighter after the darkest night, does it not? But it was always Sol that I worried about, and now things are well with her.'

'You spoke of a curse?'

'Yes. Do you wish to hear more?'

'Indeed. Very much.' This non-human sitting before him with his sad eyes could never know just how much he wanted to hear more.

Tengel paused, then nodding in agreement, he began. 'Once at the beginning of time … Well, perhaps not so long ago as that – but at least several hundred years ago – there lived a man called Tengel of the Ice People.'

'The Ice People?' exclaimed Johan rather loudly, before quickly recovering his composure.

'Yes. Have you heard of them?'

Master Johan had certainly heard of them. A man from Tröndelag had recently been travelling through Denmark proudly bragging about how he had helped obliterate an entire valley populated by witches and warlocks – but he decided in that moment not to reveal what he knew. 'No!' he replied evasively, 'I've no knowledge of them at all.'

'Well, this Tengel of the Ice People was a very wicked person. It is said that he sold his soul to Satan in return for happiness and wealth in this life. Some of his descendants would be chosen to inherit evil powers and abilities that no other could acquire in order to carry out the wishes of the Evil One. Can you believe this?'

Johan gave a calm nod of his head, but he was quivering with excitement. *This* would be something to tell the Court! The Ice People. The accursed ones, the damned!

'Not that I believe that devil's story,' said Tengel. 'There is no doubt that my forefather had a streak of evil in him that has been passed down to some of us. Look at us! I am one of the afflicted, as is my niece, Sol. All my life I have tried to fight the wickedness within me and use its power for good. Dear God – if you understood how many

238

troublesome, barren times I have known! Silje and I have tried to bring up Sol to be a good person, but it has been difficult, because she cannot grasp the difference between right and wrong – good and evil. Not until now – since you arrived – have I seen how much goodness she has within her. She is a wonderful girl, Master Johan, who is struggling to conquer the wickedness in her soul.'

Insidiously Johan asked, 'But you are surely not the only descendants of that man of the Devil?'

'Yes, we are. You see the bailiff's troops killed all the others. We were able to flee across the mountains and nobody else knows that we survived. Nobody except for the two ladies of Gråstensholm and their little boy, that is. He also endured the journey across the mountains away from the Valley of the Ice People with us. Yes and there are four old ones living in Tröndelag who know, but they will tell no one. And now you, Master Johan. But you have been so much like one of our family these past few days that we trust you implicitly. Sol is very fond of you and worries about your health.'

Master Johan swallowed. His stomach was aching so badly that he felt sick. The Inquisition Court – the burnings – a sensational tale to tell – honour and recognition! A tribute to God! A triumph! A magnificent triumph!

'Believe me, Master Johan, when I say that I have toiled hard to remedy the horror that was thrust upon me at birth. All I have ever thought of is to be kind-hearted to others. I only wish I knew whether I had succeeded.'

All those proud instruments of torture – inflicting the most exquisite pain! The reality of Tengel's voice was so far away.

'What is wrong, Master Johan? Are you feeling unwell?'

In reply, his patient mumbled indistinctly and none of

his words were clearly audible. Tengel supposed he might be trying to utter words of comfort, so did not press him. Seeing that the greenish pallor was beginning to fade from the man's taut face, he stood up quietly and left the room.

When he had shut the door behind him, Tengel stood with his eyes closed, completely exhausted. Had he achieved what he set out to do? Had it been right to reveal everything? He opened his eyes to see Sol standing, looking questioningly up at him. He placed his hands on her shoulders and silently motioned her to acccompany him downstairs.

'What's wrong, Tengel?' she asked as they moved down towards the ground floor. 'You look very worried.'

Tengel bit his lip. 'I do not know who this man is, Sol – Master Johan, I mean. But there is something about him that does not feel right, something I have sensed from the moment he arrived. You know how I notice such things, don't you?'

Sol nodded, but did not say anything. Having reached the bottom of the stairs, they carried on out into the yard, away from the house. The air was chill and the sky overcast – the fine summer weather had abandoned them for the day.

'Something is completely awry,' Tengel continued, 'which is why I decided to adopt the path of friendship. I appealed to the man's better nature and told him of the load we carry with us.'

'And if he has no better nature?'

'We can but hope, Sol,' he replied with a melancholy smile.

Sol looked at him earnestly. 'I believe you did right, Father. I sense that this will end well.'

'I am not as sure as you are,' he sighed. 'Who do you think he can be?'

'Hmm, who can say? That nasty little verger hinted at something that might have been a warning. That we shouldn't be so sure of ourselves. I thought he was talking about himself, but now that I think about it, maybe he wasn't.'

Tengel's fingers dug into her shoulders. 'Merciful God, Sol! What are we to do?'

'We shall carry on as you have started,' she answered calmly. 'I too will appeal to his better nature. And don't worry,' she gave a smile, 'I know my place now!'

'That's good. Do what you can, Sol.'

She looked down. 'I *shall* do my very best. I am a responsible girl now.'

'I know you are. You have been very resourceful. If you carry on like that everything will be well with us!'

****

It was time to bid farewell and Johan, dressed in his plain brown cloak, stood ready to leave. The two younger children had each given him a parting hug, so hard that his neck still ached. Silje had given him a basket filled with food and warm clothes and her eyes had filled with tears as she wished him well for the future.

Tengel's powerful hand reached out and those strange eyes peered trustingly into his. 'Be sure to take the medication as I have told you! Remember Master Johan that you do not have a strong constitution! Thank you for visiting our humble home, it has been a pleasure to have you here with us.'

'And for me also,' he muttered, finding it hard to say the words. 'Please accept my warm thanks for all the – food.'

Tengel handed him a small item of silver. 'Take this – and keep it about your person. It is an amulet that will protect you against all evil.' Tengel laughed and added, 'Real witchcraft! It holds all sorts of strange things – but I believe it works.'

With barely a moment's hesitation, Johan took it from him. Proof at last! The very thing he had been seeking. The perfect piece of evidence and now it was his! He could feel Sol staring at him. Her eyes had a strange fiery glow that seemed to be asking him something. Such wonderful, beautiful eyes!

Quite unexpectedly, she threw her arms around his neck and pressed herself to him. At that moment she was behaving as a child again, but Johan, seeing her also as a young woman, could not help hugging her a little closer than was appropriate and tears filled his eyes. As they drew apart she gave him one final glance. It held so much intense heartache, such endless pity – her emotions became his and he found it hard to breathe – there was a knot of deep gloom below his heart, tearing at him. Abruptly wishing them a hasty goodbye, he turned away.

The coachman from Gråstensholm took him all the way to the outskirts of the town. However, Master Johan did not go on to Akershus straight away. Waiting until the carriage had driven out of sight, he entered the first inn he came to. He asked for writing implements and while he drank a glass of wine he sat staring at his list, preparing to write down the answers. In his pocket, the amulet Tengel had given him seemed to be on fire.

He sat thinking for a long time, becoming aware that a strong pain was growing in his abdomen. The glass of wine became a bottle, yet still no words had appeared on the paper lying in front of him. Deep pools of despondency, melancholy and gloom surrounded him. They called to him and drew him to them, dragging him down, deeper and deeper, clutching at him with talons of uncontrollable sadness.

Visions drifted past him – the innocent faces of the

children, the pure image of the wife, the huddled figures standing on the steps waving him farewell. They were an unusually happy family – and heathen! He took the burning amulet from his pocket. This was Satan's artefact and it was enough to convict all of them. Oh, yes, he could convict the messengers of the Devil – he knew what to do – and he had been highly praised for his strict, unbending ways.

Two men were engrossed in conversation in the booth behind him. He had been half-listening to them for a while and the vague thought had crossed his mind that he recognised one of the voices. He listened more closely, because they were discussing a subject about which he knew a great deal.

'Yes, it was one of the Inquisition's henchmen! He ordered a terrible punishment for the woman.'

'How was she condemned?'

'Neighbour's wife informed against her. Cows had stopped milking.'

'That's evidence enough! What was her punishment?'

'The funnel.'

Johan gave a start. He had often ordered the use of the funnel – it was his favourite method of torture. A funnel was thrust into the mouth of the condemned and water poured in. She was forced to swallow, it was impossible not to – and those great tubs of water …

Johan shuddered from head to toe. The pull of the depths was there again, dizzying, enticing – Sol's eyes. So sad – beckoning. Triumph. Honour! Then suddenly nothingness! It was all gone. His mind was a void.

Then he heard the voice from behind him again. 'She stayed alive for a long time in the flames. It was an extraordinary sight to see!'

Johan was becoming more light-headed. Suddenly he grabbed his pen and began scribbling frantically. He was answering all the questions with an emphatic 'No!', pressing so hard each time that the pen almost broke in two. Underneath he added, 'There are no signs that any person in the house has ever practised witchcraft. I have received an urgent summons to Denmark and must leave this very day.'

He left his booth quietly so that the men would not see him, paid for the wine and once outside he called to a young lad in the yard.

'Here! I want you to take this letter to the Principal Judge of the Inquisitional Court. It is very important and you will be paid well for your trouble. Wait, you shall have a coin from me and this amulet as well. It is of silver and has the power to protect you from evil.'

The boy was only too pleased to take both the charmed amulet and the coin. He promised, on the sanctity of his soul, to complete the errand and ran off at once.

Master Johan gave a tired sigh and walked away from the town in the opposite direction. He handed the basket of food and clothes to a poor beggar he found at the roadside, then left the road and set off across country towards the fjord. He stopped when he had reached the edge of a high precipice and looked down across the water. Directly beneath him the waves were breaking in a creamy foam over the rocks at the foot of the cliff. The pull of the depths – it was there waiting!

Johan said a prayer begging for God's mercy on his tormented soul. Then he jumped off the cliff. It was quick and he didn't feel much.

****

Young Klaus was also in prayer, on his knees in the procurator's hayloft. He begged and begged, repeating over and over, 'God, please help me, please help me! They will come for me! She will tell – she will surely tell someone – and they will come for me. Please God, hide me! I didn't mean to do anything to her – I should have killed her then and there, God. Strangled her! Oh no, I don't mean that – I couldn't kill anyone, You know that Lord, not even a fly. Oh help me! What am I to do, now that my life is destroyed? I shall never know happiness again!'

Someone shouted for him and he jumped up with a yelp. 'They're coming for me – where can I hide? I know – a rope! I'll tie a rope round that beam and hang myself.'

At that moment, a voice from below shouted, 'Have you given that mare more hay yet?'

Klaus breathed a sigh and felt his shoulders relax. Saved, this time at least. But what about the next time? Or the time after that? Or the next? He felt his life from now on would always be lived in terror.

****

Sol was dancing in the moonlight. She had woken about midnight and seen the moon shining with a cold golden glow. Stealthily she got out of the bed she shared with Liv and went out to the meadow. Dressed in her white shift with her hair hanging loose down her back, she resembled a beautiful nymph dancing over the flowers.

It was not the moonlight that appealed to her so much, but the shadows that it cast. At night in her world there were so many exciting things hiding in the depths of the forest – so many grotesque and wonderful creatures that might emerge and she had only to call for them. But she would not do that now – not yet. Not for a few years. She had made a promise. So instead she stood and stretched her arms up towards the blue-white light.

'Forgive me, Hanna! You know that it is only for a time. A few short years. Then, when I am grown, I shall once more serve you and our own Master. I shall be skilled in our craft, Hanna, and then I shall meet Him – just as you did on your wild rides through the sky to his mountain. To the great Witches' Sabbath.'

She laughed at the night and danced across the meadow again – then she stopped.

'It doesn't count of course, what I did with Master Johan,' she murmured to the coldness of the moon. 'You know I remember hearing Silje and Tengel whispering about how I once made a nasty boy cut himself with a knife. It didn't surprise me at all, because I knew all the time that I could do such things. So that's what I did with Master Johan. I forced my will on him and convinced him he was unhappy and overcome with mortal anguish. Not because I thought it was needed – he was already finished. He was so filled with regret and remorse as he was. But still it was not a bad thing to give him a little shove. I did nothing that was forbidden, did I Hanna? I used neither powder nor thorn. I just had the feeling that his presence on this earth was no longer required. Of course, you do understand?'

Then she resumed her rapturous dance, spinning around faster and faster, feeling as though she was floating above the sleeping, dew-covered flowers.

'Life is so beautiful,' she whispered. 'And it won't be very long now! Just a little while to wait.'

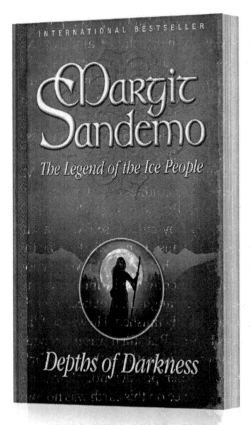

ISBN: 978-1-903571-79-8

*Book 3 of The Legend of the Ice
People series,* Depths of Darkness, *is
to be published on 4 September 2008*

Further Information

Publication for the first time in the English language of the novels of Margit Sandemo began with *Spellbound*. The first six novels of *The Legend of the Ice People* are being published monthly up to Christmas 2008 and further editions will appear throughout the following year.

The latest information about the new writing of Margit Sandemo and worldwide publication and other media plans are posted and updated on her new English-language website at www.margitsandemo.co.uk along with details of her public appearances and special reader offers and forums.

All current Tagman fiction titles are listed on our website www.tagmanpress.co.uk and can be ordered online. Tagman publications are also available direct by post from: The Tagman Press, Media House, Burrel Road, St Ives, Huntingdon, Cambridgeshire, United Kingdom PE27 3LE.

For details of prices and special discounts for multiple orders, phone 0845 644 4186, fax 0845 644 4187 or e-mail sales@tagmanpress.co.uk